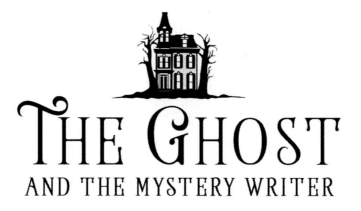

The Ghost
and the Mystery Writer

HAUNTING DANIELLE

The Ghost of Marlow House

The Ghost Who Loved Diamonds

The Ghost Who Wasn't

The Ghost Who Wanted Revenge

The Ghost of Halloween Past

The Ghost Who Came for Christmas

The Ghost of Valentine Past

The Ghost from the Sea

The Ghost and the Mystery Writer

The Ghost and the Muse

The Ghost Who Stayed Home

The Ghost and the Leprechaun

The Ghost Who Lied

The Ghost and the Bride

The Ghost and Little Marie

The Ghost and the Doppelganger

The Ghost of Second Chances

The Ghost Who Dream Hopped

The Ghost of Christmas Secrets

The Ghost Who Was Say I Do

The Ghost and the Baby

The Ghost and the Halloween Haunt

The Ghost and the Christmas Spirit

The Ghost and the Silver Scream

The Ghost of a Memory

The Ghost and the Witches' Coven

HAUNTING DANIELLE - BOOK 9

THE GHOST

AND THE MYSTERY WRITER

BOBBI HOLMES

The Ghost and the Mystery Writer
(Haunting Danielle, Book 9)
A Novel
By Bobbi Holmes
Cover Design: Elizabeth Mackey

Robeth Publishing, LLC

robeth.net

ROBETH PUBLISHING, LLC

ISBN-13: 978-1536809664
ISBN-10: 1536809667

To Elizabeth, who has shared this journey with me. Thank you for creating the inspired covers for the Haunting Danielle series— and for all the support you've given me during this adventure. I could never have done it without you.

ONE

Jolene Carmichael didn't make a practice of arranging late night rendezvous under the Frederickport Pier. It was all very spontaneous. While on her way home from the movies, she had decided to stop at Pier Café for a late night snack. The moment she entered the diner she spied him sitting at a booth.

Jolene viewed this as her opportunity to settle the matter. Unfortunately, once she realized Carla was working the late night shift, she knew it would be difficult to say much with the nosey woman hovering about. Jolene suggested they leave the restaurant separately. She would go first, he could wait a few minutes before leaving, and then they could meet under the pier to conclude their business.

Had she been in her prime, Jolene might have described the night air as brisk. But she was no longer a young woman. Her joints ached. The damp salt air savagely permeated her bones. Stubbornly, she continued to wait for him in the darkness, the only light coming from the moon beyond the shelter of the pier. Unable to stop her shivering, wishing she had worn a heavier jacket, she cursed him for making her wait. When he didn't show up within fifteen minutes, she began to wonder if he had stood her up. *He's deluding himself if he thinks he can avoid me indefinitely*, she thought.

Jolene wasn't afraid of the dark, nor of being alone under the pier so late at night. She had grown up in Frederickport, and while she had spent the last few years in New York, the Oregon seaside village still felt like home—and certainly a safer place for a senior citizen late at night compared to a big city.

"Jolene?" a faint voice called out in the darkness.

She turned to the approaching voice. It came from the direction she had recently walked from Pier Café. After a moment or two, she could see the shadow of his figure coming toward her.

"What took you so long?" Jolene snapped. Wrapping her arms around her waist, she hugged her lightweight jacket closer to her body.

"I had to pay my bill. As it was, I didn't get to finish my pie. I don't know why you insisted on coming down here. I thought I made it perfectly clear on the matter. We really have nothing left to discuss."

Jolene laughed. "Oh really? And yet, here you are."

"If you do this, Jolene, it's not going to make you look good."

"As if I really care at this point."

"What will you accomplish if you do this? What?"

She smiled at the sound of his desperation. "I'm counting on you giving me what I want, and then neither of us will be embarrassed."

"You don't care how this might hurt Melony?" he asked.

"I'm doing this for Melony."

"I doubt she'll see it that way."

Nearby, waves crashed along the shore, and the evening breeze intensified, making it impossible for him to hear Jolene's next sentence. He took a step closer to her so they could talk without shouting. The last thing he wanted was for their voices to carry and for someone on the pier to overhear their conversation.

When he took another step toward her, he felt his foot kick something in the sand. He paused a moment and looked down. Jolene was still talking and hadn't noticed he was briefly preoccupied by something at his feet. She continued to prattle on as he leaned down to pick up whatever it was he had kicked. He found an empty wine bottle.

Jolene turned to face the ocean. The moon cast a shimmering streak of gold across its surface. Determined to get her way, she broke into an enthusiastic rant, explaining exactly what she intended to do and say if her demands were not met in the morning. This was the first time she had issued a deadline. Until now, they had been in negotiations. Jolene was no longer willing to negotiate. She knew exactly what she wanted, and if she didn't have it by tomorrow at noon, she would make good on her threat.

Clutching the bottle's neck, he slowly stood back up while listening to Jolene recite all the nasty things she planned to say about him the next day should he refuse to give in to her demands.

Laughing, Jolene turned from the ocean and faced him, never noticing the bottle in his right hand, dangling limply at his right side.

She sounded pleased with herself. "I really don't know why I let this go on for so long. You're going to give me what I want eventually—you really have no other choice. There's no reason to put off the inevitable any longer." Jolene shivered. "It's cold out here. No more playing this silly game." Turning her back to him, deciding to return to her car, she said, "I expect you to give it to me—"

Jolene didn't have the opportunity to finish her sentence. But he gave it to her. It wasn't exactly what she was asking for, nor what she expected. The wine bottle didn't break when it crashed over Jolene's head, but it sent her crumpling to the ground after making a most unpleasant cracking sound.

The bottle slid from his hand a moment later, landing back in the sand. He rushed to Jolene's side, kneeling by the still body.

"Jolene?" he whispered.

There wasn't even a groan.

He placed his fingertips along her neck. There was no pulse. His own pulse raced as he rested his head on her chest, listening for a heartbeat. There was none.

Taking a deep breath, he told himself it was a blessing. Had Jolene been teetering between life and death, another bash or two over the head would be required, and that could get messy.

He hadn't planned to kill her tonight. Hell, he hadn't even intended to see her tonight. Although, he had to admit, the thought of murdering Jolene Carmichael had been lurking in the back of his mind.

Letting out another deep breath, he asked, *Who am I kidding?* The idea hadn't been lurking, it had been driving recklessly throughout his mind for the last few days. He had imagined grinding up oleander leaves and spiking her morning coffee. He considered backing over her with his car and claiming it was an accident, but then he remembered his car had a backup camera.

He never really imagined he would have the guts to carry through, yet now Jolene was as dead as her poor husband and his miserable business partner, Clarence Renton. Standing up, preparing to leave, he glanced down at Jolene, her dead eyes stared blankly at him. Suddenly, he remembered Carla.

"Damn, Carla saw me talking to Jolene. She saw me leaving the restaurant." Now starting to panic, he glanced around and then looked back to Jolene, trying to figure out what to do next. Dragging the body out to the water was one option, but there was no guarantee it would be washed out to sea and not show up on a nearby beach. After a moment of consideration, the only reasonable option—make it look like a robbery gone bad.

Smiling, he remembered the ridiculous number of gold and diamond rings Jolene liked to wear—one ring on every finger. Glancing around to make sure they were still alone on the beach, he knelt beside Jolene, intending to remove her jewelry. He started with the ring on her right index finger, giving it a little tug, but it stubbornly refused to budge. Letting out a curse, he gave the ring a twist and turn, but he couldn't get a firm grip. Reaching into his pocket, he pulled out a handkerchief and used it to obtain a better grip on the ring. Finally, it slipped off the dead finger.

One by one he removed her rings. It took a great deal of twisting and tugging. When the dead woman's fingers were bare, he stuffed the jewelry in his coat's pocket with his handkerchief and reached for Jolene's purse, which lay abandoned by her side. Rummaging through the purse, he grabbed all the cash he could find and then tossed the purse aside.

Standing up, he looked down at Jolene, whose lifeless eyes continued to stare up, the angle of the moon now casting light over the gruesome corpse. A shiver ran down his spine. On impulse, he leaned down and rolled Jolene over onto her belly, and then he frantically began shoveling sand over the body in an attempt to conceal it. Whether the morning tide would undo the camouflage, he gave it no thought. Instead, like a dog furiously digging for a bone, he shoveled sand, sending it flying in all directions, until all that appeared to be left of Jolene was a suspicious sand dune.

He remembered the bottle. Hauling it away from the crime scene was one option, but he was afraid someone might see him carrying it. Since he had only touched its neck, he quickly retrieved it and used his handkerchief to wipe his fingerprints from the bottle's neck before tossing the murder weapon back onto the beach. With the toe of his shoe, he kicked sand over the bottle.

Turning from the grizzly scene, he dug his hands into his coat pockets—and then he felt them—Jolene's rings. "Damn, I don't want your rings. And I sure as hell don't want anyone to find them on me."

He considered throwing them into the ocean, but he was never much of a pitcher, and with his luck, they would wash up on shore and the cops would find them when investigating Jolene's murder. Tossing them in some trash can was not an option. If anyone found the rings and turned them in to the police—and if someone identified them as belonging to Jolene—the police would realize this wasn't a mugging gone bad. What mugger steals jewelry, kills the victim, and then dumps the loot? No mugger.

Walking faster, putting distance between him and Jolene's lifeless body, his mind raced, trying to come up with a solution to the unwanted rings weighing down his coat pocket. Just as he reached the sidewalk, the solution presented itself.

"You idiot," he mumbled. "Toss them off the end of the pier. It's deep. They'll sink. No one will ever find them." Tugging the brim of his hat down over his eyebrows and his coat collar upward in an attempt to conceal himself, he turned in the direction of the pier. If he passed anyone who had seen him leave the area earlier, he would just say he had taken a walk along the beach.

Moonlight cast a muted golden glow across the weathered planks of Frederickport Pier. He stayed to the right of the wooden walkway, avoiding the doorway leading into Pier Café. He didn't want Carla to see him.

Hastily, he made his way toward the end of the pier, passing a few fishermen along the way. Fortunately, they were preoccupied and gave him little notice. One was busy reeling in a fish while another was cursing his tangled line.

Before he reached the end of the pier, he passed a young couple holding hands in the moonlight. They, like the fishermen, were preoccupied with their own business and didn't seem to notice when he walked by.

Now standing at the far end of the pier, his hand dipped into his pocket and scooped up the rings, clutching them tightly. Nervously, he glanced around to see if anyone was watching. The handholding couple was some distance away, their backs to him. He couldn't see the fishermen now concealed by shadows of the night.

Slowly, he removed his hand from his pocket and glanced behind him one more time before reaching out beyond the rail of the pier and opening his hand. The rings slipped out, falling to the water below. He didn't hear a splash, but he assumed the ocean beating against the pier muted the sound. He was confident they had found their way to the bottom of the ocean's floor beneath the pier.

Dipping his hand back into his pocket to make sure it was empty, he froze when he felt one more ring.

"Damn," he muttered. Again, he glanced around to make sure no one was watching. Certain no one could see him even if they were looking his way, he pulled his hand out of his pocket and dropped the last ring into the ocean. He heard a splash.

TWO

Danielle had left the parlor window open for Walt. In the late evening hours, he enjoyed listening to the sound of the breakers beyond the row of houses separating Marlow House from the ocean. Waves hitting the shoreline were not the only sounds filtering in through the screen. Limbs from a tree outside the parlor window brushed angrily against the house, telling Walt—had he been listening—the evening breeze was approaching gale level. However, Walt was not listening. His attention was focused on the television.

Lounging on the parlor sofa, Walt watched the late night thriller. Danielle had gone to bed several hours earlier, and Lily was in Portland with Ian for the night. Snoozing on the floor by his feet was Ian's golden retriever, Sadie. Danielle was dog sitting, but Sadie preferred to hang out with him. Walt assumed Max was roaming through Marlow House, on rodent patrol. He hadn't seen the feline for several hours.

Their only guest, Hillary Hemingway, had gone out for the evening and hadn't yet returned. Walt told himself he needed to turn the television off as soon as he heard her enter the house.

Twenty minutes later, so enthralled in the movie, Walt failed to hear Hillary enter the front door and was surprised when she walked into the parlor.

"Danielle?" Hillary said, glancing around the room. It appeared to be empty except for Sadie.

Walt watched her from the sofa, wishing she would simply go upstairs so he could continue to watch his movie. Sadie lifted her head and looked at Hillary. The dog's tail began to wag.

"Hello, Sadie, where's Danielle?"

Not expecting an answer, Hillary peeked her head out the doorway back to the hallway. There were no lights on downstairs, only a few random nightlights breaking up the darkness. Turning back to the parlor, Hillary looked at the television and let out a sigh.

"I guess Danielle couldn't sleep and must have come back downstairs to watch TV. But she forgot to turn it off." Hillary headed toward the table where Danielle kept the remote.

Panicked, Walt sat up straighter on the sofa. The movie was coming to a crucial part; he was about to find out the killer's identity. "No! Don't turn it off!"

Unable to hear or see Walt, Hillary snatched the remote from the table and pushed the off button. The television remained on.

"The batteries must be dead," Hillary mumbled. Setting the remote back on the table, she headed for the television.

The killer still had not been identified, and Walt briefly considered interfering with Hillary's attempt to turn off the television, as he had with the remote, but he preferred discretion with his ghostly powers when in the presence of Marlow House guests.

He let Hillary turn off the television and anxiously waited for her to leave the room and go upstairs so he could turn the television back on and watch the rest of his movie. But now she turned her attention to the open window, its curtains fluttering inward as the tree limbs hit the side of the house, making a steady rapping sound.

"Danielle certainly didn't do a very good job of locking up tonight," Hillary muttered.

Walt watched as Hillary walked to the open window and then tried closing it. She wrestled with it a moment, but it refused to budge. Danielle had been talking about having Bill Jones adjust the window, but she hadn't gotten around to it. Anxious for Hillary to be on her way so he could turn the television back on, Walt focused his energy on the stubborn window. It slammed shut.

Hillary lurched back, startled at the abrupt closure. She stared at the window for a moment; the curtains now hung motionless. The room seemed eerily still, with the wind no longer blowing in and the sound of the trees hitting the house muted.

Walt assumed she would now go up to her room. Much to his annoyance, she took a seat on the sofa. To make it worse, she sat on him. He leapt from his seat, and Hillary, who was now in his place, reached down to pet Sadie, who rewarded her attention with an accelerated tail thump.

"You are a fickle dog," Walt grumbled.

Sadie glanced over at Walt, silently asking him, *Who am I to turn down a good ear scratch?*

When Hillary left the parlor fifteen minutes later, she tried to get Sadie to go with her, to sleep upstairs, but Sadie stubbornly refused to budge, now feeling a little guilty over Walt, who had been impatiently pacing the room, waiting to turn the television back on.

Finally alone with Sadie again, Walt turned on the television, only to discover the movie had ended, and he still had no idea as to the killer's identity. He spent the next hour channel surfing until he finally got bored and decided to head back upstairs to the attic. First, he would make his nightly rounds, inspecting each room in the house to make sure all was well, beginning with the first floor.

Sadie trotted along by his side until they reached the library. There, she jumped up on the sofa, ceremoniously pawed the upholstery, circled the seat a half a dozen rounds, nudged the throw pillows to the floor with her nose, and finally settled down, sprawling across the length of the sofa.

"You know you aren't supposed to get on the furniture," Walt reminded her.

Sadie looked up at him. *Are you going to tell on me?*

"Don't be ridiculous. But why don't you come upstairs with me, there's a sofa up there."

Because you never sleep, and I'm tired. Plus, this is the most comfortable spot in the house. Sadie rested her chin on her front paws and closed her eyes.

"Okay. But you better get off there before Joanne comes in for work in the morning."

Several minutes later, Walt found Max coming through the pet door in the kitchen.

"Where've you been? I thought you were upstairs."

The black cat, now standing by the kitchen door, stretched lazily and yawned. His golden eyes looked up at Walt.

"Ahhh, you were out prowling," Walt said.

Max swished his tail.

"You followed our guest? Hillary?" Walt asked.

The black cat dropped to the floor and stretched out on his side, pawing the air; he looked up at Walt.

"What was she doing at the pier?"

Max pawed the air again and then rolled over onto his back and looked up at Walt, who noticed the cat had gained a few pounds since moving in with Danielle. His belly was rather impressive.

"She's back now. I wish she would have stayed away fifteen more minutes."

Max blinked his eyes at Walt.

"You wouldn't understand."

Walt left Max in the kitchen and headed upstairs. On the second floor, he was surprised to discover light coming from under Hillary's bedroom door.

"You're keeping late hours," he mumbled. He then turned his attention to Danielle's room. Its door was shut; the room appeared to be dark. He stood by her door a moment, debating if he would go in or not, until finally he moved effortlessly through the closed door. He found Danielle sleeping peacefully on her bed, curled up in a fetal position, her arms clutching the quilt. Moonlight streamed in through the window, lighting her delicate features.

Walt stood by her bedside and watched her sleep. It had been days since their last dream hop—and what a dream hop it had been. Danielle had kissed him. Walt smiled at the thought.

He reached out to brush his fingertips over her brow, but they moved through her forehead, cruelly reminding him he was not of her world. Snatching back his hand, he continued to watch her sleep while he thought about their kiss.

He had taken her to see what his yacht, the *Eva Aphrodite*, had been like before it was lost to the sea. Danielle had only seen its rusty and battered hull, destroyed after sitting under the ocean for almost a hundred years. He also wanted to give her an opportunity to say her final goodbyes to Emma Jackson.

What Walt hadn't counted on was how he would feel seeing her on his yacht's deck—making him believe for a brief moment that he was still alive—with a woman he had been waiting a lifetime for. Impulsively, he had cupped her face in his palms, preparing to claim a kiss, when he had suddenly remembered—*my* lifetime *is no longer.*

He intended to pull away, but then Danielle had seized the moment and kissed him—*she kissed him*. While he knew it was all wrong, he still couldn't help but smile at the thought. Perhaps he was no longer alive—yet that one kiss made him feel more than he had ever felt when he was a living, breathing man.

The next morning, after the dream hop on the *Eva Aphrodite*, neither he nor Danielle had mentioned the kiss. However, it was obvious she was embarrassed. Because of her apparent embarrassment, Walt was reluctant to initiate another dream hop. He would give her time—give them both time—to consider what had happened and what it meant, if it meant anything. Chris would be returning in a few days, and Walt couldn't help but wonder if Danielle would tell Chris what had happened. He hoped not.

Turning from the bed, Walt made his way back to the hall. Walking toward the stairs leading to the attic, he paused by Hillary's closed door. By the light coming from under the door, he assumed she was still awake.

"I wonder if she's working?"

Hillary Hemingway, bestselling mystery author, claimed to have come to Marlow House to write her next book. *I need some inspiration*, she had told Danielle. *My muse has been silent, and I need something to wake him up*.

As far as Walt knew, Hillary's muse was still snoozing. He hadn't seen her write a single word since her arrival. He didn't doubt she was really a writer—Ian was a huge fan of the woman's work. Considering Ian was a well-known author himself, one with a series of award-winning documentaries to his credit, Walt assumed she must be good.

Curious, Walt moved through Hillary's closed door. Danielle hated it when he went into a guest's room, but he didn't plan on telling her about his snooping.

Once in the room, Walt glanced around. Hillary's overhead light was on, as was the lamp on her nightstand. Clad in a long flannel nightgown, her gray hair in rollers and covered with a pink netted cap, she sat in the center of her bed, with sheets of yellow paper scattered around her on the mattress and on the floor. Clutching a yellow legal pad in one hand and an ink pen in the other, Hillary frantically scribbled across the pad of paper, writing one sentence after another.

Standing between the bed and the door, Walt frowned as he

noted the sheets of paper strewn all over the floor. Cursive writing covered each line of each sheet of paper. It was impossible to read what she was writing, at least not from where he stood.

The sound of paper being ripped from the pad caught Walt's attention, and he looked over to Hillary, who flung a sheet of paper—one freshly ripped from the pad—onto the floor and then started writing on a new sheet.

"Does this mean your muse has woken?" He took a seat on the edge of the mattress to have a closer look at some of the pages. He began to read one.

A woman meets a man under the pier. They argue. She is blackmailing him. While she yells at him, he finds an empty wine bottle in the sand. He picks it up and hits her over the head. It kills her. He removes all her rings. She has a ring on every finger, even her thumbs. Diamonds and gold. He covers her body with sand and leaves her there. He doesn't want the rings. He throws the dead woman's jewelry off the pier. When he puts his hand back into his pocket, he finds one of her rings he missed. He throws it in the ocean with the others and hears a splash.

THREE

Each day, Heather Donovan started her morning jog by first walking down to the Frederickport Pier by way of the sidewalks running along the road leading from her house to the pier. She did this in lieu of stretching to prepare herself for the jog.

She had fashioned her raven hair into two braids. They weren't fancy fishtail or French braids like Danielle Boatman normally wore. Heather liked to think of it as her Indian princess look, in honor of her native American great-grandmother on her father's side of the family. Ancestors on her mother's side of the family tree carried too much karma baggage—those she would rather forget.

When she reached the pier, she walked past it and then stepped onto the beach to start her morning jog, which would take her under the pier, past Ian Bartley's house and just beyond Chris Johnson's, where she would then cut back onto the sidewalk, cross the street and walk back to her house—her way of cooling off after the run.

It was a quiet, chilly morning, and so far she hadn't passed anyone on her walk, not even a car driving down the street. But the moment she stepped from the sidewalk onto the sand, she had the overwhelming sensation someone was watching her. Heather paused and looked around. To her surprise, she spied Jolene Carmichael standing some twenty feet from her, staring in her direction.

Instead of offering a greeting, Jolene turned from her and raced from the beach to the pier. Heather assumed the woman was headed to Pier Café for breakfast.

"Wow, Jolene can sure run for an old lady," Heather mumbled. *Not very friendly. I guess she's still pissed I told the world the truth about her grandfather.*

Heather continued on her way. A few moments later, she stood under the pier, fitting earphones into her ears, when she noticed a mound of sand under the pier. It hadn't been there yesterday. Remembering the wind the night before, she wondered if it were possible the wind had created a mini sand dune, yet found it implausible, considering it was tucked under the protection of the wooden structure.

With a shrug she said, "Wind tunnel maybe? Dumped all the sand in one place?" Turning on the music, she walked to the mound to have a closer look before starting on her run.

The first thing she noticed was the shoe poking out the end of the sand dune. Her initial thought was that the wind had gathered up debris from the beach—like an abandoned shoe—along with sand and had dumped it all in one place. But then she spied the leg attached to the shoe.

Without thought, Heather leapt down and shoved what she now assumed to be a person trapped under the sand. She rolled the corpse over onto its back. Horrified to discover the body was dead, Heather jumped up and stared down. There, looking up at her, was Jolene Carmichael, sand affixed to her dead eyeballs.

Heather began to scream.

HANDS ON HIPS, Police Chief MacDonald watched as they moved the body onto the stretcher. Standing next to him was Officer Brian Henderson, who had just arrived.

Absently removing his cap and refitting it back on his head, Brian asked, "Any idea what happened?"

"Appears to be a mugging. Looks like someone bashed in her head and then took her jewelry and rummaged through her purse. I think we found the murder weapon. There was a wine bottle near the body, had blood and hair on it."

Brian shook his head in disbelief. "In Frederickport? Someone would kill a little old lady over jewelry and some pocket change?"

"You probably didn't notice, but Jolene liked to wear every diamond ring she owned, all the time. That woman loved diamonds."

"I forgot, you knew her well, didn't you?"

"We weren't close. But her daughter and my wife were good friends."

"Who found her?" Brian asked.

"Heather Donovan came across the body when she was jogging this morning. At first she thought it was some sort of sand dune, but then she noticed the shoe. Freaked her out; kept yammering on about karma."

"Karma?" Brian frowned.

"Yeah, all that about Jolene's grandfather and Heather's great-grandfather being responsible for the *Eva Aphrodite* massacre," MacDonald reminded.

Brian frowned. "I don't know about karma, but how is Jolene Carmichael responsible for something that happened before she was born? I don't see how any of that has to do with her death."

"Not saying it does. But Heather tends to read more into these types of coincidences—the fact she found the body and what she and Jolene have in common. Think about it; Heather has made it her mission to make amends for her ancestor's crimes while Jolene would rather pretend hers did nothing wrong. And now Jolene is dead, murdered."

"Yeah, well, Heather Donovan is an odd one." Brian shook his head. "So what do you think happened? Why would Jolene Carmichael be under the pier alone at night? Assuming it happened last night."

"My guess, Jolene stopped to have something to eat at the diner. Her car is still in their parking lot. Maybe someone was passing through and noticed those diamond rings she liked to flash around and the fact she was an older woman, alone and vulnerable. Maybe she decided to take a late walk on the beach, and the killer followed her. Joe is up at the diner now, seeing who was working last night."

"I still can't believe something like this would happen in Frederickport. We just don't have muggers, and not someone willing to kill. Is it possible this wasn't about the rings?"

The chief glanced briefly to Brian. "You think someone wanted Jolene dead and just took her rings for good measure?"

"She wasn't the most pleasant person after she conned herself into Ian's house. Adam Nichols wanted to strangle her."

"Jolene wouldn't win any popularity contests. I know she and her daughter had a turbulent relationship." The chief cringed. "Damn, I'm going to have to call Melony and tell her about her mom. I know they had issues, but she was still her mom."

"So what do you think? Could it be something more than just a mugging?"

MacDonald shrugged. "I guess we'll have to see, find out if anyone had a motive. Adam was understandably angry at the time, but considering Danielle's probably going to end up with the gold coins Jolene found in Ian's house, I think we can confidently cross him off our suspect list."

"Maybe it's just a mugging."

FIFTEEN MINUTES LATER, Police Chief MacDonald sat with Brian Henderson in Pier Café, waiting for Carla to show up for work. When Joe had come into the café earlier that morning, he had been informed Carla had closed up the night before and would be in within the hour. Jolene's body had been removed, and Joe remained at the beach with several other officers, still processing the crime scene.

By the time Carla arrived, the chief and Brian were already eating breakfast. Without asking permission, she took a seat at their table.

"Is it true what they said, Jolene Carmichael was murdered last night?" Carla asked.

"How did you know the victim's identity?" MacDonald asked.

"So she really was killed!" Carla gasped.

"Yes, but we would prefer to keep the identity of the victim quiet until we can contact her daughter."

"Oh, I won't say anything," Carla solemnly vowed.

"But how did you know?" Brian asked.

"They were talking about it at the gas station this morning when I stopped by to fill up my car."

The chief let out a weary sigh. He set his coffee cup on the table and looked at Carla. "They told us you were working last night?"

She nodded. "I've been working double shifts lately. Trying to earn some extra money. My side job at Pearl Cove didn't work out. So is she really dead?"

"Yes. Her body was found this morning under the pier," MacDonald explained.

Carla cringed. "Oh, my god! To think I closed up last night, and a killer was lurking around!"

"Did you see her last night?" Brian asked.

"Yeah. She came in here late last night. Said something about being on her way home from the movies, ordered a piece of pie."

"Was she with anyone?" Brian asked.

Carla shook her head. "No. Came in alone, left alone. She wasn't here long, didn't even finish her pie."

"Were there any strangers in last night?" Brian asked.

"Not that I can remember. It was kind of slow last night, mostly locals. I never saw anyone suspicious looking."

"You say locals, who was here last night around the same time as Jolene?" the chief asked.

Carla considered the question a moment. "There was Adam Nichols and Bill Jones. They came in late, had some burgers. Bill left around the time Mrs. Carmichael arrived."

"Adam didn't leave with Bill?" Brian asked.

"No. He decided to have some dessert. Adam has a sweet tooth. And then there was that author lady who's staying at Marlow House."

"Hillary Hemingway?" Brian asked.

"Yeah! That's her name!" Carla smiled. "Isn't that funny her name is Hemingway like that other writer?"

"Was she alone?" MacDonald asked.

"Yes, she sat over there." Carla pointed to a booth across the diner. "She wasn't very friendly last night, spent most of her time reading. She's been in here before and was always pretty friendly, but last night she made it clear she didn't want to be disturbed. Just bring her the food, and get out of her face. Mrs. Carmichael stopped by her table, and I could tell Ms. Hemingway wasn't thrilled with the interruption."

"Do they know each other?" Brian asked.

Carla shrugged. "I guess so. Seemed to anyway. But it was pretty clear Ms. Hemingway didn't want to talk to her."

"Did they argue?" Brian asked.

"Argue? I don't think so. It was more Mrs. Carmichael stopping by her table to say hi and Ms. Hemingway giving her the brush-off. But Mrs. Carmichael stopped by everyone's table and said hello. She seemed to know everyone who was in here last night. To be honest, it was the friendliest I've seen her."

"What do you mean?" MacDonald asked.

Carla considered the question a moment. "I don't want to speak ill of the dead, but well, she always acted like she had a stick up her…well, you know. But last night, she comes in here and is all Miss Social Butterfly, stopping at everyone's table, saying hello. It just didn't seem like her."

"Who else was in here besides the people you've mentioned?" MacDonald asked.

"There was Steve Klein, the bank manager. Pete Rogers, he lives over by Marlow House. The kid that works at the gas station by the grocery store; can't remember his name. He was in here with his girlfriend. Don't remember her name either."

"Were Rogers and Klein together?" Brian asked.

"No. They each came in alone. Pete comes in a lot; he likes to fish off the pier."

"Anyone else?" Brian asked.

"Sam, who works over at the Seahorse Motel. He often stops in after his shift ends and has a piece of pie. I think that's about it."

CHIEF MACDONALD SAT ALONE at the table. Brian had left a few minutes earlier, and Carla had gone back to work. Picking up his cellphone, he placed a call and waited for his party to answer.

"Hey, Chief, what's going on?" Danielle's voice asked over the cellphone.

"I'm at Pier Café and was hoping you could get down here."

"Now?" Danielle asked.

"Jolene Carmichael has been murdered. Heather Donovan found her body under the pier this morning."

"Oh my god! That's horrible! What happened?"

"That's what I want to find out. According to Heather, she saw Jolene."

There was silence on the line for a few moments. Finally Danielle said, "And?"

"What do you mean *and*?" the chief asked.

"You already told me Heather was the one to find her body. And then you say Heather saw Jolene. I just assumed there was more to that sentence."

"Ahh…I see what you mean. Heather told me she saw Jolene running from the beach to the pier."

"Heather saw Jolene running from her killer?"

"No. This was just a few minutes before she found the body."

Once again, there were a few moments of silence. Finally, Danielle said, "Oh, Heather saw Jolene's spirit."

"That's what it sounds like. I was hoping Jolene's spirit might still be hanging around, and maybe…"

"You want me to talk to her?" Danielle asked.

"It would make this a lot easier if she could simply tell you who killed her."

FOUR

When Danielle entered Pier Café, all the tables were taken, as were all the seats at the counter. The sudden surge in business had more to do with the news a body had been found under the pier as opposed to the popularity of the restaurant's breakfast special. Word had spread quickly in the small town, and many locals had flocked to the pier to get a closer look, only to be barred from the crime scene by yellow tape.

Coffee pot in hand, Carla greeted Danielle. "Sorry, I don't have any empty tables. It'll be a few minutes."

Danielle glanced around and spied the chief sitting in the corner. "That's okay. I'm meeting the chief." Danielle nodded toward his table.

"I'll be over in a minute with coffee. You having breakfast?"

"No, just coffee. I already ate."

A few minutes later Danielle sat alone with Chief MacDonald.

"Wow, I don't think I've ever seen it this busy in here," Danielle whispered, glancing around the restaurant.

"I was hoping we could talk alone, but people keep coming up and asking me questions," the chief told her.

"So what happened?" Danielle asked.

While MacDonald told Danielle what he knew so far about Jolene's murder, Carla stopped by the table with coffee. The waitress was too busy to linger and quickly left them alone.

"I hate to think we have some killer running around, attacking women on our beaches, hitting women over the head for…" Danielle stared blankly ahead and didn't finish her sentence.

"What is it?" he asked.

Danielle shrugged and took a sip of her coffee. "I was about to say for jewelry, and then Cheryl popped into my head. She was murdered on this beach…hit over the head…for jewelry."

"Not really the same thing. Cheryl wasn't murdered for the necklace, and she knew her killer."

"Do you think Jolene knew hers?" Danielle asked.

"I suppose it's possible it wasn't a random mugging. You know as well as anyone Jolene was not a likable woman."

"She wasn't my favorite person. She hated me."

"Not something most people tell the police about someone who's just been murdered."

"Please don't put me on your suspect list."

The chief smiled. "No. One thing I've learned about you, you seem to have great tolerance for people you hate. Sometimes even turning them into friends."

"Oh, I don't hate anyone," Danielle scoffed. "I certainly didn't hate Jolene."

"You know what I mean." He downed the last of his coffee and then asked, "Do you think Heather really saw Jolene's spirit?"

Danielle fidgeted with her cup's handle and stared into her coffee. "I know Heather is sensitive to spirits. Not quite as sensitive as I am—but she did talk with Harvey, and I know she's caught glimpses of Walt. So it wouldn't surprise me if she saw Jolene's spirit so soon after her murder." Danielle glanced up into the chief's eyes. "When exactly do you think she was murdered?"

"The coroner said it looks like she was killed sometime last night. But they'll know more after the autopsy."

"When I walked up, I noticed some of your people still under the pier."

"Joe and Brian are down there with some others, finishing up. By the way, when you see them, can we just say you were on a walk, and we ran into each other? I'd rather they not wonder why I called you while we're in the middle of processing a crime scene."

"No problem." Danielle glanced over at Carla, who was taking food to a table across the room. "Although, when I got here, I told Carla I was meeting you."

"Well, hopefully she won't say anything."

Danielle laughed. "We *are* talking about Carla."

"IT WAS PRETTY GRUESOME," MacDonald said as he and Danielle stood outside the crime tape, looking in. The body had long since been removed, but MacDonald's team continued to comb the area for evidence.

"How so?" Danielle glanced briefly from the activity at the crime scene to MacDonald.

"Whoever killed her covered her with sand. She was on her stomach, face in the sand, and her poor eyes…" He shook his head.

"What about her eyes?"

He cringed. "Her eyes were open. Sand was embedded in them—it looked so damn uncomfortable."

"Well, she's dead, so I don't imagine it bothered her," she reminded him.

"Do you see her?" he asked.

Danielle glanced around. "Not yet. It's possible she moved on. Where did you say Heather saw her?"

"Heather was standing about where we are when she noticed Jolene. She ran by Heather and onto the pier. Heather told me she assumed Jolene was on her way to Pier Café for breakfast. But then she found the body a few minutes later and realized what she had really seen was Jolene's spirit."

"And she told you all this?" Danielle asked. "Did anyone else hear?" Danielle looked to Joe, who stood under the pier, talking to Brian and another officer. "Maybe Joe or Brian?"

The chief shook his head. "No. Joe and I were the first ones to arrive on the scene. We were both on our way to work when the call came in. When we arrived, Heather was understandably upset. Joe stepped away for a moment when the rest of our team arrived; she told me then about what she had seen. I have a feeling she knows more about you and me than you realize."

"What do you mean you and me?" Danielle frowned.

"She knows you can see spirits, right?"

"Yeah, that was sort of unavoidable. But she knows I prefer not to broadcast it."

"Brian thinks Heather is a little…odd."

Danielle smiled. "Yeah, I think she is too. But then again, I think all of us are a little odd."

"I get the feeling she's also observant. I think she may know you've been open with me regarding your…*gifts*. When she told me about seeing Jolene, I believe she felt she could trust me, that I wouldn't just write her off as being crazy."

"Did you ask her if she talked to Jolene? If Jolene told her who killed her?"

The chief laughed. "What, and make Heather think I'm crazy?"

Danielle smiled. "Yeah, well…we wouldn't want that. It was a silly question anyway. Knowing Heather, had Jolene's spirit said anything to her about the murderer, I'm sure Heather would have told you."

"Heather didn't realize Jolene was dead when she first saw the spirit. And she did tell me Jolene didn't say anything to her—that her initial thought was that Jolene was avoiding her because of what came out after the treasure hunt."

Danielle glanced around. "I don't see her down here, but if you say she ran up to the pier, maybe we should look up there. Assuming she hasn't moved on yet."

"THERE'S DANIELLE," Joe told Brian when he spied Danielle standing beyond the yellow crime tape, talking to the chief.

Brian glanced over toward the pair. "I bet she's not thrilled about all this."

"I don't think she and Jolene were exactly friends. From what I gathered, Jolene didn't like Danielle. According to Kelly, Jolene got pretty nasty with her."

"When was Kelly around Jolene?"

"I don't think she ever met her," Joe explained. "Ian and Lily told Kelly about Jolene after the gold coins were found. I guess Lily told Kelly Jolene was a real bitch to Danielle, even planned to sell the emerald Danielle was donating to the museum. Which is why Danielle ended up loaning it to the museum instead of giving it to them."

Brian frowned. "How could she sell the emerald if it belonged to the museum?"

"I didn't mean she was going to sell it and keep the money, but she's on the historical society board, and she was pushing to display the emerald for a short time and then sell it and put the money toward the museum's building fund. I guess Danielle wasn't thrilled with the idea. No, Jolene and Danielle weren't friends."

Brian shrugged. "I wasn't talking about Danielle being upset about who was murdered—but the fact someone was murdered in her neighborhood. Especially considering she's trying to operate the bed and breakfast. A killer on the loose can't be good for business."

"I'd be more concerned with her and Lily's safety. She doesn't have to worry about how this will hurt her business. The bed and breakfast is just a hobby. Danielle—and even Lily, don't need to worry about money."

BRIAN AND JOE were still talking amongst themselves when Danielle and MacDonald turned from the yellow crime tape and made their way back to the sidewalk leading to the top of the pier.

"Has her daughter been notified yet?" Danielle asked.

"I called Melony when I was waiting for you at the diner. I would have preferred to make the call when I was back at the office, but I didn't want to risk someone from here calling her to tell her how sorry they are—while she has no idea what they're talking about. I'm not particularly worried about her hearing it on the news, since she's in New York, and I doubt they'll report Jolene's death there."

"Isn't the victim's identity withheld until after family is notified?"

"We try. But when Carla showed up at the diner this morning, the first thing she asked, was it true about Jolene being murdered."

"She already knew?"

The chief nodded. "Small town. Word gets around quickly. There were a few people on the beach when we first arrived and many more after the rest of our team got there."

Together Danielle and the chief walked down the pier. The few people milling around were looking over the railing, trying to get a glimpse of the crime scene.

"If I don't see Jolene here, it's always possible she'll show up at her funeral. Spirits often want that last farewell before moving on. Any idea when her daughter will have the funeral?"

"According to Melony, there won't be one. Her mother wanted

to be cremated and Melony—well, I guess she's decided a funeral isn't necessary. Like I said, she and her mother had issues."

"She already decided that, just after learning her mother was dead?" Danielle asked.

In response the chief shrugged.

"No funeral? Not even a private memorial for the family?"

"There was no family. Just Melony."

Danielle let out a sigh. "Well, I guess everyone has to do what's right for them."

When they reached the end of the pier, Danielle stood by MacDonald's side. The two gazed out to the ocean. The morning breeze gusted up, making Danielle thankful for the warm jacket she wore over her pullover sweater. Her knee-high boots—with her jeans tucked in—gave her an additional measure of protection against the brisk air.

Danielle glanced around, surveying the area. "I'm really sorry, Chief, I don't think…" Danielle froze; her eyes widened. Just beyond the railing, over the water, hovered Jolene's spirit. The apparition ignored Danielle, but stared intently at MacDonald while frantically pointing downward.

Anxiously, the chief looked at Danielle. "What is it? Do you see something?"

"She's right there," Danielle whispered, motioning to the hovering spirit.

"Ask her; find out who killed her," he urged.

"Jolene," Danielle called out, "can you tell us who killed you?"

Jolene continued to ignore Danielle. Instead, her eyes fixed on the chief while she frantically pointed down to the water along the edge of the pier.

"What did she say?" MacDonald asked.

Jolene disappeared.

Danielle let out a deep breath—one she hadn't realize she had been holding since asking Jolene the question. "She's gone, Chief."

"Gone? What do you mean gone? Did she say anything?"

Danielle frowned and looked over the railing at the ocean below. "In a way."

"What do you mean?" he demanded.

"I think there's something down there she wants you to see."

FIVE

"Are you sure they're hers?" Brian asked MacDonald. He and Joe sat in the chief's office, looking at the nine diamond rings strewn across the desk. An hour earlier the jewelry had been discovered tangled in a fish netting hanging off the side of the pier.

"I emailed a photograph of the rings to Melony, and she says they look like her mother's. Several rings have engraved initials—JC. Jolene normally wore ten rings, so either the killer kept one as a souvenir, or it didn't make the netting and ended up in the ocean."

"If he tossed the rings, that can only mean one thing," Joe said.

"This wasn't a robbery," Brian answered.

"Whoever killed her wanted everyone to think this was a robbery, but he…or she…did not want to risk being caught with the rings," the chief summarized.

"I can't imagine the killer intentionally put the rings in that netting," Joe said. "Not a particularly safe place for a thief to stash his loot. One good wave and those rings could have been washed away."

"I agree," MacDonald said. "By the way they were positioned in that net, looked as if someone had dropped them over the side of the pier."

Brian eyed Jolene's rings. "So now the question, who had a motive to kill Jolene?"

"She hasn't been back in town long. Did she make an enemy

since she returned, or is her killer someone harboring a grudge from when Jolene used to live in Frederickport?" Joe asked.

"We need to get a team over to Jolene's house. If this was someone she knew, maybe we'll find something in her things that'll lead us in the right direction." The chief opened a small notepad sitting on his desk and flipped to the third page. He read it quickly and then looked up at Joe and Brian. "We also need to interview everyone who was in Pier Café last night, and see if we can find out who was on the pier fishing. According to Carla, she closed up about an hour after Jolene left. Jolene paid by credit card. So I'm pretty confident about that time frame."

"Do we know who left the restaurant right after Jolene? Maybe whoever it was saw something. Maybe noticed Jolene meeting someone on the pier," Joe suggested.

"We don't know who left right after she did. I'm counting on the other customers to fill in the blanks. According to Carla, the last customers to leave the restaurant last night were a young couple; he works at one of the local gas stations. This was about a half hour before she closed up. She can't remember when everyone else left, and they all paid in cash. Carla didn't ring up any of their bills until everyone was gone, so there's no way to be certain who might have left right after Jolene, but hopefully the customers we interview can give us answers, and maybe one of them saw something that will help," the chief explained.

The desk phone began to ring. Brian and Joe quietly waited while the chief took the call. When MacDonald finished and hung up the phone, he looked at Joe and Brian and said, "Well, I know who we'll interview first. Adam Nichols."

"Adam? Why Adam?" Joe asked.

"Results on the wine bottle are back. The blood and hair found on the bottle were Jolene's, and they found a fingerprint. One that's in our system."

"Adam?" Joe asked.

"Yes. No doubt about it. We can connect the murder weapon to Adam Nichols," the chief explained.

"I know Adam was pissed at Jolene for trying to claim the treasure, but kill her over it?" Joe asked.

"Not saying he did it, just that his fingerprint is on the murder weapon," the chief said.

"According to Carla, Adam was at the diner with Bill, and he stayed after Jolene entered and Bill left," Brian said.

"What I don't understand, if Adam did kill Jolene, is he really so stupid to drop the murder weapon by the body and just take off? I would have given Adam more credit than that. If he took the time to drop the rings in the ocean, why not get rid of the murder weapon too?" Joe asked.

"Adam's prints weren't the only ones on the bottle. Whoever they belong to, they aren't in our system. It looks as if someone wiped down the bottle's neck. Adam's print was found just below that."

"Like he tried to wipe off his prints and didn't do such a terrific job?" Joe asked.

The chief nodded. "If it was Adam, my guess, they happened to hook up after they both left the diner. Maybe they were each taking a walk on the beach. They exchanged words, and in the heat of the moment, Adam grabbed the first thing he could find and attacked her. We all saw how angry he was at her for treasure hunting on one of his properties."

"Technically, his grandmother's," Brian reminded him.

MacDonald shrugged. "Same thing to Adam."

ADAM NICHOLS SAT ALONE in the interrogation room. Yawning, he stretched his legs out under the table, leaned back in the chair, and glanced at his watch. In the next moment, Joe Morelli entered the room.

"How long is this going to take, Joe? I have a crap load of stuff to do today."

"You don't seem surprised we called you in." Joe tossed his notepad and pen on the table and sat down across from Adam.

Adam shrugged. "I heard about Jolene Carmichael this morning. Figured you had talked to Carla by now and would be interviewing everyone who was at Pier Café last night. But I'm sorry to tell you, I really didn't see anything when I left the restaurant. Nothing that can help you. But I did notice Jolene's car in the parking lot when I left. At the time, I really didn't think much about it. Figured she was still on the pier."

"What was your relationship with Jolene?" Joe asked.

"You want me to be honest?"

"No, Adam. I asked you to come in so you can lie to me," Joe snapped.

"Okay…okay…I understand this is serious. A murder and everything. You know, this is not terrific for me either. A murder on the beach can really screw with the vacation rental business. I want the killer caught as much as you do."

"My question again, your relationship with Jolene?"

"I was going to say I thought she was a bitch. But the woman was just killed, so I guess that's cold. I really didn't have a relationship with her, but I've known her for years."

"So she made you angry?" Joe asked.

"You mean when she broke into the house Ian's renting? Damn right. Maybe she didn't break in exactly, but practically. Of course, that didn't work out so terrific for her…or for me. Looks like Danielle scores another one."

"But you suspected the gold might be hidden in the house. If Jolene hadn't found it, you might have, and then you could have kept it for yourself. I could see how that would piss you off."

Adam shrugged. "Maybe I would have kept it, maybe not. I've never been terrific at keeping secrets, and the minute Grandma found out about the gold, it would have gone straight to Danielle anyway. So I suppose Jolene saved me some aggravation." Adam paused a moment and frowned at Joe. "Hey, what's this about? You don't think I had something to do with her murder, do you?"

"We're just trying to figure out who might have had a motive to kill Jolene."

"I thought this was a mugging? Someone killed her for her rings."

"Where did you hear that?" Joe asked.

"Grandma told me."

"Your grandmother? How did she know about Jolene's missing rings?"

Adam laughed. "Seriously, Joe? You know Grandma. Ask her yourself."

"I will," Joe mumbled.

"So can I go now?" Adam started to stand up.

"Sit down, Adam," Joe ordered. "We're not done."

Reluctantly, Adam sat back down in the chair and glanced at his watch. Letting out a sigh, he leaned back in the seat and looked at

Joe. In the next moment, Brian entered the interrogation room, carrying a clear plastic bag—it contained an empty wine bottle. Without saying a word, Brian set the bag on the table before Adam and took a seat. He and Joe watched Adam.

Staring at the bottle trapped in the clear bag, Adam's eyes widened. "Where did you get that?"

"You recognize it?" Brian asked.

"It can't be the same one." He looked up at Joe and Brian and frowned. "What's going on?"

"Tell us what you know about this bottle," Brian said.

"I bought one just like it."

"You touched it?" Brian asked.

"Of course, what kind of question is that?"

"This is what killed Jolene Carmichael," Brian explained.

"Wow, your killer has expensive taste!"

"What is that supposed to mean?" Joe asked.

"I bought a bottle of wine just like that. Bought it in Portland; you can't get it in Frederickport. It's pricy."

"Where is the bottle now?" Joe asked.

"I assume it's still sitting over at Gusarov Estate."

"Gusarov Estate?" Brian asked.

"A closing gift for Chris. He's not back yet, so it's still over there. Why?"

"Can you explain why your fingerprint is on this bottle?" Brian asked.

Adam bolted up straighter in his chair. "What do you mean? That's impossible."

"Like we said, this is the murder weapon. We found Jolene's hair and blood on the bottle," Brian explained.

Adam cringed. "I don't even want to think about that."

"It also had your fingerprint," Joe reminded him.

"Then it has to be the bottle I bought. Holy crap, that means someone broke into the Gusarov Estate!"

SIX

Instead of returning to Marlow House after meeting MacDonald at the pier, Danielle decided to run some errands in town. Everywhere she stopped, people were talking about Jolene, and everyone assumed she had been murdered for her jewelry, which Danielle now believed was untrue.

Danielle kept asking herself, *Who wanted Jolene dead?* When she finished her errands, she decided to make one final stop before returning home—to Marie Nichols's house. If anyone in Frederickport knew who had been harboring a lethal grudge against Jolene, it would be Marie. Marie knew all the town's sordid secrets.

"Are you playing detective?" Marie asked Danielle with a chuckle as she led her to the kitchen. When Danielle had arrived a few minutes earlier, Marie had asked her if she'd had lunch yet. When Danielle said no, Marie told her she had just mixed up a fresh batch of egg salad and insisted Danielle join her for a sandwich.

"It always makes me nervous when someone I have an issue with gets murdered," Danielle said, only half in jest. She sat at the table and watched as Marie prepared the sandwiches. Danielle had known the elderly woman long enough to know that any offers to help her prepare the food would be met with opposition.

"You plan to get your ducks in a row in case Edward comes gunning for you?" Marie teased.

Danielle laughed. "I don't think the chief will try to pin this one on me. But I am curious. Do you have any suspects?"

Marie stood at the kitchen counter; two freshly made egg salad sandwiches waited for her to cut them in half. She paused a moment and glanced over to Danielle. "I thought this was a mugging? You don't think so?"

"I guess…umm…some new information has come up. They suspect someone Jolene knew may have killed her. But why? Any ideas?"

Marie cut the sandwiches in half and set each one on its own plate. She had already added potato chips, pickles, and a cookie to each dish. She carried the plates to the table and set one before Danielle. "There were times I wanted to wring her neck."

"Yeah, me too." Danielle shrugged. She watched as Marie set the second plate on the table and then poured them each a glass of lemonade before sitting down.

"I suppose that's not exactly a kind thing to say about the poor woman. She is dead." Marie sighed.

"I didn't like her, but I certainly didn't want her dead. I assume that goes for most people who felt the same way about her." Danielle took a bite of her sandwich.

"I'm sure a few of the people her husband's law firm cheated might be holding a grudge. With Clarence dead, maybe one of them went after her."

"I was one of those. I mean, not that I wanted to vent my anger on her. But I obviously had an issue with Clarence."

"True, dear. But you ended up winning at the end—financially, that is. I suspect Jolene had far more reason to kill you than the other way around."

Danielle cringed. "I guess you're right."

"Word around town, Jolene was having serious money problems."

"I've heard that too. Which seemed odd, considering those rings she wore. If it was me, the first thing I'd do is sell off the jewelry."

"Yes, but you're not pretentious like Jolene was. Jolene liked to think of herself as Frederickport royalty. Absurd notion, really. She'd been wearing those rings for so long, removing them—selling them—to Jolene that would be as shameful as begging on the corner. No, she'd be kicked out of her house before she would've pried those rings from her fingers."

"Well, someone pried them from her fingers," Danielle muttered before taking another bite of her sandwich.

Marie sipped her lemonade and then said, "Whoever killed her, I don't imagine it was premeditated."

"Why do you say that?"

"Think about it. From what I heard, she was hit over the head with a bottle. The police have it. They found it by the body. It had fresh blood on it—probably Jolene's blood."

"How did you hear that?" Danielle asked.

Marie smiled and took another sip of her lemonade.

"Keeping secrets?" Danielle prodded.

"My friend Eleanor, her daughter works at the coroner's office. She called me this morning, but you can't say anything. I don't want to get her in trouble."

"Okay, but how does that prove it wasn't premeditated?" Danielle asked.

"If your intention is to kill someone, are you really going to rely on an empty wine bottle? It's always possible it'll break before it finishes the job. And then what do you do? Stab your victim with shards of glass?"

Danielle wrinkled her nose and set her sandwich down. "Ewww, please. I really did not need that visual."

Marie shrugged. "Well, you did ask, dear. No, you're planning to kill someone, you bring along a gun or knife. Something to get the job done."

"So you're saying the bottle was simply a weapon of opportunity?"

Before Marie could answer Danielle, her phone began to ring.

"Excuse me, dear," Marie said as she stood up to answer the phone.

Danielle picked up her sandwich and started eating again, paying little attention to Marie's phone call. Yet, just moments after answering the phone, Marie cried out, "Oh no!"

Setting what was left of her sandwich back on her plate, Danielle watched Marie's obvious distress as she talked to whomever was on the phone. Finally, Marie hung up.

She looked at Danielle. "They've arrested Adam for Jolene's murder!"

"Adam? Why would they arrest Adam?"

"That was my friend Eleanor. She just talked to her daughter, who told her they found Adam's fingerprint on the wine bottle that killed Jolene!"

Danielle stood up. "What do you want to do? Do you want me to take you to the police station?"

Frantic, Marie shook her head and began pacing in front of the kitchen counter. "No, no. I can't do that. I'm not supposed to know about the arrest. And if I go down there, they'll know, and I'll get Eleanor's daughter in trouble, and if they arrested Adam, I need to have someone on the inside who can tell me what's going on!"

"Marie, I'm sure there's a logical explanation. I can't imagine Adam killed Jolene."

"No, no. He wouldn't. I know that. But he was pretty angry with her, and they've never liked each other. And if they bring up all that stuff about Adam and Melony, well, they could pin this on him!"

"Melony? Isn't that Jolene's daughter?"

Marie nodded, still pacing.

"You need to calm down, Marie." Danielle took Marie's elbow and guided her to the chair at the kitchen table.

"I can't deal with Adam getting arrested for murder *again*."

"You want me to go down there? See what's going on? I could make some excuse. I wouldn't have to say anything about knowing about Adam's arrest. I think the chief will talk to me."

"Would you, dear?"

"Of course." Danielle leaned to Marie and gave her a hug. Gently patting the woman's shoulder, Danielle couldn't help but notice how fragile the elderly woman felt in her arms.

"WHAT DOES it prove if there's no bottle of wine at the Gusarov Estate?" Brian asked the chief.

"I was curious when Adam confessed to recognizing the wine bottle. When he started talking about how pricy it was, I decided to do a quick Google. That wine goes for over three hundred dollars a bottle," MacDonald explained.

Joe let out a low whistle. "I never figured Adam for some wine connoisseur."

"I don't think he is. Like he said, he bought it as a closing gift for Chris. Considering the commission Adam earned on that sale, he probably figured it was a good investment."

"I still don't understand what we hope to prove by going over there," Brian reiterated.

"We know Adam didn't have a wine bottle with him when he left Pier Café after Jolene. If he did kill her with it, I have to believe he found the bottle on the beach. Yet it's been my experience, the type of people who litter the beach with empty wine bottles normally don't drink the expensive stuff."

"He could have grabbed it from a trash can when he followed her under the pier," Brian suggested.

"True. It's always possible we had a tourist with expensive wine tastes. In that case, it doesn't look good for Adam. But if Adam can prove he really did purchase that wine—and the bottle has gone missing—then he has a reasonable explanation for his prints showing up on the murder weapon."

A call from the front desk interrupted their discussion. Danielle Boatman wanted to see Chief MacDonald.

"Have her wait in my office. I'll be right there." The chief hung up the phone. He looked at Joe and Brian. "This works out well; Danielle's here."

"That's convenient. And if she verifies Adam's story?" Joe asked.

The chief headed for the door. Before opening it, he looked back at Joe and said, "Then I guess you'll be taking a run over to the Gusarov Estate."

WHEN MACDONALD REACHED HIS OFFICE, he found Danielle waiting for him. She sat in one of the chairs facing his desk.

"Hi, Chief," Danielle greeted him without standing up.

"What do I owe the honor?" MacDonald asked as he sat down behind his desk.

"I was just heading home. Thought I'd stop by and see if there were any new developments."

"I was hoping maybe you'd seen Jolene again."

"No…umm…I thought I saw Adam's car in the parking lot. Is he here?"

"Yes. We brought him in for questioning. He was at the diner last night when Jolene was there. He's in the interrogation room now."

"So that's why he's here?"

MacDonald studied Danielle for a moment. Finally, he said, "I need to ask you something."

"Sure, what is it?"

"According to Adam, he left a bottle of wine over at the Gusarov Estate for Chris, as a thank you gift. He said you had to let him in because he didn't have the keys anymore. Said he had given them to you. Is that true?"

"Yeah, a couple days ago, why?"

"Do you remember anything about the wine?"

"What do you mean? It was a bottle of wine. What's this about?"

"Do you know if it's still there?"

"I hope so." Danielle laughed. "Chris hasn't gotten back yet. And I sure didn't drink it."

"Do you remember what kind of wine it was?"

"I know it was a red wine, because I teased Adam about taking it home and keeping it in my wine chiller."

"You don't chill red wine."

"Exactly. That's what Adam reminded me. But sorry, I didn't recognize the brand. Why?"

"Can you describe the bottle, such as what kind of label it had? This is important."

Danielle considered the question for a moment. "I'm pretty sure it had a house on the label, more like a chateau. Why? What is this about?"

"We're going to need you to take us over to the Gusarov Estate and let us have a look at that bottle."

"Do you have a search warrant?"

MacDonald's expression went blank. "Are you serious?"

"Sure. I mean, I can't just let you go into Chris's new house because you want to check out his wine. Not without a search warrant. Of course, if you tell me what this is about, then maybe I can work something out." She smiled sweetly.

"I really don't want to get into it now."

"Then you better get a search warrant."

"Are you blackmailing me?"

"Chief, that would be illegal, wouldn't it?"

MacDonald let out a sigh. "Fine. Adam's fingerprints were found on the wine bottle that killed Jolene. He claims the only bottle like that he touched was the one he left at the Gusarov Estate. We need to go over there to see if the bottle is still there. If it isn't, and if you can confirm he left it there, then we won't be holding him."

Danielle stood up. "What are you waiting for? Let's go to the Gusarov Estate."

SEVEN

The chief remained seated. He studied Danielle for a moment. "Where were you before you came here?"

"I was running errands here and there. Why?"

The chief didn't respond immediately, but continued to study Danielle. Finally, he said, "Before we go, I'd like you to look at something."

Danielle let out a sigh and sat back down. She watched as MacDonald turned his attention to his computer. "What are you doing?"

His eyes focused on his monitor while one hand moved his mouse on the desk. "Hold on. This will just take a minute."

Danielle let out another sigh and settled back in the chair, waiting. Waiting for what, she had no idea. Finally, the chief looked up and motioned for her to come and look at his computer monitor. Leaving her purse sitting on the floor, she stood up and walked around his desk, standing next to him. She looked at the computer monitor. He had six windows open. Each window displayed a different bottle of wine.

"I had no idea there were so many wine labels with chateaus," Danielle said.

"Neither did I. Do you recognize the one Adam took over to Chris's house?"

Danielle pointed to a red and gold label. "That one."

"Are you sure?" he asked.

"Positive."

"That's the label on the bottle that killed Jolene," the chief said.

"What was the point of me picking it out? Why didn't you just show me the bottle you have? I could have told you if I thought it was the same one or not. You had to have a bottle lineup?"

The chief turned off his monitor and stood up. "Before we go over to the Gusarov Estate, I want to know the bottle he claims to have taken over there matches the bottle we found on the beach. If you can identify it now—before seeing the bottle we found—it will be more difficult for someone to argue you were swayed in your testimony."

"Even if the wine is still at Chris's, which it probably is, I'd still think Chris's bottle would help prove Adam probably touched that murder weapon before the killer."

"How do you figure?"

"Whoever killed Jolene probably did it in a fit of anger and happened across that bottle. If it was premeditated, I'd assume they wouldn't choose a weapon that might break or not finish the job."

"What's your point, Danielle?"

"Adam probably bought that wine for Chris because it was one he liked, a brand he'd bought before. Maybe even handled other bottles at the store, which would have left his fingerprints on the eventual murder weapon."

"Adam said that was the first and only time he had bought that type of wine. Even claimed it was the only bottle like that he had ever touched."

"Maybe he forgot," Danielle suggested.

"I don't think Adam would forget buying a three-hundred-dollar bottle of wine."

"Adam spent three hundred bucks on that wine?" Danielle asked incredulously.

"I'm not sure exactly what he spent, but that was the price I found online."

"Wow, I guess Adam really does want to keep Chris as a client. I suppose I should have told Adam Chris is perfectly happy with Two-Buck Chuck."

"I think it may be about three bucks now."

Danielle grabbed her purse and headed for the door. "Yeah, but still. For that much money, he could have gotten Chris eight cases of wine as a thank you gift. That would have gotten Chris's attention."

MacDonald opened the door for Danielle. "For a rich girl, you sure are cheap."

"The term is frugal. If I was cheap, I'd have a much more interesting social life."

"DID you really spend three hundred bucks on that wine?" Danielle asked Adam as they sat in the backseat of the squad car on their way to the Gusarov Estate. Brian drove the car while Joe sat in the passenger seat.

Before he could answer, Joe asked, "Do you need to stop at Marlow House and pick up the keys?"

"No. I have them in my purse." She turned her attention back to Adam, waiting for his answer.

"Hey, it was a good commission. I couldn't be cheap," he said with a shrug.

"Knowing Chris, he would have been thrilled with a couple cases of beer," Danielle told him.

"The man is a billionaire," Adam countered.

"And billionaires don't like beer?"

"It doesn't matter now. If my fingerprint really was on that bottle they have, that means someone has broken into the Gusarov Estate and took the wine."

"Under normal circumstances, I'd want you to be wrong," Danielle confessed.

"That's the only explanation." Adam stared out the side window. "Someone broke into the Gusarov Estate."

"You know, we're going to have to stop calling it the Gusarov Estate. It isn't anymore." Danielle reminded him. A few minutes later, they pulled up in front of the property.

WHEN DANIELLE STARTED to slip the house key into the lock, Adam looked at Brian and asked, "Shouldn't one of you be doing this? If someone broke into the house, they could still be in there."

Danielle paused and looked over at Brian and Joe.

"I seriously doubt that," Brian said. "If they stole the wine, they obviously took it down to the beach to drink. It was probably teenagers. I doubt they returned."

"Great," Adam grumbled. "When I was a teenager, I drank Boone's Farm wine. I just hope whoever stole it enjoyed it!"

"If it *was* stolen," Joe said, taking the key from Danielle and opening the door. He walked in the house first and looked around. With the sunlight streaming in through the high windows, it wasn't necessary to turn on the overhead lights.

"What's that supposed to mean?" Adam snapped. He and Danielle followed Joe and Brian into the house. "You seriously think I killed Jolene?"

"Where did you put the wine?" Brian asked.

Danielle motioned to the living room. "He set it on the mantel."

The four walked into the living room. Adam's eyes fixed on the fireplace mantel first. He pointed across the room to where he had placed the bottle of wine. "See, it's gone!" They looked to the fireplace. The only thing sitting on the mantel was an envelope containing the thank you card Adam had left with the wine.

If Brian hadn't noticed motion out of the corner of his eye, the man sneaking out of the house might have gone unnoticed. Without pause, Brian turned back toward the front door and let out a shout. He took off in pursuit. Joe didn't wait for an invitation. He raced past Adam and Danielle and out the front door, behind Brian and the intruder.

Together, Adam and Danielle stood at the front window, looking outside, watching Brian and Joe chase the man down the front walk to the street.

"Damn, Brian can run for an old guy," Adam said in awe.

Still watching the chase, Danielle nodded. "I'm impressed. That other guy is pretty fast too. I wonder who he is."

"Probably the one who drank my wine. Jerk."

The three were now halfway down the street, but Brian was getting closer, with Joe on his heels.

Still watching the pursuit through the window, Danielle said, "Next time, buy Chris some cases of beer. Buy aluminum cans. Harder to kill someone with."

Adam rolled his eyes. "Funny, Danielle."

"You think they'll shoot him?" she asked.

"If he doesn't stop running, maybe."

In the next moment, Brian reached the man, slamming him to the ground.

Adam winced. "Ouch. That looks like it hurts."

ADAM AND DANIELLE sat with the chief in his office, waiting for some answers. After apprehending the intruder, they had gone through the rooms at the estate and had discovered the man had broken in through a back window and had been camping out in one of the rooms.

"He's not from around here," the chief explained. "If he's ever been arrested, he's not in our system. But his fingerprints match the other prints we found on the bottle that killed Jolene."

"Did he kill her?" Adam asked.

The chief shook his head. "The man claims to have spent last night in the ER. I called the hospital; they confirm he checked in last night around ten, before Jolene arrived at Pier Café, and didn't get out of there until this morning, after Heather found the body. He admitted to taking the bottle of wine down by the pier and drinking it. Left the empty."

"So he's a litterbug and a thief," Danielle said.

"He's also homeless. Lost his job; doesn't appear to have any family," MacDonald explained.

"What now?" Danielle asked.

"Now Adam can go home."

Danielle and Adam stood up.

"And, Danielle," the chief called out.

Danielle turned briefly to him. "Yes?"

"Tell Marie hello for me."

"WHAT WAS THAT ABOUT?" Adam asked when they were out in the parking lot.

"Your grandma sent me over here to check on you. I think the chief figured that out."

"She did?"

"One of her informants told her you'd been arrested. She was pretty upset; you should probably stop by her house on the way home and let her know what's going on."

"I wasn't really arrested. They asked me to come in for questioning." Adam opened his car door.

"If you hadn't come up with an explanation for that fingerprint, you would have been arrested."

Adam got into the driver's seat of his car, slipped his key in the ignition, turned the key, rolled the window down, and closed the door.

Danielle leaned against the car door, looked in the window, and watched as Adam hooked his seatbelt. "Who do you think killed Jolene?"

"I thought the cops figured it was a robbery gone bad? I understand questioning me because of the fingerprint, but are they really looking for someone who was out to get Jolene?"

"She wasn't killed because of the rings," Danielle whispered.

Adam looked out the window at Danielle. "How do you know?"

"I just do. The cops are looking for someone who had a grudge against Jolene."

"Well, I didn't kill her. And if I did, I certainly wouldn't use a wine bottle that could be traced to me—and leave my fingerprints behind!"

"What's this about you and Jolene's daughter?"

"What are you talking about?"

"After your grandma heard—or thought—you were arrested, she said they might pin it on you because of what went on between you and Jolene's daughter."

"That's old news. Has nothing to do with Jolene's death. I can't even imagine why Grandma would bring it up." He sounded annoyed.

"Your grandma loves you. She just worries about you."

With his hands firmly on the steering wheel, Adam revved his engine. He glanced up into the rearview mirror. "I have to go now."

"So you aren't going to tell me?"

"Tell you what?" He revved his engine again.

"About you and Melony? That's her name, isn't it?"

"None of your business, Danielle," he said impatiently, glancing back up into the mirror.

"Okay." Danielle stepped back from the car. "But you know,

she's probably going to be coming to Frederickport this week. Melony, that is."

Adam briefly glanced to Danielle and then gunned his engine. In the next moment, he backed out of the parking space and raced from the police department parking lot, without stopping for the stop sign on the corner.

Somewhat startled, Danielle watched as Adam's car disappeared down the street. "I really shouldn't have gone all Lily on him. But there's a story here."

EIGHT

When Danielle finally returned home that afternoon, she noticed Joanne's car wasn't parked in front of Marlow House, but Hillary's was. She glanced over to Ian's house before turning into her drive and noticed Ian's vacant driveway. *Lily and Ian aren't back from Portland.*

It suddenly dawned on Danielle that she had been so busy all day, she hadn't called or texted Lily. Since she hadn't heard from Lily, she had to assume her roommate didn't know about the murder, which she found peculiar considering Ian's sister, Kelly, was dating Sergeant Morelli. She would have assumed Joe had already filled Kelly in on all the details, which Kelly would then relay to her brother.

Sadie greeted Danielle the moment she entered the kitchen, with a wet nose eagerly sniffing and a wagging tail. Hillary Hemingway sat at the kitchen table, eating a sandwich, while Walt lounged against the kitchen counter, his arms folded across his chest.

"Where have you been all day?" Walt asked the question in spite of the fact Danielle couldn't directly answer it—not with her guest sitting in the kitchen.

Hillary set her sandwich on her plate and smiled up at Danielle. "You just missed Joanne. She left about ten minutes ago."

"It's been an insane day." Danielle tossed her purse on the kitchen counter and grabbed a glass from the overhead cabinet.

"Did you hear about the murder?" She filled her glass with water and then turned to face the older woman.

"Oh yes. One of Joanne's friends called her, told her someone was mugged on the beach last night. Have you heard if they've caught him yet?"

Danielle took a seat at the table. "Unfortunately, no."

"I hope you have more information. Joanne didn't tell us anything. Or should I say, she didn't tell Hillary much," Walt said.

"I must say, it was comforting having Sadie here. What with a killer on the loose. I kept all the doors locked while you were gone," Hillary explained.

"Who was murdered?" Walt asked. "Were you off helping the chief? Is that where you've been all day?"

"I don't think we're in any danger, but it's always good to keep the doors locked," Danielle said. "I knew the woman who was killed—Jolene Carmichael." Danielle glanced up to Walt; their eyes met.

"I'm sorry, was she a good friend of yours?" Hillary asked.

Danielle sipped her water and then said, "No. She was more an acquaintance than a friend. In fact, I only just met her a short while ago."

"You loathed the woman," Walt smirked.

Ignoring Walt's comment, Danielle said, "I met her through the historical society. She was a board member. I think I've mentioned her before. She was the one who found the gold coins at Ian's house."

Abandoning the partially eaten sandwich on her plate, Hillary looked over at Danielle with keen interest. "She was the one who thought she should be able to keep them, right?"

"Yeah, that's what she thought. But now the poor woman is dead."

"Do you know the details?" Hillary asked.

Danielle shrugged. "Not really. Probably no more than what Joanne told you."

"I don't believe that," Walt scoffed.

"So what did you do today?" Danielle asked.

"My muse finally spoke to me!" Hillary said brightly.

"You started your book?"

"Oh yes. I've been writing all day. It's so exhilarating. Nothing like it; when a story grabs me, I can do nothing but write."

"She's not kidding," Walt said. "She was still up when I went to the attic last night after midnight, and this morning, when I came back downstairs, I could hear her clicking away on a typewriter. I thought you told me people don't use typewriters anymore?"

"I've been meaning to ask you, I noticed the typewriter in your room. Don't you write on a computer?" Danielle asked.

"I don't like writing on a computer," Hillary told her. "Stifles my creativity. Mr. Royal has been my loyal assistant for over fifty years."

Danielle frowned. "Mr. Royal?"

"My Royal typewriter. It belonged to my father."

"I didn't realize you could still buy typewriter ribbon," Danielle muttered.

"Certainly."

"I saw her typewriter," Walt told Danielle. "It isn't even an electric one."

"Can you tell me what your story's about?" Danielle asked.

Hillary's thin pale lips crinkled as she broke into a sly smile. "I never talk about my story during the early stage. It's bad luck. But I must say, I feel good about this one. I knew coming to Marlow House was the right thing for me."

"How do you mean?" Danielle asked.

"I've been experiencing such a bad case of writer's block. Something told me coming here would prime my creative pump and it has! When I returned from my walk last night, I felt exhilarated! I just knew my dry spell was over!"

"I'm happy for you." Danielle smiled.

Hillary stood up and carried her plate to the sink. "If you'll excuse me, Danielle. I need to get back to work. I'll keep my door closed, but if my typing bothers you, please let me know. I could always come downstairs and write."

"No, your typing doesn't bother me. I've never even heard it."

"Wonderful." Hillary started to rinse her plate off, but Danielle told her to leave it, she would take care of it. Grateful, Hillary flashed Danielle a smile, set the plate in the sink, and hurried from the kitchen.

"How can you not hear the typing? I could hear it up in the attic," Walt asked.

Danielle went to the sink and finished rinsing Hillary's plate before placing it in the dishwasher. "I don't know. Maybe I'm just a heavy sleeper."

Walt watched Danielle for a moment as she wiped down the

counter with a paper towel. Finally, he asked, "So there's a killer on the loose in Frederickport?"

"Afraid so." Danielle tossed the paper towel into the trash can and turned to face Walt.

"Perhaps whoever killed Jolene has already left town. No reason to stick around and risk getting arrested."

"The chief seems to feel it wasn't a mugging—that the killer targeted Jolene specifically."

"From what I heard Joanne tell your guest, Jolene was robbed."

"Maybe she was robbed, but that's not why she was killed. Whoever killed her wanted her dead."

"Are you a suspect?" Walt asked.

"Me?" Danielle frowned. "Why would I be a suspect? I barely knew the woman!"

Walt laughed. "I know you didn't kill her. I just wondered if you were a suspect since it was no secret you disliked the woman. And you seem to be the favorite suspect when someone gets killed in Frederickport."

"It was more that she didn't like me. But no, I'm not a suspect. But Adam was for a while this afternoon—which is one reason I was late getting home."

Before Danielle could elaborate, her cellphone began to ring. She slipped it out of her back pocket. It was Lily.

"Hey, Lily, I thought you'd be home by now." Danielle sat down at the table while Walt silently listened to her side of the conversation.

"We're getting ready to head back now. Why didn't you tell me about Jolene?" Lily asked.

"So you heard?"

"Yeah. We just got back to Kelly's, and she told us all about it."

"Where did she get her information, the news or Joe?" Danielle asked.

"Joe. He called her about thirty minutes ago. Told her all about it."

"I'm surprised you didn't hear something about it on the radio."

"We've been at the tattoo parlor all afternoon so—"

"Tattoo parlor?" Danielle interrupted.

"I finally did it, Dani. I claimed the dragon," Lily told her.

"Did you tattoo over it?"

"No. Like I told you before, I didn't want to do that. I…well, you'll see. But I have to tell you, it hurt! Damn! I should have made them knock me out like before!"

Danielle laughed. "Yeah, I'm kind of a wimp. When Lucas got his second tattoo, he tried to convince me to get one, but I hate needles."

"Unfortunately, I have to go back for them to finish it. But I've gone this far, I can't wimp out now."

Danielle heard Ian in the background. Lily then said, "Ian wants to talk to you for a minute."

"Hey, Danielle, we heard about Jolene," Ian said after he took the phone from Lily.

"Crazy, isn't it?"

"Kelly said Adam was almost arrested, but you helped him out," Ian said.

"I suppose I did. Poor Marie was really freaked. But we straightened it out quickly. I suppose Joe told Kelly about the bottle?"

"Yes. I was wondering, what does Hillary think about all this?" Ian asked.

"Hillary? In what way?"

"I just thought she might be down at the police station, asking questions. Checking out the crime scene. Going all Jessica Fletcher."

"Why would she do that? As far as I know, she's been holed up in her room since last night, working on her new book."

"I just figured, with her history, she'd be in the middle of things."

"Her history, in what way?" Danielle asked.

"You haven't read her books, have you?"

Danielle glanced up at the ceiling, imagining Hillary in her room on the second floor, busily working on her new book. "No, but please keep that to yourself. I keep sidestepping that question. I need to read one of her books in case someone comes out and asks me in front of her."

"Every Hillary Hemingway interview I've read or watched, she's asked if her stories are based on real events—which she continually denies. I've read a couple interviewers who've come out and called her a liar. Of course, her fans don't care. They love her. She has loyal fans."

"I would imagine most authors steal their ideas from real life. So what does this have to do with Jolene?"

"I just figured, with a murder in such close proximity, she'd be out there soaking up story fodder for future books."

"From how she's been glued to her typewriter, I think she already has her next book worked out."

"WHAT'S THIS ABOUT A TATTOO?" Walt asked when Danielle was finally off the phone.

"Lily finally did it. She's making the tattoo hers."

Walt understood what Danielle was talking about. After kidnapping Lily, in his attempt to make the world believe the comatose young woman was his niece Isabella, Stoddard Gusarov had Lily's arm tattooed—a dragon tattoo exactly like the one his late niece had worn.

Lily had contemplated removing the tattoo, but because of the ink used, the painful process would leave her arm severely scarred. Instead of removal, Lily decided to make the tattoo hers by adding additional artwork.

"I'm curious to see it. But I still can't get used to how women of your generation mark up their bodies."

"Times have changed."

"So you keep reminding me," Walt said as he followed Danielle from the kitchen to the hallway, with Sadie trailing behind them.

They made their way to the parlor, where they found Max dozing on the sofa. Danielle promptly picked up the feline and put him on her lap as she sat down. Max yawned and opened his eyes.

Spying the cat on Danielle's lap, Sadie rushed to the sofa and nosed the feline, only to be greeted by a scolding swat of a paw across her nose. Uninjured, as no claws were involved, Sadie gave another sniff, endured another swat, and then curled up on the floor by Danielle's feet.

"So tell me about today—what you know about the murder. Did you see her spirit?" Walt asked.

"Yes, I did. But she didn't talk to me. In fact, she ignored me." Absently, Danielle scratched under Max's chin. He closed his eyes and began to purr.

"Are you saying she hasn't warmed up to you in death?" Walt chuckled.

"More like I don't even exist. But she tried awful hard to get MacDonald's attention. She showed him where her rings were."

"Rings?" Walt frowned.

"Whoever killed Jolene hit her over the head with a wine bottle. They were under the pier. He…or she…took off Jolene's rings. She wore a diamond ring on every finger, even her thumbs. The killer dumped the rings off the end of the pier. We figure he did that because he didn't want to be caught with her jewelry, but had to take them so the police would think it was a robbery. Unbeknownst to the killer, the rings got tangled up in some fish netting that was stuck to the side of the pier. They recovered nine of her rings. The chief assumes one of the rings didn't make it into the netting and is probably at the bottom of the water under the pier. I think it's possible the killer kept one ring as a souvenir."

Walt stared blankly at Danielle.

"What is it?" she asked.

"No…the killer didn't keep the tenth ring," Walt said in a low voice.

"Why do you say that?" Danielle frowned.

"I think our mystery writer is the killer."

NINE

"What are you talking about?" Danielle watched Walt from her place on the parlor sofa.

Agitated, he paced the room. The jacket of his gray three-piece suit suddenly vanished—as did his tie—leaving him wearing just his vest with his white shirt—its sleeves now rolled up (they hadn't been a moment earlier)—and his slacks, socks and black dress shoes.

"What you just told me." Walt stopped pacing and turned to face Danielle. "All of that, Jolene getting killed under the pier, being hit with a wine bottle, having her rings removed. I didn't know the rings landed in a net, just that the killer tossed them off the pier. And I didn't know it was Jolene, just some older woman."

"What do you mean you knew the killer tossed the rings off the pier? How would you have known that? And why would you accuse Hillary of being the killer?"

"Last night, I read all that—everything you just told me—up in Hillary's room." Walt started pacing again.

Perplexed, Danielle frowned, considering Walt's words. She looked up at him. "Please sit down. You're making me dizzy."

In the next instant Walt was sitting on the chair facing Danielle, a lit cigar now in his hand.

"Okay, run this by me again. You were in Hillary's room last night?"

"I know you don't like me going into the guests' rooms, but I saw she was still up when I went to the attic last night. I was curious to see if she was writing."

"You know I hate it when you go into the guests' bedrooms. She could have been getting dressed or something, and that's just so creepy. I'd hate to think of a ghost lurking around in my room while I'm taking my clothes off. Couldn't you have just listened for the typewriter?"

"I suppose I could have, but that's hardly the point right now," Walt snapped.

"What is your point, and why would you make some crazy accusation about Hillary being the killer?"

"I think she killed Jolene."

"She didn't even know Jolene."

"Danielle, listen to me, and forget for a moment I broke your rule about invading a guest's privacy."

Danielle let out a sigh and leaned back in the sofa, crossing her legs while folding her arms over her chest. "I'm listening."

"When I went into her room last night, she was completely dressed in a flannel nightgown, from her chin to her toes. And trust me, if I decide to become a ghostly peeping tom, hers is not the room I would invade."

"I didn't say you went in there with prurient intent, it's just that—"

"Yes, yes. I understand," Walt said impatiently. "When I went into her room, she was writing on a legal pad of paper. By the looks of her room, it was not her only legal pad."

"What do you mean?"

"There was paper strewn all over the place. She'd fill up a page, rip it off, toss it to the floor, and then write some more."

Danielle shrugged. "So? What does this have to do with her being the killer? Sounds to me like she was getting all her ideas down. She did say she'd been experiencing writer's block, and it suddenly ended."

"I read some of what she'd written."

"I imagine for Hillary she'd be more offended knowing you peeked at her notes rather than peeking up her nighty."

Walt scowled. "I may be dead, but even suggesting I'd want to peek up her nighty makes me want to kill myself."

"That's not nice," Danielle scolded.

"She's old enough to be my grandmother."

"You mean granddaughter," Danielle teased.

"Do you want to hear this or not?"

"I'm sorry. It's just been a long day, and I'm getting loopy. But Hillary did say she considered it bad luck to tell people about her storyline when she's early into a project."

"Her story is Jolene's."

"Jolene's? What do you mean Jolene's?"

"Everything you told me about the murder—even the rings being tossed off the pier—I already knew all that because Hillary had written about it. I read it. Her next book is about Jolene's murder."

"That's impossible. When did you read her notes? This morning?"

"I told you, last night. Before I went up to the attic."

Danielle shook her head. "No. That's impossible. You know how you are with time. I bet it was this morning. Hillary probably went out for an early morning walk, stopped by the pier, saw all the commotion, and then came back here and wrote down everything she had overheard and seen."

"If that's true, why didn't she tell you she'd been to the pier this morning and seen the crime scene? I was there when Joanne told her about the murder. She pretended she knew nothing about it. In fact, she hasn't left the house since she got up this morning."

"She did say she doesn't like discussing what she's working on. Ian suggested she writes about real-life murders, but never admits her ideas come from real life. You have to be wrong about her leaving the house."

"Danielle, did Joanne arrive before you left this morning or after?"

"Before, you know that. She prepared breakfast. You sat there and watched us eat."

"Didn't you tell me you discovered Jolene's rings—the ones tossed off the pier—after Jolene's spirit showed you were to find them?"

"Yes, but technically, she showed MacDonald. But he couldn't see her."

"And until then, what did everyone think had happened to the rings?"

"That the killer had them. So?"

"Danielle, I may sometimes get confused about time, but I know

I read Hillary's notes before Joanne arrived this morning—before you ever found those rings. Before anyone knew the killer had tossed them off the pier. As I said, Hillary was wearing her nightgown. She wasn't wearing a nightgown when she came down for breakfast this morning, was she?"

Danielle opened her mouth to say something, but closed it again. She sat quietly on the sofa, considering all that Walt was telling her. "You're saying Hillary wrote about the murder before it happened?"

"Or minutes after. Do you know when Jolene was killed?"

"I'm not sure. I know Jolene stopped in Pier Café about an hour before it closed. I'm pretty sure it closes at midnight. If so, she was killed sometime after eleven. Exactly what time, I don't know."

"I know it was around midnight when Hillary came home last night."

"Came home? She went out last night? When I went to bed, she was watching television in the living room. She didn't say anything about going out."

"After you went to bed last night, Hillary left the house. She was gone for a couple hours. I was watching television in here when she got back. I know it was a little before midnight because I was watching a movie—it was almost over. It ended at midnight. I still don't know the killer's identity."

"I thought you just said it was Hillary?"

Walt shook his head. "I was talking about the movie I was watching. I was just about to find out who the killer was when Hillary came home. When she finally went upstairs—after making me miss the end of the movie—I stayed down here for a while flipping through the channels. When I went upstairs an hour or so later, I noticed the light on in her room, and that's when I went in and read some of what she wrote."

"That's just a creepy coincidence."

"I hardly think it's a coincidence."

"It has to be," Danielle insisted. "I can't imagine that nice little old lady killed Jolene in cold blood."

"Perhaps she just witnessed the murder and wrote about it. According to what she wrote, the killer was a man."

"And not report the murder? Just come back here and start using it as—what is it Ian calls it? Oh—story fodder."

Walt shrugged. "I just know what I read."

They sat in silence for a few minutes, each lost in his or her private thoughts. Finally, Danielle looked up at Walt and asked, "When I mentioned the rings being tossed over the pier, why did you say the killer didn't keep the tenth ring?"

"Because according to Hillary's notes, after the killer removed Jolene's rings—although she does not refer to the victim by name—she wrote that the killer put all the rings into his pocket. He goes to the end of the pier, throws the rings into the ocean, and then discovers one ring still in the pocket, which he then throws off the pier."

Danielle shivered. "That is so creepy."

"I don't see how this can be a coincidence. Under the pier—a wine bottle—ten rings—the killer gets rid of the rings. No, if Hillary wasn't involved in the murder, at the very least she witnessed it."

"You said she wrote all this on a notepad? I thought she typed her stories?"

"She probably does. What I read weren't lines from a book—they were notes. Ideas, thoughts. Perhaps part of her creative process."

Danielle stood up.

"Where are you going?"

"Upstairs to talk to Hillary."

"Do you think that's a good idea? Perhaps you should instead talk to the chief."

"I'll talk to him tomorrow. But I need more. If I call him now, he could interview her, but I doubt she'll admit she witnessed a murder and failed to report it."

"He could read what she wrote."

"I seriously doubt he'd be able to obtain a search warrant to look through her notes or read the manuscript she's working on."

"It's your house," Walt reminded her. "You can give him permission."

Danielle wrinkled her nose. "I don't know about that. I don't think I've the legal right to let the police search my guests' private property. I'd probably end up getting sued, and if it was illegal, he couldn't use anything he found anyway."

"What are you going to do?"

"I don't know. Wing it for now, I suppose. But you can come with me and be my bodyguard. Although I should be safe as long as Hillary doesn't have any bottles of wine up in her room."

TEN

Before heading upstairs, Danielle stopped in the kitchen, placed a slice of chocolate cake on a small plate, and poured a glass of cold milk.

"You're eating cake now?" Walt asked. "I thought you were going to talk to Hillary."

"This isn't for me. I have to have some reason to interrupt her writing."

Walt silently followed Danielle from the kitchen and up the stairs to the second floor. When they got to Hillary's door, Danielle juggled the glass of milk and small plate in one hand while using her free hand to knock on the door.

"Come in," Hillary's voice called out.

"I thought you might need a little nourishment," Danielle told her when she entered the room, carrying the cake and milk.

"Oh, chocolate cake!" Hillary said brightly, turning from the small desk where her antiquated typewriter sat. "That's so sweet of you!"

Danielle smiled, set the plate of cake and glass of milk on the desk, and glanced around the room. She spied a stack of yellow sheets of paper sitting on the corner of the bed. Cursive handwriting filled the top page of the stack, but from where Danielle stood, she couldn't read what was written.

"This cake is so moist," Hillary said after taking her first bite. "I love chocolate."

Danielle nodded to the stack of papers. "Do you write out your story before typing it?"

Hillary glanced to the papers and then shook her head. "No. But writing my ideas out by hand, it seems to get my creative juices flowing. If I have writer's block, it can help."

"You mentioned your writer's block ended."

"Yes, it certainly has!" Hillary cheerfully announced. "Last night this story just came to me, and I grabbed my pad of paper and just started jotting down notes. Before I knew it, I had worked out my plot. At least the important parts."

"How did you get your idea for this story?" Danielle asked, still standing.

Hillary took a sip of milk before saying, "It just came to me. Like they always do. I guess I just have a wild imagination."

"Where does this story take place? I know you don't like to talk about your work when you first begin writing, but I thought perhaps you could tell me at least that."

Hillary set the glass of milk back on the desk and smiled up at Danielle. "Well, you did bring me up this delicious piece of cake, so I suppose I can at least tell you that. But I don't think it will be much of a surprise. My story will take place in a little town just like Frederickport. Of course, I'll give it another name, make it a fictional place. I don't like to write about real locations." Hillary took another bite of the cake and then another.

"Why is that?"

"For one thing, people are always trying to say my stories are based on real events—which they aren't. They come from my imagination. The minute I use a real location, I'll have to be careful what I write about my characters or someone will insist I've based those on real people from the town."

"Since you're a murder mystery author and your next story is taking place in a town based on Frederickport, I don't suppose your victim gets killed under the pier. Now that would be a little creepy."

Hillary set her fork on her now empty plate and looked up at Danielle. "Why is that, dear?"

Danielle shrugged. "Well, that's where poor Jolene—the woman who was killed last night—was murdered. Under the pier."

"Really? I thought Joanne said she was murdered on the beach."

"Yeah, but under the pier." Danielle studied Hillary.

"You know what it says in Ecclesiastics," Hillary said brightly.

"Ecclesiastics? Umm…no…what?"

"There really is nothing new under the sun. Which means all stories have already been told. So it's not unusual for a fictional murder mystery to have some similarities to a real-life case. It doesn't mean the author borrowed from the real-life events."

Hillary picked up her empty plate and glass and handed them to Danielle. "This was really sweet of you, dear, but I really need to get back to work."

Reluctantly, Danielle took the plate and glass. She glanced over to the pile of papers on the bed before leaving the room with Walt.

"EXACTLY WHAT DID THAT ACCOMPLISH?" Walt asked as he followed Danielle back down the stairs.

"Nothing really. I was hoping to have more to tell the chief," Danielle whispered.

"Are you going to say something to him?"

"I have to. I'd love to get my hands on her notes first. But I don't see that happening."

"I could probably help you there," Walt suggested.

Danielle shook her head. "No. If you spirited away the pages she wrote about Jolene's murder—"

"Spirited away?" Walt laughed.

"Isn't that what you'd be doing?" Danielle entered the kitchen and set the dirty dishes in the sink before turning to face Walt.

"I suppose so."

"Anyway, that would practically be stealing them from her room, and all it would do is verify what you said you read. The chief couldn't use them to force Hillary to admit she knew something about the murder, not if they were obtained illegally. So what's the point?" Danielle glanced nervously at the kitchen door leading to the hallway.

"I suppose you're right."

Danielle turned back to the sink. "I just can't believe she had something to do with the murder. It just feels all wrong—in spite of what you read."

"Perhaps I overreacted," Walt suggested. "The more likely

scenario, she witnessed the murder and, for whatever reason, decided not to come forward."

Turning on the water faucet, Danielle began rinsing the dirty dishes. "If she did witness the murder, I find her attitude extremely bizarre…and creepy."

"So what are you going to do?"

"Call the chief. See if I can go back down there and talk to him before he goes home for the night."

When Danielle got off the phone fifteen minutes later, she told Walt her talk with the chief would have to wait; he had left the office for the night and was not answering his cellphone.

MACDONALD SPIED Steve Klein's car parked down the street from the bank, at the diner. Instead of going home, MacDonald pulled behind the bank manager's vehicle and parked. Inside the restaurant, he found Steve sitting alone at a booth. When the waitress greeted him and asked if he would like a table, he waved her away and headed toward the bank manager.

"You're a hard man to get ahold of," MacDonald said when he reached Steve's booth.

Steve, who was just about to take a bite of his burger, set it down on his plate and smiled up at MacDonald. "Sorry I didn't get back to you, but it's been a crazy day."

Without asking, MacDonald took a seat at the booth. "I've had a crazy day today too."

Sheepishly, Steve picked his burger up and, before taking a bite, said, "Yeah, Jolene. I can't believe that."

"I understand you saw her last night."

"Yes. At Pier Café. I would have gotten back to you after you called, but it really has been a crazy day at the bank, and I figured you wanted to talk to me because I was at the pier last night, but I really didn't see anything that might be of help." He took another bite of the burger.

"Why don't you let me be the judge of that."

Steve picked up his beer and took a drink. "Okay. What do you want to know?"

MacDonald started to say something and then paused a moment and then asked, "Why are you eating alone?"

Steve smiled. "The wife is in California, visiting her sister. I'm batching it."

"Ahh. Pier Café last night, diner tonight?"

"Pretty much. The wife is always nagging me about eating red meat. When she's home, all we eat is fish and chicken." Steve took another bite of the burger.

"Carla told me Jolene talked to everyone who was in the diner last night."

"Yeah." Steve set his burger on his plate and picked up his napkin. He wiped off his mouth and looked over at MacDonald. "She stopped by my table. Didn't stay long."

"Carla said she wasn't with anyone last night."

Steve shook his head. "No. She came in alone. Didn't stay long. But she seemed to know everyone in the diner. I noticed her going around the tables, saying hello to everyone."

"Did you notice if she argued with anyone last night?"

"Argued?" Steve frowned.

"When she went around talking to everyone, was it all friendly? Or did you notice anyone who might have been unhappy with Jolene?"

"You don't think someone who was in Pier Café last night murdered her, do you?"

"I'm just trying to cover my bases."

"From what I understand, Jolene was mugged last night. I heard her rings were taken. I can't believe someone from Frederickport, someone Jolene knew, killed her. Not for her jewelry."

"Jolene wasn't an easy person to get along with."

Steve let out a snort and said, "Tell me about it." He picked up his burger and took another bite.

"What can I get you, Chief?" a waitress asked. She held a pitcher of water. MacDonald hadn't noticed her approach the table.

"Some water would be good. I won't be eating, just keeping Steve company while he eats."

She smiled and filled the empty glasses on the table.

When they were alone again, the chief asked, "You have a problem with Jolene?"

"Problem?" Steve shrugged. "She was on the museum board with me. Millie thought she'd make a good replacement for the board member we lost."

"She didn't?"

"I think her attitude made Danielle Boatman change her mind about donating the Thorndike emerald. We're a nonprofit, and we can't afford to be alienating any wealthy members."

"I heard something about that."

Steve shrugged. "I suspect Jolene's attitude toward Danielle was out of jealousy. Danielle has money, and Jolene had lost hers."

"I heard she was having money problems."

"She came to me for a loan. She was about to lose her house."

"That bad?"

Steve nodded. "Yeah. Her estate was tangled up with Renton's. Money she had loaned to the law practice. Whoever wrote up the loan agreement didn't protect Jolene's interests."

"Renton maybe?"

Steve shrugged again. "Doug was still alive back then. It doesn't matter now. Jolene's dead. I imagine her daughter will have to sort it all out."

"You said she came to you for a loan? I assume your answer was no?"

Steve picked up his beer and took a sip before answering. "There was no way I could give her a loan. She simply didn't have the assets or the income."

"Last night, did you see who left after Jolene?"

Steve downed the rest of his beer. "That would probably be me. I don't remember anyone else leaving the restaurant after Jolene. But I could be wrong." He picked up what remained of his hamburger.

"When you went outside, did you see Jolene? Maybe walking on the pier?"

"When I went outside, she was nowhere around."

"Did you see anyone on the pier?"

"There were a couple of guys fishing."

"Do you know who they were?"

He shook his head. "I really didn't pay any attention, and there wasn't much light. Might have been someone I knew, maybe not."

"And you never heard anything suspicious?"

"No. Nothing. Like I told you before, that's why I didn't think it was a big deal if I didn't get right back to you. Nothing really to tell."

ELEVEN

The next morning, Chief MacDonald sat at his office desk, reading the newspaper and drinking his coffee, when he heard a knock at his open door. He looked up and saw Joe Morelli standing in the doorway.

"I see you're reading the paper," Joe said as he walked into the office and took a seat.

MacDonald shook his head and slammed the paper on the desk. "Can't we ever keep anything out of the damn paper?"

"It's—"

"Don't say it!" MacDonald snapped. "If I hear *it's a small town* one more time, I'm going to do something we'll all regret!"

"Well, it is," Joe said with a shrug.

"How did the paper find out about Jolene's rings?"

"Come on, Chief, there were people on the pier when you recovered them. You didn't really expect to keep that under wraps."

"It would have been nice. At least for a while. Now the killer knows we're onto him." MacDonald downed the last of his coffee.

"I wish they could have found something at Jolene's house. Anything."

MacDonald set his empty cup on the desk and shoved it to the side. "There really wasn't much in the house. She had hardly any furniture and relatively few personal items. It didn't take them that long to go through it."

Joe frowned. "I don't understand that."

"I called Melony to tell her we were going to go through her mother's house. She told me her mom had practically emptied the house when she moved to New York. I guess she sold everything before she moved back. Might have figured shipping it all a second time was too expensive."

"I know when the guys first got over there, they wondered if someone had been in the house because the back door was unlocked," Joe noted. "And then there was hardly anything inside."

"It's entirely possible the killer got into the house and removed any incriminating evidence before we arrived. I know some of the longtime residents never lock their doors, and it's possible Jolene left that back door unlocked. There were some smudged fingerprints on the doorknob, but it wasn't wiped clean," the chief explained.

"If the killer figured we wouldn't be looking for someone Jolene knew, he—or she—may not have even considered going through her house, looking for any possible connection. But now—"

"Which is why I've someone keeping an eye on her place," MacDonald said. "And what I don't want is for the killer to go after someone he thinks might be a witness now that everyone knows the killer probably dumped Jolene's rings off the pier."

"Like the fishermen who were on the pier when he tossed the rings," Joe suggested.

"We need to figure out who they were and quick, before the killer does. And he has the advantage; he probably saw who they were. If he's afraid one of the fishermen can identify him as the person who tossed something off the pier, we might have more dead bodies to deal with."

The office phone began to ring. MacDonald answered it. When he hung up, he said, "Pete Rogers is here. I'm going to go ahead and talk to him in my office. Check with Brian and see if he's made any progress tracking down whoever was on that pier when Jolene was murdered."

"SORRY I WASN'T able to come in yesterday," Pete said when he walked into MacDonald's office. The two men briefly shook hands and then each took a seat, MacDonald behind the desk and Pete facing it.

Peter Rogers had moved to Frederickport thirty years earlier with his new bride. Just six months after exchanging vows, his wife was diagnosed with a terminal illness. She did not make it to their first wedding anniversary. In all those years, he had never remarried.

"I understand. How was Portland?"

"It was fine. Just a doctor's appointment. When your office called me, I was shocked to hear about Jolene."

"I understand you saw her that night in Pier Café."

"Yes. I stopped in late to grab something to eat."

"Did you talk to her?"

"Yeah. She stopped by my table. Said hello. We didn't really have a long conversation."

"I understand she made her rounds, chatting with the other diners. Did you happen to overhear anything, maybe a disagreement? Anything."

Pete shifted uncomfortably in his seat. "You know, Chief, I didn't really think anything about it yesterday. But when I read the paper this morning and heard the killer threw Jolene's rings off the pier—that it probably wasn't a mugging…"

"Did you see something, hear something?"

"I'm sure it really is nothing…" He shook his head, not sounding convinced.

"What?" the chief urged.

"Steve Klein from the bank was sitting in the booth across from me when Jolene first came in. She stopped and said something to him. I don't know what she said, but when she walked away from his table, if looks could kill."

"What do you mean?"

"The minute she turned her back to him and walked away from his table, his smile disappeared, and he gave her the most hateful look. It was pretty obvious to me he couldn't stand the woman."

"Was there anything else?" MacDonald asked.

Pete let out a sigh. "After I left the diner, I saw him again. He was walking up from the beach. He'd left Pier Café a few minutes after Jolene. I figured he was out for a walk and decided to come back up on the pier."

"Do you remember what time you left the diner?"

Pete shook his head. "I didn't really pay any attention to the time. Sorry."

"Do you think you left the restaurant maybe fifteen minutes after Jolene, thirty minutes, forty?"

"After Jolene?" Pete shrugged. "Like I said, I didn't pay attention to the time. Maybe thirty minutes, more or less."

"When you saw Steve on the pier, after leaving the restaurant, did he say anything to you?"

"No. I don't think he saw me. To be honest, he seemed preoccupied. I was standing in the shadows; I doubt he would have seen me had he looked my way. But I was watching him. He kept looking around like he was nervous. I thought it was odd."

"Where did he go?"

"I assume to the end of the pier, since that's where he was heading." Pete shrugged.

"Did you see him again?"

Pete shook his head. "No. I went to use the bathroom on the pier. When I came out, I hung around for a while before walking home. I didn't see him again."

"Did you happen to notice who was fishing on the pier that night?"

"There were a couple of fishermen, but I don't know who they were."

"Did you see Jolene again after you left the restaurant?"

Pete shook his head again. "No."

"You said Jolene stopped by your table."

"Yes. After she left Steve's table, she stopped by mine."

"Did she say anything, maybe mention anything about meeting someone later?"

"No. She just stopped, said hi."

"Did you know Jolene very well?"

"I've known her for years. Her husband was my wife's attorney; he was one of the first people I met when I first moved to town. We used to do a lot socially when Doug was alive."

"So you and Jolene were friends?"

"Yes, but after Doug died, Jolene left town, and we really didn't keep in touch. I've run into her a few times since she moved back, but honestly…"

When Pete didn't finish his sentence, the chief asked, "Honestly what?"

Pete shrugged. "She really wasn't the same Jolene I remembered. I don't recall her ever being so—bitter. She just wasn't pleasant to be around. Of course, one of the first times I saw her again since she moved back was after the *Eva Aphrodite* washed up on the beach, and the historical society had the ridiculous notion to keep it there as some tourist attraction. I suppose I didn't hold back when expressing my opinion. I sure as hell did not want to look at that eyesore from my back patio. That thing would have destroyed local property values. But fortunately it seemed to take care of itself."

"Did you notice anyone else milling around the pier that night?"

"Not that I noticed. Just a couple of fishermen and Klein."

"And you don't recall Jolene acting strange—maybe even anxious? Nervous?"

Pete let out another snort. "She was acting strange, for Jolene. But not anxious or nervous. Like I said, since she's moved back, I don't think anyone would accuse her of being Miss Sunshine. But that night, she seemed particularly happy—giddy maybe. Upbeat."

"I don't think her evening turned out quite as she expected," MacDonald muttered.

Pete let out a sigh and shook his head. "No, I don't imagine it did. This is just a horrible thing. I can't believe it happened here, in Frederickport. Seems like we've had more than our share of tragedies this past year."

"Is there anything else you can remember about that night?"

"I really can't think of what else to tell you. Other than noticing Steve's reaction to Jolene and seeing him on the pier later, I can't think of anything else that might be helpful. But in fairness to Steve, his wasn't the only eye roll I noticed that night."

MacDonald frowned. "What do you mean?"

"After Jolene stopped by to say hello, she continued to make her rounds, stopping by each table. No one seemed particularly welcoming, and when she moved on, the expressions weren't much different from Klein's—just not as severe. Of course, he was the only one I noticed hanging around on the pier."

DANIELLE PASSED Pete Rogers in the hall of the Frederickport Police Department on her way to Chief MacDonald's office. She said a brief hello to her neighbor and then continued on her way.

"I passed Pete in the hallway," Danielle said when she entered MacDonald's office, closing the door behind her.

"He was at Pier Café the night Jolene was murdered. We tried to talk to him yesterday, but he was in Portland." MacDonald settled back in his chair while he absently rapped the end of his pen against the desktop. "This thing just keeps getting stranger."

"Tell me about it." Danielle plopped down in a chair and let out a sigh.

"Unless you've seen Jolene's ghost, I really don't have time to chat. Sorry, Danielle."

"I haven't seen Jolene's ghost again—but I have something stranger to tell you."

"Stranger than seeing a ghost?"

"Actually, this does involve a ghost, Walt. And what he tells me he saw."

"Does it have something to do with my murder?" he asked wearily.

"Yes. But I'm afraid it's going to raise more questions than answer any."

He tossed the pen aside and said, "Just what I need!"

Danielle then went onto explain everything Walt had told her—about Hillary going for a walk the evening of Jolene's murder, returning late that night, and then Walt reading the notes for her new book.

When Danielle finished passing on Walt's information, she and MacDonald sat quietly for a few moments. Finally, MacDonald said, "I knew Ms. Hemingway was at the café that night."

"You did? She never mentioned it to me."

"Carla told us when we first interviewed her after finding Jolene's body. In fact, she was on my list of people to interview. If she wrote all that, she must have witnessed the murder. But why hasn't she come forward and said anything?"

"The entire thing is bizarre. I don't know Hillary very well, but I liked her—at least until Walt told me what he'd read. I know she's one of Ian's favorite authors; he's quite taken with her. But this. I just can't understand how anyone can just witness a murder and then walk away and not report it. Maybe Jolene was still alive when the killer left her on the beach. Maybe she could have been saved."

"Unfortunately, it's not all that uncommon for someone to

witness a crime and say nothing. It happens all the time," MacDonald said.

"I know, but a high-profile person like Hillary Hemingway? And if Walt's right, she's planning to use Jolene's murder in her next book. That is…well, macabre."

"People are strange."

She let out a weary sigh. "No kidding. Now what?"

"I know who's next on my list. I was going to have Brian interview her, but I think I better."

"Yeah, it would be sort of difficult to explain to Brian about Hillary's notes—which I didn't read, but Walt did."

"If it's okay with you, Danielle, I think I'll stop by Marlow House and interview her there. If I call her up and ask her to come to the station, then she'll have time to think about what she wants to say."

"What if she denies seeing anything? Unless I can get my hands on her notes, we can't very well tell her Walt was in her room, looking over her shoulder."

"Unfortunately, I expect her to deny witnessing the murder. Considering who she is, it wouldn't be good for her public image if it got out that she witnessed a murder taking place and failed to report it."

"What if she didn't witness the murder?" Danielle asked.

"Are you suggesting Walt exaggerated what he read in her room?" he asked.

Danielle shook her head. "No, on the contrary. What if she was the one who murdered Jolene? Maybe she didn't witness the murder, but was the killer."

"I thought you liked Ms. Hemingway. Now you suggest she might be the killer."

"I liked Clarence Renton when I first met him, and look how that turned out."

TWELVE

Easing the attic door open, Lily sniffed the air. The distinct scent of sweet cigar smoke drifted out from the room. Stepping into the attic, she closed the door behind her and glanced around.

"Walt, are you in here?" she whispered.

In response, the spotting scope spun around on its tripod and then came to a stop.

"I'll take that as a yes," Lily said as she approached the attic window. "I should have gone with Dani to the police station. I wish she'd hurry up and get home. I'm dying to hear what the chief said." Lily looked outside. Across the street the blinds to Ian's front window were open. She assumed he was somewhere in the house.

Lily looked to where she imagined Walt stood. "Hillary's still in her room. I can hear her typing." Looking back out the window, she leaned against the windowpane and let out a sigh. "Who uses a typewriter these days? Do you realize what a pain that would be, no word processor?"

Lily stood at the window a few minutes, looking out. "It's not much fun talking with you when you never answer me."

The spotting scope twirled once and stopped, barely missing Lily. She giggled and turned around, now leaning back against the edge of the windowsill. "I suppose that's something." Lily smiled.

Pushing away from the windowsill, she walked to the sofa bed. It hadn't been made out into a bed since their one attic guest over

Christmas week. Lily sat down and crossed one leg over the opposing knee. "You know, this is killing me not saying something to Ian. But what could I tell him?"

There was no response.

Lily sighed and leaned back, staring up to the ceiling. "After Dani left this morning, I looked through the trash."

The room was quiet.

"I was hoping Hillary might have tossed some of her notes, and then I could show them to Ian. But even if I find them now, he'll just assume she wrote them after hearing about the murder in the paper this morning, and what will that prove?"

Lily lifted her head and glanced to the window. "Walt, do you really think Hillary was there when Jolene was murdered?" The spotting scope rocked gently up and down—like a nod.

"Hmmm, I never knew spotting scope could be its own language. Do you think Hillary was involved with the murder or just witnessed it?"

There was no response.

"I have to assume you don't have an opinion on that," Lily said.

A persistent knock came at the window and then stopped.

Lily turned and faced the window. "What? Is that supposed to be Morse code or something?"

There was another knock.

Lily frowned. "I don't know Morse code."

The spotting scope twirled again, and when it stopped, it was pointing out the window. Lily watched as it tilted to one side. The rim around its lens gently rapped the glass pane before the instrument settled back quietly on its tripod.

Jumping up from the sofa, Lily dashed to the window and looked outside. A police car had just parked in front of the house, and she spied Danielle's red Ford Flex turning into the side driveway.

"Oh, you're trying to tell me Dani is back. Sorry, I guess I can be dense."

The spotting scope moved again, nodding up and down.

Lily glared at where she imagined Walt stood. "You don't have to agree with me." Turning her attention back to the window, she watched as MacDonald got from the police car and started toward the walkway leading to the front door.

"I wonder why the chief came back with her. You think he's

going to take Hillary in?"

IF THE PROSPECT of an interview with the police chief was making Hillary Hemingway nervous, Walt thought she was doing an excellent job concealing her emotions. In his opinion, she looked more grandmotherly than like a bestselling mystery author. But he had never known a mystery author before, so he wasn't certain what one was supposed to look like.

Walt sat on the edge of the small desk in the parlor and watched as Hillary settled onto the sofa. MacDonald took a seat on the chair facing her.

"What's this about, Chief MacDonald?" Hillary asked in a calm tone.

"I understand you were at Pier Café when Jolene Carmichael was murdered."

"Was that the woman's name?" Hillary asked. "Now that you mention it, I think Danielle told me…or did I read it in the paper?"

"I was under the impression you knew her." MacDonald studied Hillary's expression.

"The woman who was murdered?" Hillary shook her head. "Not that I know of, although the name is familiar, but then I believe Danielle mentioned it. I'm not very good with names." She flashed him a smile.

"You knew all about her murder," Walt scoffed.

"According to witnesses, when she came into Pier Café before her murder, she stopped and talked to you."

Hillary gasped. "The woman who was murdered was in the restaurant that night?"

"Yes, and she stopped at your table. You two exchanged words."

"Oh my, was that nice woman the one who was killed?" Hillary paused a moment, her forehead drawn into a frown. Finally, she said, "Now that you mention it, there was something familiar about her. I don't remember thinking it at the time, but now that you mention it…"

"But you talked to her?"

"Yes. She stopped by my table. Asked me what kind of pie I was eating."

"Pie?"

"She asked me if it was good, what kind it was. I assumed she was thinking of getting pie herself and wanted to know if I liked the piece I was eating. Oh my, you say she's the one who was killed?"

"So you didn't know Jolene Carmichael?"

"No. Not personally. She was the one who found those gold coins across the street, wasn't she?"

"Yes, that was her. So you never met Jolene before that evening at Pier Café?" the chief asked.

"Didn't I already answer that question? I haven't been in Frederickport long, and I haven't met that many people since I got here."

"Why were you at Pier Café that night?"

"Having pie. Didn't I just say that?" Hillary asked.

"It was rather late to be out alone, wasn't it? Or perhaps you weren't alone?" MacDonald studied Hillary.

"I suppose it was late, but I feel safe in Frederickport. Of course…now…now with there having been a murder, I suppose that was foolish of me."

"Can you tell me about that night?"

"Oh…of course. You're wondering if I saw anything. Anything that might help you solve the murder."

"Did you?"

"I suppose I might have seen something that I wasn't aware of seeing." Hillary leaned forward and flashed him a smile. "Something that might help you solve the murder. At least, that's how it works in my books." Hillary sat up straight again.

"Why don't you tell me what you remember about that night."

"I've been having the worst case of writer's block. That's why I decided to come to Frederickport and stay at Marlow House. I thought it might help get my creative juices flowing."

"Has it?"

Hillary smiled again. "I suppose it has. But it didn't work immediately. In fact, that's why I went out that night. I was frustrated, discouraged. Danielle had already gone to bed, and Lily was in Portland with Ian. I was bored—antsy. I tried watching some television. Finally, I decided to take a walk, clear my head."

Hillary leaned forward again, hands resting on her knees. "I wish I could tell you something that might help you, Chief. But I don't remember seeing anyone—or anything—on my walk down to the pier. In fact, I don't think any cars drove by. It was pretty quiet out."

"What happened once you reached the pier?"

"My first thought was to get some ice cream at that little shop down there. They make marvelous homemade ice cream, you know. But it was closed. So I decided to go into Pier Café instead. I really didn't talk to anyone in there, just the waitress who took my order and—well, your murder victim. But aside from our brief discussion over pie, that was the extent of our conversation. I'm sorry."

"What did you do after you left the restaurant?"

"Don't you want to know what happened in the restaurant?"

"I thought you just said you only had a brief conversation with Jolene and the waitress."

"Perhaps I saw your victim talking to someone. Or perhaps arguing with another customer—or the server. Maybe I saw someone follow her out of the restaurant."

The chief arched his brows. "Did you?"

Leaning back again, Hillary shook her head. "No. But shouldn't you be asking those types of questions? That's what I have my detectives ask. But no, I didn't notice anything like that. In fact, I hadn't even noticed her walk into the diner. I was reading and eating my pie when she approached me and asked what kind it was. She took a seat after that, and I went back to eating and reading. I didn't really notice her again, or when she left."

"You noticed something," Walt voiced to deaf ears.

"Tell me about when you left the restaurant."

Hillary shrugged. "I walked back here. Nothing much to tell."

"Did you go right home, or perhaps you walked down to the beach?"

"No. I left the restaurant and just came straight back here."

"Did you walk along the beach side of the street?" he asked.

"No. I crossed the street at the entrance of the pier and walked back on the sidewalk, on Marlow House's side of the street, not the beach side."

"You're not telling the truth. You were there. You saw everything," Walt grumbled.

"You didn't walk down the pier or on the beach?"

Hillary frowned. "Didn't I just say that?"

"When you left the restaurant, did you see anyone on the pier?"

"I noticed a couple fishermen. I think there might have been some other people on the pier, but I honestly wasn't paying attention. I'm sorry, Chief, I wish I could help you."

THIRTEEN

"She's upstairs in her room, typing away," Danielle said when she entered the parlor after Hillary ended her interview with the chief and went back upstairs. In the parlor, Danielle found Lily, MacDonald, and Walt.

"Just like I expected, she admitted seeing nothing," MacDonald said after Danielle closed the door behind her.

"She obviously saw something. There is no way she just happened to come up with a murder scene identical to what actually happened," Danielle said.

He shook his head. "I don't know what to tell you. I wish I could see what Walt actually read."

Walt narrowed his eyes at the chief. "Is he implying I might not have read what I claimed to have?"

"I don't think that's what he's implying," Danielle said.

"It's possible Walt read more into those notes than was actually there. He may be imagining similarities that are nothing more than explainable coincidences."

Danielle cringed and looked apologetically at Walt. "Or maybe that's what he's implying."

"Excuse me?" MacDonald glanced from Danielle to where he imagined Walt stood.

"Walt's pretty clear about what he read, Chief. The fact you don't believe him, well…" Danielle began.

"It's not that I don't believe him, Danielle. I'm sure he's sincere in what he thinks he read. But let's face it, Ms. Hemingway writes murder mysteries, and she came here to write her next novel. Frankly, it's no surprise to me she chose to use this setting in her book. We all knew she would be writing a murder mystery before Jolene was killed."

"What about her killer and the real killer both removing Jolene's rings?" Danielle asked.

"I can't honestly say Ms. Hemingway's killer removed Jolene's rings—but I see what you're saying. Fact is, when someone is murdered, it's common for the killer to remove anything of value."

"True, but for both killers to toss the valuables off the pier?" Lily asked.

MacDonald glanced at Lily. "That's one reason I'd like to read those notes myself. Maybe her killer tossed the weapon off the pier, not the rings."

"I know what I read!" Walt said angrily before disappearing.

"You've insulted Walt," Danielle said with a sigh. "He just left."

"I'm sorry. Without being able to read those notes myself, there's really nothing I have to go on. It's possible she did witness the crime. But I seriously doubt she was involved with the murder." He stood up. "And since I have a murder to solve, I need to get going."

"I think the whole thing's creepy," Lily said as she followed Danielle and the chief to the entry hall.

MacDonald paused at the front door a moment before exiting. He looked at Danielle. "Maybe you might consider taking a walk on the beach, perhaps you'll see Jolene again?"

"Or the killer," Lily reminded.

MacDonald opened the door. "My gut tells me this killer was after Jolene. But Lily is right. There is a killer out there, and I want you both to be careful."

SHE HATED TO FLY. But the sooner they got into the air, the sooner she could have a drink. That was one thing she liked about flying first class—they kept the beverages flowing. Shifting uncomfortably in the seat, she shoved her purse under the seat ahead of her and fastened her seatbelt. Fidgeting nervously, she wished the other passengers would step it up and get boarded so they could get off the ground, and she could get a cocktail.

Wringing her hands nervously, she stared out the side window. A moment later a male voice said, "Hello, neighbor."

Melony glanced to her immediate right and found herself staring into an incredible set of deep blue eyes.

"I guess this is my seat," the male passenger with the incredible blue eyes said as he took the place next to her. He flashed her a smile, showing off straight white teeth. Once seated, he extended a right hand in greeting, "I'm Chris. I guess we'll be flying together."

Melony wondered if she had been living in New York for too long, considering she wanted to recoil from the friendly greeting rather than embrace it. Unprepared for such a cheerful hello from a handsome stranger, she had been primed—and preferred—a quiet uninterrupted flight. The only interruption she wanted was when the steward brought her another cocktail.

Her first thought, *He has to be gay*. It wasn't that he was feminine looking—just the contrary. But in her experience a man this good looking was inevitably gay. Reluctantly, she accepted his brief handshake and watched as he settled into the seat next to her and buckled his seatbelt.

"I'm headed to Oregon, what about you?" he asked in a friendly tone after buckling his seat.

Without thought she responded, "Oregon." Her gaze swept over him. At first glance, she was so captivated by his eyes—that smile—that face—she hadn't really looked at what he wore. Now noting his clothes, she was fairly certain he was no New Yorker, not with those worn denim jeans and colorful T-shirt. He reminded her of a surfer—or a beach bum. *A beach bum riding in first class?*

He broke into a wide smile. "Then we'll be flying the entire way together, great." He settled back into his seat, his eyes still on her. "I take it this is a business trip for you?"

Melony frowned, "Umm…business? No, why do you ask that?"

Boldly, his eyes looked her up and down, taking in her silk business suit. "Not exactly vacation wear. Nice though." He smiled again.

"I take it this is a vacation for you?" she countered, without answering his question.

"I'm heading home now—but no, it wasn't a vacation. But I wrapped up business a little earlier than I expected, and I'm heading home a little earlier. Hope to surprise someone." He leaned back in his seat and smiled.

Glancing at his left hand, she didn't see a wedding ring. She almost asked if he had a girlfriend waiting at home. *Is that who he intends to surprise?* It might answer her gay question. From her experience, gay men tended to be more open about their sexual orientation these days. At least that was true in her circle of friends.

"You have a girlfriend you're surprising?" Melony asked.

He arched his brows and smiled over at her. "Girlfriend…no…"

Aha, I was right, he is gay! I can always tell.

"Maybe," he added.

Melony frowned. "Maybe?"

"I think I'd like her to be…maybe she already is." Chris let out a sigh.

"You don't know?"

Chris shrugged and then looked at Melony, studying her for a moment. "What about you? You traveling alone, or did you ditch your guy for first class?"

Melony smiled. "No, I'm traveling alone."

"So it is business?"

Melony glanced away and looked out the window. "In a way. Family business."

"Depending on the family, that can be good times or bad. Hope yours is good."

"Not particularly good. My mother just died. I'm going back to settle her estate."

Chris's smile immediately vanished. His hand reached out and briefly touched hers. "I'm sorry."

Melony shrugged and looked from the window back to Chris, who had just removed his hand from hers. "My mother and I weren't particularly close."

"I don't imagine that makes it any easier for you. Sometimes, it can make it harder."

Melony let out a sigh. "I suppose you're right."

"If you're settling her estate, I assume your father's not in the picture."

"He passed away a number of years ago."

"I'm sorry. Do you have any brothers or sisters waiting for you in Oregon?"

Melony shook her head. "No, it's just me. I'm an only child."

Chris smiled. "I'm an only child too. I think it would have been nice to have a brother or sister, but then when I see how some of my friends fight with their siblings, I think maybe I had the better deal."

"Are your parents still alive?"

Chris shook his head. "No, I lost them both."

"I'm sorry. I guess that makes us both orphans?" Melony said sadly.

"I suppose it does. Although, I once heard you're technically an orphan if you've lost just one parent."

"Interesting…I've been an orphan all this time and didn't realize it," Melony said dully, looking back out the window.

"So where in Oregon are you headed? Portland?"

"My first stop. But from there, I rent a car and drive to my mother's place a couple hours from Portland," Melony explained.

"Are you returning to your hometown?"

"Yeah, I suppose I am. It's where I grew up."

"Maybe you don't have siblings waiting for you, but I imagine you've lots of old friends there," Chris suggested.

"I really never kept in contact with anyone. It's been years since I've been back. I don't imagine I'll see any old friends while I'm there. I intend to take care of business and then head home."

"Not even at the funeral?" Chris asked.

"There won't be a funeral."

From the speaker the stewardess's voice blared, telling the passengers the plane was preparing to take off, but first she wanted everyone to make sure they were properly buckled up, and items securely stored, before explaining the flight's safety procedures.

FOURTEEN

Since he had been the one to talk to Pete Rogers, Chief MacDonald decided he would talk to Steve Klein himself instead of having Joe or Brian conduct the informal interrogation. After leaving Marlow House, he headed for the bank. Once there, the chief stopped at the desk of Susan Mitchell.

"What can I help you with, Chief?" Susan asked brightly.

He glanced from Susan to the teller windows. "I'm not used to seeing you out here. I thought Klein kept you tellers locked up."

Susan laughed and said primly, "I was promoted."

"Congratulations."

"So if you need a personal loan, you know who to come to."

"I'll remember that." MacDonald grinned. "Is Steve in? I saw his car out there."

"Yes, he's in his office, but he's with someone. He should be out in a minute. You want me to tell him you're here?"

"No, I'll wait."

Susan pointed to a chair by her desk. "You're welcome to wait here."

MacDonald smiled and took a seat. "Thanks."

Susan leaned toward MacDonald and said in a hushed voice, "It was just awful about Jolene Carmichael. Have you arrested anyone yet?"

He shook his head. "I'm afraid not."

Susan reached over to a stack of papers and gave them a pat. "I was just gathering up Jolene's paperwork. I guess I won't need it now."

"Paperwork?"

"For her loan. Well, for the loan she wanted." Lowering her voice, Susan glanced around the bank and then said in a whisper, "Jolene was trying to get a personal loan. Of course, Mr. Klein told me there was no way she could qualify. I thought it was so sad. I always heard how wealthy her family was, but the poor woman lost everything." Susan then added in a hasty whisper, "I would never talk about a client's business—not even one who just died—but you are the police chief and I assume you need to know everything about Jolene in order to find her killer. Maybe someone she owed money to killed her."

"Did she mention owing money to anyone?"

Susan shook her head. "No. But she seemed so desperate to get the loan. I just wondered if maybe it was a life-or-death situation for her. She wanted it so bad. Of course, Mr. Klein said there was no way. His loyalty is to the bank shareholders. I totally understand his position and respect him for it. That's why he's the bank manager. But still, I couldn't help but feel sorry for her."

"If she wasn't going to get a loan, why did you still have her loan papers sitting on your desk?"

Susan smiled. "One thing I can say for Mrs. Carmichael, she was persistent. She told me to keep her application on my desk because Mr. Klein would be giving her the loan, and if she had to fill out the forms again, she would not be happy with me." Susan then whispered, "I'll admit, she scared me a little."

"Jolene could be a formidable woman."

"Yes, she could. And frankly, I rather expected her to get her way. She seemed so sure of herself. But I certainly never expected this—that someone would kill her!"

TEN MINUTES later Chief MacDonald sat in Steve Klein's office with the door closed.

"I assume this is about Jolene again?"

"Yes. I have a few more questions."

"Certainly. However I can help."

MacDonald studied Klein's face, watching for the slightest change of expression. "The night of the murder, when Jolene stopped at your table, what did you talk about?"

Klein let out a sigh. "We really didn't have a conversation. She stopped by my table and told me she'd be seeing me in the morning about the loan."

"I thought you said you weren't going to give her the loan?"

"I wasn't. But Jolene wouldn't take no for an answer. I told her not to waste her or my time, that the answer would still be no."

"What did she say to that?"

"She smiled, said she would see me in the morning."

"What did you say?" MacDonald asked.

"I don't think I said anything. I just went back to eating my pie."

"Someone mentioned that when she left the table, you gave her a pretty dirty look when her back was turned."

Klein let out a sigh. "I didn't mean to. But it's very possible I did. She had been badgering me about that loan. She just wouldn't give up. I don't know how she expected to pay it back. She had no collateral, and her monthly income could barely cover her living expenses."

"It was that bad?"

Klein nodded. "I'm afraid so. When Renton's law firm toppled, it landed on Jolene."

"After you left the diner that night, where did you go?"

"Home."

"Did you go right home?" MacDonald asked.

"You mean immediately after leaving the diner? No. I walked around a bit, but then the wind started kicking up, so I decided to go home."

"Walking around? You mean on the beach, the pier?"

Steve shook his head. "I didn't go on the beach. But I did walk down the boardwalk a bit, then came back up on the pier. I didn't stay long. With the wind, I decided to call it a night."

"Someone mentioned they saw you walking up from the beach that night."

"They're mistaken. I certainly wouldn't be walking on the beach in the shoes I was wearing. Like I said, I walked down the boardwalk a bit that night. They probably assumed I'd been on the beach when I returned to the pier."

"When you were walking around, you never saw Jolene—or

noticed anything suspicious? Maybe heard someone cry out? Anything?"

"Sorry, Chief. I'll be honest. I was pretty preoccupied that night. Had a lot on my mind. I really wasn't paying much attention to my surroundings."

"But you did walk down the pier?"

"Yeah."

"You know the killer threw Jolene's rings off the end of the pier."

"I read that in this morning's paper."

"When you were on the pier, you didn't see anyone standing on the end of it, maybe see someone toss something into the water?"

Klein shook his head. "No. Sorry. I didn't see anything."

"Did you walk to the end of the pier?"

Steve shifted in his chair. "Yes. What is this about, Chief? Certainly you don't think I had anything to do with Jolene's murder?"

"I'm just talking to everyone who was there that night. Someone mentioned seeing you walking down the pier and that earlier, in the restaurant, you looked angry with her."

"I wasn't angry with Jolene. I was annoyed with her. She wouldn't stop pressing for that damn loan."

"Did you have any other issues with Jolene?"

"Not really. Just the loan. I wasn't thrilled with how she handled herself on the historical society board, but it was nothing that I'd kill someone over."

"Do you know of anyone else who might have an issue with her?"

"Not really. The only one who I ever saw her exchange words with was Danielle Boatman."

"Danielle?"

"It wasn't anything like they wanted to kill each other. But they obviously disliked each other. Jolene seemed to really have it in for Danielle."

"Did Danielle have it in for Jolene?"

Klein shrugged. "I could tell she didn't like Jolene, but I wouldn't say she had it in for her."

IN THE KITCHEN, Danielle measured soft butter into the bowl of her KitchenAid mixer.

"What are you doing?" Lily asked when she entered the room.

"I was thinking we need some chocolate chip cookies." She turned her attention to the sugar canister.

"Yum." Lily took a seat at the kitchen table. "Where's Joanne?"

"She went home about ten minutes ago. Not much for her to do around here, with only one guest. But, I think she's coming back later." Danielle dumped the sugar she had just measured out into the mixing bowl.

"If we hadn't had those last minute cancelations, we'd have a full house." Lily watched as Danielle broke eggs into the mixing bowl.

"I'd rather they not bring the flu here, so I'm fine with refunding their deposit." Danielle measured out some brown sugar and added it to the bowl.

"Have you talked to Chris lately? Told him about Jolene?"

Danielle paused a moment and looked over at Lily. "No. I tried calling him a little while ago, but I keep getting his recording. I figure he must be stuck in meetings. But he didn't know Jolene anyway."

"That's right, he never met her." Lily got up from the table and fixed herself a glass of water while Danielle turned on the mixer.

"When he called me yesterday morning, I hadn't heard about Jolene yet," Danielle explained after she turned the mixer off.

"I thought he'd be back by now." Lily sat back down at the table.

"He had to take that side trip to New York. When he left here, he only planned to go to Chicago. But his plans changed."

"Next time Ian goes to New York, I want to go with him," Lily said wistfully.

Danielle smiled. "That would be fun."

"So when do you think Chris's coming back?"

Danielle abandoned her cookie batter and took a seat at the table with Lily. "I'm not sure. When we spoke yesterday, he said it might be another week or less."

Lily frowned. "What does that mean, or less?"

"Now with this side trip to New York, I have no idea how much longer he's going to be."

Lily's cellphone began to buzz. She picked it up, looked at it briefly, and then stood up. "That's Ian. He's ready to go. You sure you don't want to grab something to eat with us?"

"No, thanks. I've got cookies to bake."

Just as Lily dashed out the kitchen door, Walt appeared in the room. "You haven't heard from Chris today?"

"You were eavesdropping?" Danielle asked as she stood up and went back to her cookie batter.

"I wasn't eavesdropping, exactly. I just overheard your conversation." Walt stood a few feet from Danielle and watched as she assembled more ingredients for her cookies. "You don't know when he's coming back?"

"I thought you overheard the conversation." Danielle turned the mixer on.

When Danielle turned the mixer off, Walt asked in a soft voice, "Will you tell Chris about what happened?"

Licking her lips nervously, she looked over to Walt. "I don't know what you mean."

"Yes, you do. Will you tell Chris about that thing you and I never discuss?"

"It's really none of Chris's business." Danielle opened the bag of chocolate chips and dumped them into the bowl.

"Does this mean you and Chris are…just friends…pals?" Walt asked.

Danielle took a deep breath before turning to face Walt. "Honestly, I don't know what Chris and I are. It's been a long time since I've seen him."

Walt laughed. "Danielle, he's been gone for just a few weeks. I've been dead for ninety years; that's a long time."

Danielle looked up into Walt's eyes. "I like Chris…I like him a lot. We've so much in common, and he understands me. I think the only one who understands me more than Chris…is…is you."

Walt smiled softly. "But you and I, we can't actually have a future together, can we?"

Licking her lips again, Danielle's gaze fell briefly to the floor and then looked up to Walt's blue eyes. "I'm sorry for what I did in the dream hop. It was foolish of me."

"Are you really sorry?" His voice was barely a whisper. "I'm not."

Blinking her eyes in an attempt to keep the tears at bay, she said, "I guess I'm not either. But I know it was foolish."

"Did you tell Lily?" Walt asked.

"No. I didn't tell her."

"Are you going to?"

Danielle shook her head. "No. Never."

"Why? Do you regret it so much you're ashamed?"

Danielle smiled softly. "No. But I don't really want to share it with anyone."

FIFTEEN

Steve Klein noticed his first gray hair on his thirtieth birthday. He immediately plucked it out. But then the second, third, and fourth quickly showed up, and he soon realized if he kept destroying the evidence of his progressing age, he would soon be bald. Before anyone else noticed the changing color of hair, he picked up a package of hair dye during a business trip to Portland. Purchasing the dye locally seemed too embarrassing, and he wasn't about to tell his wife what he intended to do.

What Steve didn't realize was that if just the tiniest speck of solution splashed on the counter or on the floor, it would eventually darken. He hadn't noticed the stray drops dribbled here and there over the counter, but his wife did when she came home that evening. By that time, he had gotten rid of the evidence—or so he thought.

She had panicked at first, wondering if their house was suddenly developing mold or some other deadly fungus. He stood by silently and said nothing as she frantically washed down the bathroom.

He didn't keep his secret for long—his wife discovered the rest of the evidence buried in the bottom of the trash can. If the neighbor's dog hadn't gotten out of his yard and decided to go rummaging through their trash, she might never have learned her husband had started coloring his hair.

Mrs. Klein found it amusing and didn't berate her husband for not saying anything while she freaked over imaginary mold. But she did enjoy inflicting an occasional sarcastic jab in his direction, reminding him he was no longer a young man. While she would prefer he let his hair gray naturally, she graciously purchased his next box of dye locally, sparing him the embarrassment. But she did lecture him on being more careful when applying the solution. That had been twenty-three years ago, and Mrs. Klein continued to keep her husband in hair dye. It was no longer a secret he colored his hair; everyone who knew him had already figured it out.

Steve was just about to take a bite of his burger when he heard a woman's voice say, "Pier Café has better burgers." He looked up and saw Carla hovering over his table. She glanced around and then hastily took a seat at Steve's booth, sitting across from him. Carla scooted over the bench seat and dropped her purse in the empty space between her and the wall.

"I thought you were working," Steve asked before taking his bite.

"If you thought that, then why are you here?" she asked.

Steve set the burger on his plate and glanced around before looking back at Carla. "I think you know why. We already went over all that."

"Does it really matter now? Jolene Carmichael is dead."

"Can you say that any louder?" Steve hissed. Picking up the burger again, he bit into it and chewed angrily.

"I don't think anyone liked her anyway," Carla said, her voice now lower than before.

Steve shrugged in response and took a sip of his soda.

Carla sent the server away when she showed up a moment later, telling her she was just stopping by to say hi to Steve and wouldn't be ordering any food.

Twirling a lock of her hair—recently dyed red with streaks of light blue—between the fingers of her right hand, Carla studied Steve as he finished his burger. "You know, according to the paper, Jolene wasn't killed by a stranger."

"How do they know that? No one knows who killed her." Steve popped a French fry in his mouth.

"The killer—or killers—know."

Steve looked up into Carla's face, noting the way she was staring at him. He ate another French fry. "Now you're saying there was more than one? A gang of killers roaming the beach of Frederickport?"

Carla shrugged and let go of the lock of hair she had been twisting. She reached across the table and helped herself to Steve's glass of water and took a sip. "Well, whoever killed Jolene probably knew her, according to the newspaper. They took her rings and then dumped them off the end of the pier. What robber does that?"

"Jolene knew how to rub people the wrong way." Steve pushed his now empty plate to the edge of the table and picked up his napkin. He wiped his mouth and then tossed the used napkin onto his plate.

"You didn't like her," Carla reminded him.

"I don't think we need to talk about that."

"Doesn't it bother you?" Carla asked, her voice a whisper.

"Bother me, how?"

"She was brutally murdered. And we were right there."

"We were hardly right there. We were up on the pier in the restaurant; she was murdered below the pier."

"You know what I mean." Carla shivered at the thought.

"Actually, I don't know what you mean," Steve said sharply.

"What if someone finds out? They might think we had something to do with it."

"Carla, why would someone find out? Have you said anything?"

She shook her head while her right hand nervously fidgeted with the rim of Steve's pilfered water glass. "I haven't said anything to anyone—I promise."

"Which is exactly why I didn't have lunch at Pier Café today."

Carla shrugged. "I'm not working today anyway. So it would have been okay."

Steve narrowed his eyes and studied her. "Why aren't you working today, by the way?"

"I've been working all those double shifts—and then with Jolene's murder and all the questions the police have asked me…"

"You were questioned again?"

Looking up into Steve's eyes, she shook her head. "No. I meant that one time. Still, it was nerve-racking. And with all the people showing up at the pier, trying to see the murder scene. It has just been too much. I got the afternoon off. I needed some time to myself."

With an expression devoid of emotion, he asked, "So why are you here?"

She shrugged. "I saw you. I missed you."

"We talked about this."

"I know, but now with Jolene dead—"

"*Exactly*. With Jolene dead, we have a *reprieve*."

"You have a reprieve; I have nothing."

Steve let out a sigh. "What do you want from me?" In the next moment, he felt the toe of Carla's foot run up his leg, settling by his groin. It was obvious she had slipped off her shoe. She wiggled her toes.

"Stop that!" Steve gasped, nervously glancing around the diner to see if anyone was watching.

Slowly she slid her foot off his lap until it was no longer touching him. Carla laughed and then flashed Steve a pout. "What will it hurt? I'll meet you at my place."

"I have to go back to work."

"No, you don't. You're the boss. Come on, Steve, one more time. I miss you."

Swallowing nervously, Steve picked up the napkin from his plate and wiped perspiration from his brow. "Fine. You go now. I'll be there shortly. Leave the door unlocked. I don't want one of your neighbors to hear me knocking."

Quickly slipping her shoe back on, Carla grabbed her handbag and slid out of her seat. "Thanks for the information, Steve," Carla said, her voice louder than before. "I'll have to stop at the bank and pick up that brochure you suggested." Turning from the table, she sashayed from the diner.

HER TRAVELING PARTNER had fallen asleep just moments after takeoff. She was grateful. Aside from being exceedingly handsome, he seemed like a nice man, but she did not feel particularly social. An hour into the flight—and starting her third cocktail—she was beginning to feel mellow. Smiling, she glanced over to Chris and noticed he was waking up.

Rubbing his eyes and sitting up, Chris glanced around. "Have I been sleeping long?" He unhooked his seatbelt and stretched, making himself more comfortable.

"About an hour." Melony sipped her drink.

It wasn't long before Chris was being served his own cocktail—a bloody Mary. "These always make me feel like I'm drinking something healthy."

Melony laughed. "What, the tomato juice as your vegetable for the day?"

Chris grinned. "Something like that."

"I'm a purist. I prefer my vodka with nothing to get between me and my buzz. Plus, flying terrifies me."

Chris studied her for a moment. "You don't look terrified."

She flashed him a silly smile. "I know. Vodka does that to me."

"Where in Oregon are you going, exactly?" Chris asked. "You never mentioned. Where's your hometown?"

She sipped her drink and then said, "A little beach town below Astoria called Frederickport. You've probably never heard of it."

Chris sat up abruptly and looked at Melony. "Frederickport? Seriously? That's where I live!"

"Nahh…" She waved her drink dismissively in his face. "I'd remember someone who looks like you."

"I've only lived there since Christmas," Chris explained. "I bought a house in the north end of town."

"No kidding?" Melony cocked her head slightly and studied Chris. "Whatever attracted you to Frederickport? It's a nice little village, but not a lot of work there unless you're into the tourist thing."

Chris shrugged. "I stayed at Marlow House over Christmas—I don't know if you're familiar with that place."

"Sure, one of the first houses in town. I understand the new owner turned it into a bed and breakfast."

"That's right. I came for Christmas and decided to stay. I basically work out of my home, so I can pretty much live anywhere."

"Nice. I wish I could do that."

"What do you do?" Chris asked.

"I'm an attorney." She finished her drink and waved to the steward, motioning for him to bring her another cocktail.

"Impressive." He sounded sincere.

"Don't be," she said wearily. "Some major jerks in my line of work."

"Oh…sorry to hear that. But I've found every profession has its share of jerks."

Melony shrugged. In the next moment, the steward appeared and took Melony's empty glass while giving her a fresh drink. When she and Chris were alone again, she said, "Marlow House, are the rooms nice there?"

"Sure, really nice. And the breakfast is amazing."

"Hmmm…I guess there's zero chance they have any vacancies."

"You thinking of staying there?" Chris asked.

"I hadn't—not until you mentioned it. The thing is, the more I think about staying at my mother's house while I'm in town, the more I hate the idea."

"Yes, that can be hard when someone has just passed away—staying in their home."

"It's the house I grew up in, but still, that doesn't make me want to stay there. My mother moved from Frederickport after my father died. She took everything with her, didn't want to sell her house in Oregon—didn't want to rent it either. When she decided to move back, she sold all her furniture, figured it would be cheaper just to buy new stuff. So I'm fairly certain the only bed in that big old empty house is the one she's been sleeping in, and I really don't want to sleep in it."

"Then you should stay at Marlow House. They're good people. And then you wouldn't have to be alone."

"I don't care about being alone," she said with a shrug. "I've gotten used to it."

"I take it you're not married?" Chris asked.

Melony glanced down at her left hand—she wore no rings. "Separated."

"Sorry."

Melony shrugged again. "One of those jerk attorneys I told you about."

"Your ex-husband is also a lawyer?"

"He's not ex yet—but will be. But yeah, he is." Eyeing Chris over her drink, she asked, "You ever been married?"

He shook his head. "No."

Melony let out a sigh. "Marriage is overrated."

After a few moments of silence she said, "I imagine Marlow House probably doesn't have any vacancies."

"I'm pretty sure it does. I'm friends with the owner, and we spoke on the phone yesterday morning. She mentioned she had some cancellations—they came down with the flu right when they were supposed to leave on their vacation. There's a good chance you can get a room."

SIXTEEN

Peeking her head into the parlor, Danielle spied Walt lounging on the sofa and reading a book. "I'm going to check on Chris's house. If you hear Hillary coming downstairs, do something with that book."

Looking over to Danielle, his feet propped on one arm of the sofa while he leaned against the opposing arm, Walt released hold of the book. It floated over his head. "Something like this?" He grinned.

"Oh, funny, ha-ha." She tried not to smile but found it impossible.

The book floated back into Walt's hands. "I promise I'll behave."

"Thank you." Danielle flashed Walt a smile and then turned back to the hall.

"Danielle!" Walt called out.

She turned to the open doorway and looked back into the parlor. "What?"

"Be careful. Promise me."

"Careful?" Danielle frowned.

"There's a killer on the loose and Chris's house is empty. A perfect place for someone to be holed up."

"I promise, Walt, I'll be careful."

A few moments later, Danielle stepped out onto the front porch and was about to close the door behind her when she heard Hillary call out, "Yooohooo! Danielle!" Pausing, her hand still on the doorknob, Danielle looked into the house and watched as Hillary scurried toward her.

"Did you need something?" Danielle asked when Hillary reached the doorway.

"Not exactly," Hillary said, slightly out of breath. "I noticed you going out the front door, not the kitchen door where you park your car, and I wondered if maybe you were going to take a walk."

"Actually, I was going to walk down to Chris's house and check on it. I haven't been down there for a few days."

"Would you mind if I went with you? I really need to get away from my typewriter and get some fresh air. A walk would be good for me, and I hate walking alone…especially now. Would you mind?"

Since learning what Walt had read in Hillary's room, she had been a little leery with her houseguest. Yet looking at her now, Hillary reminded Danielle a little of her own grandmother. She began to wonder if maybe the chief was correct. It had all been a bizarre coincidence.

"I'd love to have the company," Danielle said brightly, finding she actually meant it.

"When is your friend Chris returning?" Hillary asked a few minutes later as they walked down the street.

"I'm not really sure. He was in Chicago on business and then unexpectedly had to go to New York. Maybe a week or so."

"Now what does he do exactly? I asked Lily, but she didn't seem to know."

Danielle's eyes darted briefly to Hillary and then looked back down the street. "Umm…well…it's sort of complicated."

"It's very neighborly of you to keep an eye on his house for him while he's away on business."

"Considering what happened the other night, I suppose none of us can be too careful."

"Ahh yes, that poor woman's murder." Hillary shook her head while muttering a few *tsk, tsk, tsks*. "I know the police chief is a friend of yours, but I'm wondering if perhaps something like this is a bit out of his league."

Danielle stopped walking a moment and glanced over at Hillary. "What do you mean?"

Hillary stopped walking and looked back at Danielle. "The questions he asked me. He wasn't very thorough. I must say, if my detective was interviewing a potential witness, he would ask more questions. Sometimes a witness doesn't even realize he's seen something."

Danielle started walking again, Hillary by her side. "What didn't he ask you?"

"For one thing, he didn't seem particularly concerned about what I saw when I was in the café. But what if the killer was in there? Maybe I happened to see someone watching her, following her out of the restaurant."

"Did you?"

"No. But that's hardly the point."

They were quiet for a few minutes. Danielle then asked, "How long have you been writing murder mysteries?"

"Ten years now."

"Really? I was under the impression you've been writing longer than that."

"I have. You asked me about murder mysteries. I used to write romance. My books did fairly well, but then romance readers seemed to get younger while I was getting older, and my publisher began losing interest in me." Hillary let out a sigh. "But to be honest, I was getting a trifle bored writing romance."

"You just shifted to murder mysteries? Your publisher was okay with that?"

Hillary laughed. "No. My publisher wasn't interested in giving me a shot in another genre, but my agent had faith in me, encouraged me, and eventually found me a new publisher willing to give me a chance."

"Nice. So you're not self-published like so many authors today?"

Hillary wrinkled her nose. "Certainly not. I'm a real author."

When they reached Chris's house, Hillary went inside with Danielle, who gave her a tour of the property. Everything appeared to be in order. After looking through the bungalow, Hillary unlocked the sliding glass door and stepped onto the back patio. Standing at the edge of the patio, she looked out to the ocean and watched the waves breaking along the shore.

"It's beautiful, isn't it?" Danielle said when she joined Hillary a few minutes later.

"Lovely, just lovely. Marlow House is wonderful, but I must

say, being right here on the ocean would be a writer's dream. Imagine looking at this all day while working. Stunning. Simply stunning."

"It is pretty nice. When Marlow House was initially built, it was practically beach front. But then the Hemming house was built—smack dab in front of Marlow House." Danielle chuckled. "Amazing really that George Hemming and Walt were such good friends. I'd think blocking someone's view might put strains on a friendship."

"Certainly Frederick Marlow realized someone would eventually block his view."

"I'm sure he did. And he obviously didn't care, or he wouldn't have built where he did," Danielle said.

"I thought I heard voices," a man interrupted.

Danielle and Hillary glanced to the right of the patio. There, standing on the beach, was Chris's neighbor Pete Rogers.

"Hey, Pete, how are you doing?" Danielle asked the older man.

"I heard voices, but didn't see a car out front," Pete said as he stepped up onto the patio.

"I was just checking on Chris's house. Making sure everything was okay."

"So he's not back yet?" Pete asked.

Danielle shook her head. "No. Pete, have you met Hillary Hemingway? She's staying with us."

Wearing a frown, Pete looked Hillary up and down. "You look kind of familiar."

Hillary smiled. "I was thinking the same thing. Have we met before?"

Pete shrugged. "I doubt it. But you do look familiar."

"Hillary's a well-known murder mystery author," Danielle explained. "Maybe you've seen her picture on a book jacket or on television?"

Pete shook his head. "Nahh, I don't read mysteries. Only watch fishing shows on TV."

"Even if you had," Hillary said, "that wouldn't explain why you look familiar to me. And I've definitely seen you someplace before… I just can't place where."

Pete shrugged again. "Small town." He looked at Danielle. "I haven't seen a bunch of strange cars parked at your house this week. Just one. You still running Marlow House as an inn?"

"A B and B, but yes. Like I just said a minute ago, Hillary is one of our guests."

Pete shook his head and grumbled. "I don't know why they let you run a business in a residential neighborhood. Just doesn't seem right to me."

Danielle let out a weary sigh. "If any of my guests ever cause you a problem, Pete, just come talk to me, and I promise I'll take care of it."

"I'd think you'd be more concerned about a killer running around in the neighborhood!" Hillary told Pete.

"I'm sure whoever killed Jolene is long gone by now," Pete said.

"You knew the poor woman too?" Hillary asked.

"Oh, that might be where you recognize each other from," Danielle said.

Pete frowned at Danielle. "Excuse me?"

"I saw you at the police station. I know the chief interviewed you because you were at Pier Café the night Jolene was murdered. Hillary here was at the café that night too. I bet you saw each other there."

Pete looked Hillary up and down again. "Yeah, I remember now. That's where I saw you."

With a frown, Hillary looked at Pete and shook her head. "I'm afraid I don't remember seeing you there. Of course, I was wearing my reading glasses that night; anything over a couple feet away is a blur if I'm wearing those. No, I've seen you before, but it wasn't from the diner."

"IT'S GOING to be after ten before we touch down in Portland. Surely you don't plan to drive to Frederickport tonight?" Chris asked.

"I might have—if I hadn't drank all those martinis." Melony giggled. "But without the martinis, I would never have gotten through this flight. I plan to spend the night in a hotel in Portland, and then I'll rent a car in the morning."

"I imagine your mother has a car you can use when you get there?" Chris asked.

"Sure, but it's not going to get me from Portland to Frederickport."

"I was just wondering—you want to drive in with me in the morning? I'm planning to get a room tonight too."

"I assume your car is at the airport?"

Chris smiled. "No. Actually, I'm picking up my new car in the morning, or should I say, they've agreed to drop it off at the motel then."

"You're getting a new car?"

"Yep. I've been without wheels for a while, figured it was about time I buy one."

"I can certainly understand getting along in New York without a car, but in Oregon?"

Chris shrugged. "I got by. But it was starting to get to be a hassle, relying on other people; figured it was time to get one. Knew what I wanted, called a few dealers when I had some downtime on my business trip, and bought a car."

"Sight unseen? Without a test drive?"

Chris grinned. "I like to live dangerously."

Thirty minutes later, after finishing their dinner, Chris glanced over to Melony and asked, "Was your mother sick long?"

"Sick?"

"I just assumed she was sick." Chris sighed. "Although, not sure why I'd jump to that assumption. My own parents were killed in a boating accident."

"You lost them both at the same time?" Melony asked in a quiet voice.

Chris nodded. "Yes. So was it an accident?"

"My mother was murdered."

Chris sat up abruptly in his seat and looked over at Melony, who sat next to him, her eyes closed.

Chris reached over, placing his hand over hers. "Oh my god, I'm so sorry, Melony. Did they catch him?"

Melony shook her head and then opened her eyes, looking over at Chris. "No. At first they thought it was a robbery. She was on the beach late at night—which is a crazy thing for a woman to do even in a small town like Frederickport. Whoever killed her took her jewelry. My mother was partial to diamonds." Melony shook her head. "I always thought those damn rings she flashed were an invitation to be hit over the head—which is exactly what happened to her."

"You said at first they thought it was a robbery? Are you saying she wasn't robbed?"

"Oh, she was robbed; the killer removed her rings. But he didn't keep them, which is why the police are certain the motive wasn't robbery."

"What do you mean the killer didn't keep the rings?" Chris asked.

"Apparently, the killer dumped them off the end of the pier. Eddy told me they got tangled in a fishing net and were recovered. He doesn't think the killer intended them to be found, but he—or she—wanted the authorities to assume the motive for murder was robbery."

"Who's Eddy?" Chris asked.

Melony smiled. "Oh, Eddy MacDonald. He's the police chief in Frederickport."

"Eddy? His name is Eddy? I was beginning to think MacDonald didn't have a first name."

SEVENTEEN

W*hen had it stopped being fun?* Carla asked herself that question for what seemed like the hundredth time. Sitting on a stool at her breakfast bar, she watched Steve hastily comb his hair and straighten his clothing as he prepared to leave her apartment.

"We can't do this again," Steve said as he checked his pockets to make sure he had his wallet and keys.

"You seemed fine with everything a few minutes ago," Carla reminded him.

Steve turned and looked at her. Carla, no longer dressed in street clothes, wore a floor-length satin robe over her nude body. Her bare feet rested on the barstool's lower rung.

"My wife's coming home. I have to drive to Portland in the morning and pick her up at the airport."

Carla frowned. "You never said anything about that. I thought she was going to be gone for another week at least."

Steve shrugged. "Plans change. She emailed me an itinerary this morning, with her flight schedule and when I have to pick her up."

"When will I see you?"

"I just said we can't do this again," Steve reminded her.

"You mean…never?"

Combing his fingers through his hair, he inched toward the front door, his eyes darting anxiously from Carla to his impending exit route.

Carla stepped down off the stool, her balled hands now resting on her hips. "I don't get it. Fifteen minutes ago you were all over me. Couldn't keep your hands off me. And now, now you say it's over?"

"I'm married, Carla."

"That didn't stop you from coming here today," Carla snapped.

Taking a step toward the door, he said, "I like you, but this is just a bad idea. I told you before, I've no intention of leaving my wife."

"I know you said that, but I can't believe you're willing to walk away from what we have. I make you happy."

"I can't leave my wife."

"She doesn't make you happy. I do," Carla insisted.

"I don't want to talk about this anymore, Carla. It's over." Without another word, Steve turned and hurried out the door.

Instead of tears, Carla picked up the closest thing she could find—which happened to be a mug of coffee—and hurled it at the front door. Her aim fell short, and the mug landed unbroken on the carpet, leaving behind a trail of coffee.

Snatching a dishtowel off the breakfast bar, she tossed it on the coffee now soaking into her carpet. Using her foot, she pressed the towel over the wet surface and haphazardly wiped the area. Instead of picking up the towel, she turned and made her way to the bathroom.

Once in the bathroom she stood before the mirror and looked at her reflection. "I'm going to be one of those old ladies waiting tables at some truck stop."

Leaning toward the mirror, she inspected the fine lines starting to show around her eyes. Pressing a finger against one line, attempting to flatten it out, she said, "Bankers' wives don't have to wait tables."

Letting out a sigh, she stood up straight, narrowed her eyes, and stared intently into the mirror. "Okay, be honest, Carla, you don't love the guy. But it would make things a hell of a lot easier if he left his wife."

Slipping off her robe, she let it fall to the floor in a silky heap. Her hand reached into the shower and turned on the water. While she waited for the water to reach the desired temperature, she considered her options.

"I could swear off married men—if there were more single guys in Frederickport." Reaching out, she put her hand under the showerhead to check the water's temperature. She then remembered what Steve had said about the email. Quickly, she turned off the water, snatched her robe up off the floor, and slipped it back on.

"What do you mean she emailed you her itinerary?" Carla said aloud as she hurried from the bathroom, fastening the robe's belt along the way. "You told me once your wife doesn't know how to use a computer."

Several minutes later, Carla sat at her kitchen table and turned on her laptop.

"I bet your wife isn't even coming home tomorrow," Carla mumbled as she logged on to the computer and opened the page for Yahoo Mail. She knew Steve's personal email address—yet she didn't know his password.

"Considering your lack of imagination in the bedroom, I bet your password is something lame like your pet's name."

Carla was correct. She managed to log into Steve's email account on the first try.

As she suspected, she couldn't find an email from Mrs. Klein to her husband, regarding her trip home. By the size of his trash folder, Carla figured if Mrs. Klein had sent that email and her husband had deleted it, it would still be sitting in the trash bin.

Carla opened the trash file and glanced through the emails. "I knew it. You liar. Your wife isn't coming home early. Fine. You have stupid-looking hair anyway."

Just as she was about to log out of Steve's email account, a name on one of the trashed emails jumped out at her—Jolene Carmichael. According to the date associated with the email, it was sent the same day Jolene was murdered.

Carla shivered. "That's just too strange." Curious, she opened the email.

I HOPE *your wife is enjoying her visit with her sister.*

So nice of Carla to keep you company.

Please call me when I can come in and sign the loan papers.

We need to have it wrapped up this week.

Have a nice day.

Jolene

. . .

"THAT'S WEIRD..." Carla mumbled, rereading the email.

ON HER WAY to the parlor from the kitchen, Danielle noticed someone had left the light on in the downstairs powder room. The door was ajar, so she slipped her hand inside and flipped the wall switch, sending the small room into total darkness.

"Hey!" came Lily's shout from inside the powder room.

Hastily, Danielle turned the light back on. "I'm sorry," she said with a laugh as she opened the door wider. Lily stood at the mirror, the sleeve on her tattooed arm rolled up. "I thought everyone was upstairs."

Lily resumed what she had been doing before Danielle plunged her into darkness—inspecting her tattooed arm.

Now standing in the bathroom with Lily, Danielle leaned against the door jamb and watched her friend. "It looks red. Does it hurt?"

Lily shrugged. "Not really. A little tender."

"I'm curious to see what it'll look like when they add the colors."

Turning from the mirror, Lily showed Danielle her arm and pointed to the new addition to her tattoo. "I think he did a pretty good job." Two figures had been added—one an angel and the other a woman riding the dragon. When Lily had shown Danielle the tattoo when she had first returned home from Portland, Danielle knew without being told who the two figures represented. The one riding the dragon was Lily, and the angel was Isabella.

When they finished examining Lily's new tattoo, they left the bathroom and walked to the parlor.

"You still haven't heard from Chris?" Lily asked as they stepped into the room.

"No. And it's kind of late there now. But I talked to him yesterday morning. It's not like we have to talk every day." Danielle flopped down on the sofa and leaned against one armrest. She kicked off her shoes before propping her feet on the opposing arm.

Lily sat in a chair facing the sofa. "But you have talked every day."

Danielle shrugged. "I checked on his house this afternoon."

"Was everything okay?"

"Yeah..." Danielle chuckled and then said, "but right before I left to go up there, Walt told me to be careful. Reminded me it would be a good place for a killer to be hiding out. Kinda freaked me out."

"We're not that far from where Jolene was murdered. It probably wasn't wise to be checking out vacant houses alone."

"I wasn't alone. Hillary went with me. We ran into Pete Rogers when we were on Chris's patio. He's kind of a nosey busy body."

"Speaking of Hillary..." Lily glanced from Danielle to the closed door leading to the hallway and then back to Danielle. "I can't believe the chief isn't doing something with what you told him."

"I'm not sure what he can do. Hearsay from a ghost doesn't seem to carry a lot of weight."

"What if we could find the notes Hillary wrote—the ones Walt read," Lily asked.

Danielle looked to Lily. "We can't go through her room. Even if I let Walt do it, whatever we find won't help the chief. It will just put us all in an awkward position." Danielle glanced up to the ceiling, thinking of Walt, who was probably in the attic. "And maybe the chief was right. Maybe it is all a coincidence, and Walt read more into it."

"But maybe Walt didn't—and the only way we'll know for sure is to read those notes," Lily insisted.

"We can't rummage through a guest's things."

"I'm not suggesting that."

Danielle sat up in the sofa and put her feet on the floor. "What are you suggesting?"

"Tomorrow is trash day." Lily smiled.

Danielle frowned. "So?"

"The day before trash day, Joanne goes through the house and rounds up all the trash—from all the rooms. What if Hillary threw those notes away?"

"Why would she do that?"

"Because she's been writing on that typewriter for hours. All I know, when Ian is working on one of his projects, he starts jotting down ideas—sort of like what Walt said Hillary seemed to be doing, judging by her notes. But Ian doesn't keep the notes forever. Some he does, but I've seen him toss out notes not long after he's written them. Sometimes it's just a way to get ideas flowing."

"That's sort of what Hillary told me when I asked her about them."

"It's possible the notes Walt read are sitting outside in the trash cans."

Danielle groaned. "Wouldn't it have been easier to go through the trash if you had thought of this before Joanne dumped it all in the outside cans?"

"I suppose that's true." Lily shrugged. "If we would've thought of it earlier. But the fact is, if they're out there in the trash, this is our last chance to see what she really wrote."

"If they're out there."

"They might be, Dani."

Danielle glanced to the parlor window. It was dark outside. "We're going to need a couple of flashlights."

"Or we could wait until the morning," Lily suggested.

"They pick up the trash early. Even if we wait until the morning, it'll still be dark out if we want to go through the cans before the trash man shows up."

Lily stood up. "So we're going to do this?"

Danielle groaned again and reluctantly stood. "I suppose so. You think we have any rubber gloves around here?"

EIGHTEEN

Walt Marlow, Danielle Boatman, Lily Miller, Ian Bartley, Chris Glandon aka Chris Johnson, Heather Donovan, and Pete Rogers all had one thing in common. They resided on Beach Drive in Frederickport, Oregon. Beach Drive had no streetlights. A few of the houses on the street had installed their own security lighting, which helped illuminate the area on a moonless night.

Every Thursday evening the residents of Beach Drive dragged their trash cans to the curb in preparation for Friday morning's trash pickup. Those who forgot to remove their trash can lids before taking them to the curb the night before often discovered in the morning that the lids had rolled down the street, been run over by a vehicle and flattened, or sometimes they simply vanished.

Each week Joanne hauled lidless trash cans to the curb in front of Marlow House. While this saved Danielle from having to buy new trash can lids, the exposed trash was occasionally pilfered by roaming animals, resulting in garbage strewn along the street. At one time, Max had been a dumpster-diving feline, yet he had changed his way since moving into Marlow House and getting regularly fed.

Danielle stood by her trash cans, fidgeting with the flashlight she had brought with her. It had worked when she had left the house, yet died a few minutes after coming outside. Fortunately, there was a full moon overhead, and she wasn't standing in total darkness. She waited for Lily, who was inside tracking down rubber gloves and another flashlight.

THE BRIEF FLICKERING light from the sidewalk in front of Marlow House caught Walt's attention. When he stepped to the attic window and looked outside, the light was gone, but he could see a shadow standing not far from the gate.

"Is that Danielle out there?" Walt asked.

Max, who had been inspecting the attic's perimeter for possible rodent infestation, paused and looked over at Walt. Curious, he meowed and then leapt onto the windowsill. With his tail swishing, he looked outside.

DANIELLE DIDN'T SEE Lily coming, but she could hear the approach by the crunching sound of Lily's shoes making their way across the yard.

"Here, put these on," Lily ordered as she handed Danielle two large plastic storage bags.

"Put these on where?" Danielle asked, reluctantly taking the bags from Lily while holding her nonfunctioning flashlight in the other hand. She looked at the bags.

"On your hands, of course," Lily told her as she shook out a large empty trash bag she had also been carrying.

"You expect me to use these as gloves?" Danielle asked, dropping the flashlight to the ground.

"I suppose you don't have to if you don't mind going through the trash barehanded."

"I thought you were going to get some gloves?"

"I couldn't find any. But those should work." Lily gave the trash bag she was holding another shake, clutching it by its opening, waiting for Danielle to fill it. "I figure you can empty the trash from the can and put it in here. Hopefully, Hillary's notes aren't at the very bottom."

"If they're even in here."

"I bet they are," Lily said.

"We should have had Walt just keep an eye on the notes and then tell us when she tossed them," Danielle said with a groan.

"Great, now you think of that!"

"Why do I have to do it?" Danielle asked, begrudgingly slipping the gallon-sized storage bags on her hands.

"They're your trash cans."

"But it was your idea," Danielle reminded her.

"Hey, if I came up with the idea, you can do your share and sort through the trash."

Digging into the can and awkwardly pulling out garbage with her now covered hands, she said, "You know, I'm rich. I shouldn't have to do stuff like this. I should be able to pay someone to dig through my trash."

"Yeah, yeah, yeah," Lily said as she watched Danielle dump a handful of garbage into her bag. "Where's your flashlight?"

"I thought you were going to bring one?" Danielle asked, taking another handful.

"I couldn't find one. Where's yours?" Lily glanced around, but it was difficult to see what was on the ground.

"It doesn't work. But I think we have enough moonlight. I should be able to tell when…if…I get to Hillary's notes."

SADIE STOOD at the living room window and started barking.

"What is it, girl?" Ian asked, stepping from the kitchen into the dark living room. Without turning on the overhead light, he walked across the dark room and looked out the window. He could see the silhouettes of two people in front of Marlow House. They were doing something—what exactly, he couldn't tell.

Ian pulled out his cellphone and dialed Lily. There was no answer. Then he dialed Danielle. Still no answer. Glancing to the windows of Marlow House, he could see the lights were all off.

"Sadie, it looks like someone is trying to break into the side gate at Marlow House, and I think they're all in bed over there."

Without hesitation, Ian dialed the Frederickport Police Department.

"WHY DON'T you see what those two are up to," Walt told Max. The cat didn't move, but continued to stare out the window.

"Come on, Max, be a sport. I want to know what they're doing out there."

Max meowed, jumped off the windowsill, and headed for the door.

UNDER THE FIRST heap of garbage Danielle removed from the can, she found a number of smaller trash bags, each stuffed full and shoved tightly into the can. One by one, she pulled out a bag and ripped it open, transporting its contents to the bag Lily held.

"Oh dang, this stinks," Danielle groaned as she leaned into the can, trying to retrieve the last bag. As she did, it tore apart, scattering its contents on the bottom of the can and forcing Danielle to reach down into its depths.

It was impossible for Danielle to grab hold of whatever remained on the bottom of the can, so she slipped the bags off her hands and gingerly touched whatever it was with her fingertips.

"It's sheets of paper!" Danielle said excitedly.

Lily had been just about to suggest picking up the almost empty can and dumping its remaining contents into the bag she held, instead of practically climbing in, but she withheld comment, believing they might have found what they were looking for, and Danielle almost had it in her grasp.

What neither Lily or Danielle noticed was Max slinking out from the side yard after exiting Marlow House via the pet door in the kitchen. The black cat focused his attention on the trash cans, wondering what tasty treats they held. Danielle and Lily also did not notice the vehicle driving down their street, which had turned its headlights off and approached slowly.

Just as Danielle took hold of a piece of paper on the bottom of the can, Max leapt into the receptacle, landing soundly on Danielle's back. She let out a scream and jumped up, tipping over the can, sending Max charging off under Lily's feet—which in turn frightened Lily, who took off in a run in the opposite direction.

JOE MORELLI WATCHED the shadowy pair as his squad car moved slowly down Beach Drive. He was about ten feet from the drive into Marlow House when one of them took off in a run, charging away from him. He immediately turned on his headlights and siren.

LILY COULDN'T STOP LAUGHING. She found the entire situation hilarious. Danielle was not as amused. During her flight, Lily had dropped the garbage bag she had been holding, scattering its contents on the sidewalk before Danielle landed on her backside in the sludge. Joe offered her a hand to get up, but when Danielle realized her right hand was now covered in three-day-old bacon grease, she declined his offer and managed to stumble to her feet without his assistance.

By the time Ian made it across the street, Danielle had wiped her hands off on the sides of her jeans and gathered up what she could find of the yellow sheets of legal-size paper—each covered with Hillary's scribbly handwriting. The headlights from Joe's car continued to light the area, making it easier for Danielle to see what she was doing.

"You obviously lost something," Ian said when he saw the mess.

Danielle protectively held the stack of papers to her chest, unwilling to let either Joe or Ian catch a glimpse of what she held. "I accidentally threw out some important paperwork," she lied.

Feeling sorry for Danielle, Lily quickly scooped up the trash, shoving it back into the now empty can. Soon Ian and Joe were helping until all the trash was back in the container.

"Are you done dumpster diving?" Joe asked with a chuckle. They glanced to the second can.

"I think so," Danielle said, still clutching the papers to her chest. "I found the sack they were in, so I don't imagine there's any more of the papers I was looking for in the other can."

"Why did you run off?" Joe asked Lily.

"I'm not sure." Lily laughed. "Dani screamed, and then something ran through my legs. Scared the crap outa me. I think it was a raccoon or something."

"I think it was Max," Danielle said as she spied her black cat sitting by the fence, watching.

"I'M DYING to see if you got what we need," Lily told Danielle as they approached the back door.

The light in the kitchen flashed on. Danielle froze. They could see Hillary inside through the window.

"I can't let her see these," Danielle said as she hastily tucked the bundle under her shirt.

"You look like you were just in a mud wrestling match—and lost."

"Thanks, Lily. This was your idea, may I remind you."

"And maybe it worked."

"I need to take a shower first. I feel gross."

"I tell you what, when we go in there, just run to the bathroom; I'll tell Hillary you accidentally threw out some paperwork—which is the same story you told Ian and Joe—and that we had to look in the trash, and you got crud on you, and you have to take a shower because you feel so gross. Pretend like you're holding something."

"All true—except for the paperwork part. And I am holding something; it's just under my shirt."

A few minutes later, Danielle managed to race by Hillary, shouting something about feeling gross and needing to jump in the shower.

Lily stayed behind in the kitchen to wash her hands and tell Hillary what they had been doing outside, skipping over the part about them snooping for any notes she might have thrown out.

Just as Danielle reached the stairway, she met Walt, who was coming down from the attic. "I think we found Hillary's notes you read. I'll explain later! I need a shower!" Not waiting for Walt's response, Danielle continued on her way.

Walt was about to call out a question when he noticed Max trailing behind Danielle. He looked down at the cat and asked, "What's going on, Max?"

DANIELLE TOOK A QUICK SHOWER, and by the time Lily made it back upstairs, she found Danielle's bedroom door closed. Walking to the door, she knocked softly. A moment later it opened.

"Where's Hillary?" Danielle whispered, peeking out into the hallway.

"She's watching television in the living room. I think Walt's watching with her."

"Why do you say that?" Danielle opened the door wider, let Lily in, and then shut and locked it after her.

"I could smell his cigar," Lily explained.

"I've been straightening out the pages over here." Danielle pointed to the dresser, where a stack of crinkled legal-sized paper sat.

"You don't think we should have gone through the other can?" Lily asked.

"I don't think Joanne would have dumped the trash from Hillary's room in more than one bag. I suppose we could always look at the other one if we don't find anything."

"I don't want to go back out there," Lily groaned.

Danielle laughed. "*You* don't?"

Danielle divided the stack and gave Lily half. They both started reading.

"I feel like such a sneak," Lily said as she finished her first page and went on to the second.

"I know what you mean, I—" Danielle didn't finish what she was saying, but instead grabbed hold of Lily's arm and said, "This is it!" She showed the page to Lily.

A WOMAN MEETS a man under the pier. They argue. She is blackmailing him. While she yells at him, he finds an empty wine bottle in the sand. He picks it up and hits her over the head. It kills her. He removes all her rings. She has a ring on every finger, even her thumbs. Diamonds and gold. He covers her body with sand and leaves her there. He doesn't want the rings. He throws the dead woman's jewelry off the pier. When he puts his hand back into his pocket, he finds one of her rings he missed. He throws it in the ocean with the others and hears a splash.

SLOWLY, Lily and Danielle lifted their heads and looked into each other's eyes.

"Holy crap!" they gasped.

NINETEEN

Getting his sons to school on time Friday morning prevented Edward MacDonald from having his first cup of morning coffee at home. He was just sitting down at his desk to enjoy his first cup of the day when he was informed Carla, the waitress from Pier Café, needed to speak to him—and only to him. It was urgent.

"How can I help you, Carla?" MacDonald asked after she was shown to his office and sitting in a chair facing him.

Dressed in her waitress uniform from Pier Café, she wore her hair pulled back in a haphazard bun. It looked as if she had fixed her hair on the run, and now strands were escaping, making her look sloppy rather than untidy chic. Dark circles shadowed her eyes. MacDonald had never seen Carla look so haggard.

"I think my life might be in danger," she said nervously.

Setting his mug on the desk, MacDonald asked, "How so?"

"I think Steve might have killed Jolene Carmichael, and I could be next."

"Steve?" MacDonald frowned.

"Steve Klein, the bank manager," Carla explained.

"Why would Steve kill Jolene—why would he want to kill you?"

Fidgeting with the purse on her lap, she looked from it to MacDonald. "He obviously wants to kill me because I know he killed Jolene. Well…I don't know exactly. But I think it's possible."

"Let's back it up a little, Carla. Why do you think Steve killed Jolene?"

"He was there that night at the restaurant. He left right after Jolene." Carla reached back and tucked some of her escaping hair back into her bun.

"A number of people were there that night and left after Jolene," MacDonald countered.

"Yeah, but I'm pretty sure Mrs. Carmichael was blackmailing Steve."

"Blackmailing him? Where did you get that idea?" MacDonald picked up his cup and sipped his coffee.

Closing her eyes for a brief moment, Carla chewed her lower lip nervously and then opened her eyes and looked at the chief. "Steve and I have been having an affair."

Slowly, MacDonald set his cup back on his desktop while his eyes fixed on Carla.

"I know it makes me look awful," she groaned. "And I hate coming here and having to admit it all. He is a married man, after all. But gee, there are no decent single men in town." Realizing what she had just said, Carla stammered a moment and then added, "I didn't mean you, Chief. You're a real decent guy…but you aren't single anyhow, not really. You have a girlfriend. The thing is…I really don't want to be next. I don't want to end up dead because I made a stupid relationship choice. Hell, if that was some rule, I'd be dead by now."

When Carla finally stopped talking, MacDonald asked, "Are you saying Jolene knew about the affair, and she was blackmailing Steve over it?"

Carla nodded. "I don't know how she found out. I thought we were being careful. But I know she's been trying to get a loan from the bank, and Steve turned her down. We…umm…one time he came over to my place, it was after talking to her, and he was so annoyed. I guess he needed to vent. Told me Jolene Carmichael was broke. Lost everything because of that deal with Clarence Renton and the court making him pay restitution. He said no way his bank would loan her the money. That he wasn't about to jeopardize his career for her."

"How do you know she was blackmailing him?"

Still fidgeting with her purse, she shifted uncomfortably in the chair. "The night she was killed, Steve came into the diner and told me we needed to stop seeing each other, that Jolene knew about our affair. I didn't think he meant we needed to end it for good, just cool it for a while."

"Did he tell you he was being blackmailed?"

Carla shook her head. "Not exactly. But last night he came over to my place, and when he left, he told me his wife was coming home and that we couldn't see each other. I figured with Jolene dead, we didn't have to cool it anymore." Carla's eyes widened, and she looked into the chief's face. Hastily she added, "Not that I was glad she was dead or anything, or that I even suspected Steve might be responsible—not then."

"What made you start wondering if Steve killed Jolene?"

"Last night…umm…I…well, I sorta hacked into Steve's email account." She stopped fidgeting with her purse and opened it. After pulling out a folded piece of paper, she stood up and handed it to MacDonald. "I printed the email out so you can read it."

Carla sat back down in her chair while MacDonald read Steve's email from Jolene. When he finished, he set the sheet of paper on his desk and looked up.

"What's Steve done to make you think your life could be in jeopardy?"

"If he killed Jolene to keep her quiet about our affair, then isn't it obvious?"

CARLA HAD BEEN GONE ABOUT thirty minutes when Danielle arrived at the chief's office.

MacDonald greeted her with, "Danielle, with your money, is it really necessary to rummage through the neighbor's garbage?" He laughed.

"It was my trash, and how do you know…oh, Joe…right." Danielle shook her head and opened her purse.

"I guess Ian thought someone was breaking into your side gate and called us." MacDonald chuckled. "What were you doing going through your trash in the dark, anyhow? Joe said something about you tossing out some paperwork."

Removing the folded piece of yellow paper from her purse, she handed it to the chief. "I was looking for this."

Taking the paper from Danielle, he asked, "What's this?"

"It's what Walt read in Hillary's room; what I told you about."

MacDonald unfolded the paper and began to read while Danielle continued to stand at the side of his desk.

"I didn't want to go through Hillary's things in her room," Danielle explained when he finished reading. "But Lily reminded me anything in the trash would be fair game. If I found something she put in the trash—in my trash can—she really couldn't claim it was obtained illegally. You could use it, couldn't you?"

MacDonald set the paper on the desk and looked up at Danielle. "I appreciate your help—and it's exactly what you claimed Walt read, but—"

"After I went digging through my garbage in the middle of the night and humiliated myself, there is a but?" Danielle flopped down in the chair and tossed her purse to the floor by her feet.

He picked up the paper and looked at it again. "You're exaggerating a little there. According to Joe, it was a little after nine o'clock."

Danielle glared at MacDonald.

Waving the paper at her, he said, "There's no date on this, and even if there was, we couldn't prove anything. As far as we know, Hillary wrote this after she read the newspaper about fishing Jolene's rings off the pier."

"But we know she didn't. Walt read it that night. I believe him," she insisted.

"I understand. I'm just saying, when I question Hillary, I imagine that's just what she'll tell me."

Sitting up straight in the chair, Danielle leaned forward. "So you're going to talk to her?"

"At first, when you told me about what Walt read, I wondered if he had read it wrong. A lot of times, someone will read something and interject a meaning or even a word that's really not there. This is pretty much exactly what Walt claimed to have read. And if he did read this the night of the murder, before you found those rings, I have to wonder how in the hell did Hillary Hemingway know all this."

"I don't believe she had anything to do with the murder. It just doesn't feel right. But…"

MacDonald tossed the yellow piece of paper back onto the desk. "At this point, I suspect she witnessed the murder—and followed the killer back onto the pier and watched him toss the rings into the water."

"So you think the killer's a man?"

MacDonald pointed to the yellow sheet of paper. "According to this it is. I also have a suspect—he has a motive, and he was there."

"Who?"

When he didn't respond, Danielle said, "Come on, Chief. I thought we were sort of informal partners. I get you information from the spirit world, and you keep me in the loop."

"You're just being nosey," MacDonald said with a chuckle.

"I climbed in the trash can for you. Ruined a perfectly good pair of jeans with bacon grease."

MacDonald smiled. "Okay, but this goes no farther than this office."

"Can I tell Walt?"

"Can I stop you?"

Danielle smiled. "Probably not."

"Don't say anything to Lily—and I mean it."

When she didn't respond, he asked, "Do you want to hear this or not?"

Danielle sighed. "Okay. I promise. I won't say anything to Lily. Who is your suspect?"

"Steve Klein."

"Steve? The bank manager?"

MacDonald nodded.

"Are you serious? What reason would Steve have to kill her? I know they were on the board at the museum together, but they seemed to get along okay."

"Apparently, Steve and Carla have been having an affair."

"Not Carla the waitress at Pier Café?"

He nodded again.

Danielle couldn't help it—she laughed.

"What's so funny?" MacDonald asked.

"Seriously? Dippy Carla and buttoned-up Steve from the bank? He's old enough to be her father. Or at least her much older brother."

MacDonald shrugged. "No accounting for taste. I certainly never imagined those two together."

"She told you?" Before he could respond, she said, "But Steve's married! He has a couple of kids!"

"Which is the reason for killing Jolene. Apparently Jolene found out about the affair and decided to blackmail Steve. She's been trying to get a loan from the bank, but Steve turned her down."

"Wow…so you think he really killed her? Was Carla an accomplice?"

MacDonald went on to tell Danielle about his morning's interview with Carla. When he was done, he picked up the paper and looked at it. "Maybe I can use this to get Hillary to talk. If she witnessed the murder—watched the killer throw the rings off the pier—then she should be able to identify the killer."

"Before you talk to her, I have a favor to ask you."

"What's that?"

"I don't want Hillary to think I went digging around in my trash looking for her notes. If she thinks I wanted her notes, she'd have to assume I'd been poking around in her room and snooping."

"How do you want me to explain this?"

"I told Joe I had accidentally tossed some paperwork. I'd like to stick with that story. Say I found my papers in the trash—and some other papers were stuck to them, and I didn't realize it until later when I went back to my room. Tell her when I was sorting through the papers, I read hers—realized it sounded like Jolene's murder and felt I had to turn them over to you."

MacDonald considered her request for a moment. "Okay. But you know, this will probably still cause a problem with her. Don't be surprised if she checks out after she finds out you turned her incriminating notes over to me."

Danielle shrugged. "If she does, she does."

TWENTY

It was a few minutes after 9 a.m. when Danielle returned from the police station. Lily greeted her at the front door, informing her a new guest would be arriving that morning.

"She called right after you left. Said she understood we might have some vacancies and wanted to make a reservation."

"And she's coming the same day she made the reservation?"

"Yep. She said a friend recommended Marlow House," Lily explained as she walked with Danielle to the parlor. "Joanne's upstairs now, getting the room ready."

Danielle tossed her purse on the parlor desk. "How many people?"

"Just one. Her."

"Really?"

"This place is starting to feel like a sorority," Lily said with a laugh. "Except for Walt, of course."

"Where's she from?"

"I didn't get all the details. She mentioned something about flying into Portland last night and staying at a motel by the airport. Our conversation got cut short when her ride showed up. I figured she could give me her credit card information when she gets here."

Danielle sat down. "Obviously not someone who likes to plan out her travel itinerary in advance."

"Maybe someone with an adventurous spirit—or it's just a last minute trip, and she decided to make reservations when she got here." Lily sat on the sofa with Danielle and drew her bare feet up on the cushion, tucking them under her.

"You said her ride showed up? You sure it's just her, and she's not coming with someone?"

"She said a reservation for one. I figured the ride was probably a shuttle to the car rental place. She told me she wanted to stay for a week, so I imagine she rented a car."

"Did she say who her friend was? The one who recommended us?"

"No, I didn't get a chance to ask her."

"Did you get her name at least?" Danielle asked with a laugh.

"Melony Jacobs."

"Melony?" Furrowing her brow, Danielle considered the name a minute. "Why does that name sound familiar?"

"You think you know a Melony Jacobs?"

Danielle shook her head. "No…oh, wait…I remember now. Melony is the name of Jolene's daughter. I remember Marie and the chief mentioning it."

"You think Jolene's daughter is our new guest?"

Danielle shook her head. "I seriously doubt it. Why would she? I imagine Jolene's daughter will stay at her house when she comes to town."

Lily stood up from the sofa and walked to the doorway. She looked out into the hall and then closed the door. Returning to Danielle, she asked, "So what did the chief say?"

"He's going to talk to Hillary."

"When? I figured he might come back with you."

"He has someone else to interview first."

"Who? I can't imagine it's more important than talking to Hillary." Lily sat back down on the sofa.

"I did what I had to do. I passed the information on to the chief, and now he has to handle it."

"I suppose." Lily let out a sigh.

Danielle glanced up at the ceiling. "Is Hillary in her room?"

"Typing away. She never did come down for breakfast."

"When I left, Joanne mentioned something about taking her up a tray if she didn't come down."

Lily glanced up to the ceiling. "She took her up one. Should we start advertising Marlow House has room service?"

"Perhaps." Danielle smiled. "I imagine after the chief talks to Hillary, she's going to be pretty annoyed with us for giving him her notes. I wonder if we'll have another vacancy before the weekend."

Lily shrugged. "If we do, we do."

"That's pretty much what I figure too."

"By the way, have you heard from Chris yet?"

"No. I decided not to call him again." Danielle leaned back in the sofa and propped her feet on the coffee table.

"Maybe something's wrong. Aren't you worried?"

Danielle shrugged. "Not really. It hasn't been that long, and I know he's busy. It's not like he's my boyfriend or anything."

"But he—" Before Lily could finish her sentence, Danielle reached over and grabbed Lily's wrist, giving it a gentle squeeze. She nodded up to the ceiling. Danielle knew what Lily was about to say: *he kissed you.* But it had only been a spontaneous parting kiss at the airport. Since his absence, their almost daily phone conversations remained on the level of good friends—pals—not would-be lovers. Like her brief kiss with Walt, it hovered in her subconscious, yet remained virtually a taboo topic for discussion.

DANIELLE HAD BEEN BACK from the police station for about an hour when the doorbell rang. She and Lily were in the kitchen with Joanne, discussing the feasibility of installing an outdoor kitchen in the side yard before summer. Lily loved the idea, but Joanne warned that Frederickport's weather was not what they were used to in Sacramento, and the northwest coastal climate might not be conducive to what they had in mind. Lily disagreed, citing several outdoor kitchens she had seen in Astoria when she and Ian had gone there to interview Emma Jackson.

"I bet that's our new guest." Danielle stood up from the kitchen table.

"Her room's all ready," Joanne told her.

When Danielle opened the front door a few minutes later, she was shocked to find herself looking into the smiling face of Chris Johnson, aka Chris Glandon.

"Surprise!" he cheerfully greeted her.

Danielle broke into a broad smile and then realized Chris wasn't alone. Standing to his right was a tall, blond, stunning-looking woman. Noting Danielle's look of confusion, Chris quickly put his arm around the woman's waist and nudged her closer to the doorway, in clearer view of Danielle.

"Danielle, I want you to meet my friend Melony. Melony, this is Danielle Boatman. She owns Marlow House."

"Hello, nice to meet you," the beautiful blond woman said, extending her hand in greeting.

Momentarily speechless, Danielle accepted the greeting and forced a smile. Melony—her new guest—was the epitome of what Danielle—in her insecure youth—had longed to be. Tall, slender, obvious natural blonde, with vivid blue eyes and curly dark lashes. That insecure girl of Danielle's youth had returned.

"You're our new guest?" Danielle said with a smile, silently telling her former insecure self to go back into the shadows.

"Chris said I'd love it here. I'm just grateful you had a vacancy."

With one arm still around Melony, Chris used his free hand to pick up the suitcase sitting by his side. Danielle glanced down at it. She remembered Chris's luggage—she had been with him when he had purchased it. When initially coming to Marlow House, Chris's luggage had been a duffle bag. Danielle assumed the suitcase belonged to Melony.

She opened the door wider and stepped aside, making room for Melony and Chris to enter. "This is a surprise, Chris. I thought you were going to be in New York for a few more days."

Together, Chris and Melony walked into Marlow House. Danielle couldn't help but notice the pair looked like models—*a matching set.* She couldn't remember the last time she had felt so inadequate with her appearance. She remembered that insecure teenager she had been—the one who brought boyfriends home only to have her cousin, Cheryl, snatch them away and later cast them off when she grew bored.

Setting the suitcase on the floor and dropping his arm from Melony's waist, Chris stepped toward Danielle, preparing to give her a hello hug, when Walt appeared in the room, standing next to Danielle.

"So you've returned?" Walt asked, his tone reserved. He looked Melony up and down. "And you've returned with a friend?"

"I met Melony on the airplane," Chris explained, his eyes shifting from Danielle to Walt and then back to Danielle. "When I heard she was coming to Frederickport and would need a place to stay, I thought this would be perfect for her."

"Why not have her stay with you at your place?" Walt snickered.

Flashing a smile at Melony, Danielle said, "Your room's all ready. I hope you like it here."

"How about a welcome home hug?" Chris asked, ignoring Walt.

Without waiting for a response, Chris stepped to Danielle and wrapped her in a hug. Feeling a little less insecure, Danielle leaned into the embrace and closed her eyes for a moment.

"I missed you," Chris whispered in her ear right before releasing her.

"Now I know why I couldn't get you on the phone yesterday," Danielle said, regaining her emotional footing.

"Yeah, I spent most of the day on the airplane." Chris turned to Melony and smiled. "Fortunately I had good company."

"Is this your first time in Frederickport?" Danielle asked her new guest.

Melony shook her head. "No. I grew up here."

Danielle froze a moment and stared at Melony. She looked nothing like Jolene Carmichael, and yet…"Your mother wasn't Jolene Carmichael, was she?"

Melony nodded. "I guess you knew my mother?"

Danielle let out a deep breath and looked from Melony to Chris. "Yes, I did. A little. I'm so sorry for your loss."

"You knew her mother?" Chris asked with a frown. "Did I know her?"

Danielle shook her head. "I don't think so. I only met her recently—when you were in Chicago."

Walt noted the questioning looks exchanged between Danielle and Chris. He decided to fill in the blanks. "What Danielle isn't saying, your friend's mother is the woman who found the gold coins over at Ian's. I'm sure Danielle told you all about it when you two spoke on the phone."

Unaware of Walt's presence or the fact he was explaining the identity of her mother to Chris, Melony picked up the suitcase Chris had brought into the house and said something about how her mother had only recently returned to Frederickport. Chris wasn't listening to what Melony was saying, but was instead listening to Walt explain how Jolene Carmichael was the woman whose husband was the business partner of Clarence Renton—the attorney who had embezzled from Danielle's inheritance and had murdered Danielle's cousin, Cheryl.

"Chris, you're back!" Lily shouted from the hallway as she made her way from the kitchen to the foyer. Walt and Melony stopped talking, and they, along with Danielle and Chris, turned to face Lily.

"It's good to be home!" Chris greeted her. "How's Ian doing?"

When Lily reached the group, she gave Chris a brief hug. "You can ask him yourself. He's supposed to be on his way over here." She glanced at the blonde. "Hi, are you Melony?"

Before Melony could respond, another voice called out, "Melony Jacobs, is that you?" The group looked down the hallway and watched as Hillary Hemingway approached.

"Hillary? What are you doing in Oregon?" Melony asked.

In reply, Hillary gave Melony a brief, perfunctory hug and said, "My muse told me to come." Danielle and Lily exchanged glances.

Taking a step back from Hillary, Melony arched her brows and asked, "You think that was wise?"

"You two know each other?" Lily asked.

"Yes, we do. You know what they say about it being a small world." Hillary smiled. "So what brings you to Oregon?"

Without thought, Danielle blurted out, "Melony is Jolene's daughter. The woman who was murdered."

TWENTY-ONE

Steve Klein did not expect to spend his lunch hour in the Frederickport Police Department's interrogation room. When Chief MacDonald had called and insisted he come down to the station, Steve assumed their conversation would take place in Edward MacDonald's office.

Glancing around the small windowless room, he noticed the mirror on the far wall. He knew what it was: a two-way mirror. Steve remembered when it had been installed back when they had remodeled the police station.

In the early days, there was no security wall segregating the front lobby from the inner offices—no bulletproof glass separating the outside world from the office space of local law enforcement officers. Back then, the installation of the two-way mirror had caused a bit of a stir in town, as many locals disliked the idea of their community emulating the ways of a larger city.

He wondered if there was anyone watching him from the other side of the mirror. Sitting at the table in the center of the room, he glanced up at the wall clock adjacent to the mirror. He had been in the room—waiting—for five minutes.

Restless, he pulled his cellphone from his pocket, looked at it, and then set it on the tabletop and glanced around, shifting in the chair, trying to get more comfortable. Just as he was about to pick his phone up again, the door opened, and Chief MacDonald walked in, carrying a manila folder.

"What's this about?" Klein snapped. "You demand I come down here and keep me waiting forever. I'm sure whatever you needed to ask me could have been asked on the phone."

MacDonald closed the door behind him and briefly glanced to the wall clock. "Sorry about the wait, but it was my understanding you got here just a few minutes ago. I was on the phone when you arrived and came here as soon as the call ended."

"It doesn't matter if you kept me waiting five minutes or fifty. There's no reason I had to come down in the first place. Like I said, you could have easily asked me what you needed to know over the phone and saved us both some time. I have a busy schedule today."

MacDonald walked to the table and sat down across from Steve. "I really didn't want to ask you this on the phone."

"Ask me what?"

"If you killed Jolene Carmichael."

Steve stood abruptly. "What in the hell kind of question is that?"

MacDonald motioned for Steve to sit back down. "Before you answer that question, you might want to have your attorney present." He went on to recite the Miranda rights to the stunned bank manager.

Steve sat back on the chair. "Am I under arrest?"

"No." MacDonald studied Steve.

"Then what the hell was that all about?" he snapped.

"I just wanted to make sure you completely understand your rights before we continue. Do you want to call your attorney?"

"This is ridiculous. I didn't kill Jolene."

"Then you're waiving your right to have an attorney present?"

"Sure—fine—whatever—why am I really down here? You know I didn't kill Jolene."

"Is it true you were having an affair with Carla?"

Steve stared at MacDonald. Finally, he asked, "What does my personal life have to do with Jolene?"

"A great deal if Jolene was blackmailing you over your personal life. Threatening to go to your wife if you refused to give her that loan she so desperately needed."

Absently combing his fingers through his hair, Steve shook his head. "I don't know where you get the idea she was blackmailing me."

Opening the folder he had carried into the room, MacDonald removed a piece of paper and slid it across the table.

"What's this?"

"Looks a little like Jolene blackmailing you." MacDonald leaned back in the chair and watched. "Of course, one does need to read between the lines."

With a frown, Steve started to read what appeared to be a computer printout from an email account. The moment he realized what he was looking at, he snatched the paper from the table and waved it in the air. "Where did you get this?"

"Jolene sent that the same day she was murdered."

"You have no right to go looking through my email. Did you have a search warrant? If you didn't, you have no right to this!"

"I didn't go through your email, Steve. I had no reason to—at least, none that I knew of until I saw that." MacDonald nodded to the paper in Steve's hand.

"Where did you get this?"

"Carla was afraid. She brought it to me."

Dropping the paper to the table, Steve slumped back in his chair. "Carla? Carla thinks I killed Jolene?"

"She didn't until she read that."

Staring down at the paper on the table, Steve shook his head. "I didn't have anything to do with Jolene's death." He looked up at MacDonald. "I don't want my wife to know."

"That will be a little hard to keep from her if I have to charge you with murder."

"I didn't kill anyone! What do you need to know? I'll cooperate with you, but please don't say anything to my wife. Keep her out of this."

"You can start by telling me what you didn't the first two times I talked to you about Jolene's murder. Start with Carla and you, and how Jolene knew."

Closing his eyes briefly, Steve took a deep breath and then exhaled. He stared across the table at MacDonald. "About a month ago, Carla and I sort of hooked up. It started as harmless flirting, and then…well, one night when I was alone, I stopped at Pier Café and had something to eat. My wife was out of town, so I wasn't in any big hurry to get home. After I left the restaurant, I decided to walk down the pier. See if anyone was catching anything. By the time I went back to the parking lot to get my car and go home, the restaurant had closed down. Carla had locked up that night and was the last one to leave. I ran into her in the parking lot."

"So you started talking, one thing led to another, and you went home with her? And then sometime during your affair Jolene saw you?"

"Actually, I didn't go home with her that night." Steve confessed. "She was upset about something, so I sat in her car with her for a while and listened to her. And well…one thing led to another…"

"Are you saying you and Carla hooked up the first time—in her car—in the parking lot of Pier Café?"

Steve shrugged. "It seemed pretty exciting at the time."

"And cramped," McDonald mumbled under his breath. He then remembered another time—back in February—when Carla had admitted to him about hooking up with a customer in the back of her car after work. *I really need to have someone patrol that parking lot more frequently.*

"I can't believe Carla thinks I murdered Jolene." Steve picked the paper back up off the table and looked at it a moment. Glancing up to MacDonald, he asked, "If Carla brought you this, she obviously got into my email account someway. I never gave her my password."

"I can't see Carla as a skilled hacker. My guess, if you didn't give her your password, she figured it out. Do you use something obvious like your pet's name?"

Steve didn't respond.

"Tell me about you and Jolene."

"She came to the bank for a loan. When she was turned down, she came to me. Thought I could pull some strings. I told her I couldn't help her. She had no collateral. What she brought in each month barely covered her living expenses."

"So she discovers your little secret, she sends you that email in the morning, and that night, she's dead."

Steve shook his head. "No. Ask Carla. Before Jolene ever came into the restaurant that night, I told her we had to cool it. I got that email and figured Jolene must have seen me and Carla together around town, maybe noticed something in our body language and imagined we were fooling around. She always had a dirty mind."

"Umm…well…you *were* fooling around."

"True. But I don't believe Jolene knew that for sure. I certainly never intended to confirm it. I figured, when Jolene came to me, expecting to get the loan, I'd just play dumb, deny it, tell her she was crazy. Figured if she intended to make good on her threat, she'd give me some final ultimatum. Then I'd go to my wife and tell her how bat-shit crazy Jolene Carmichael was and how she was trying to blackmail me over an affair I wasn't having."

"What did Jolene say to you that night when she came into the restaurant?"

"Pretty much what I told you before. Although, she asked me if I got her email."

"What did you tell her?"

"I played dumb, told her I hadn't gotten anything—pretended I thought she was talking about my work email. She said no, she meant my private email. I lied and told her I hadn't had time to check it yet."

"What did she say?"

"Told me I needed to go home and read it and to expect her in the morning so she could finalize the loan."

"What did you say?"

"She just got up and walked away. I didn't have a chance to say anything. I just figured when she came in the next morning, I'd keep playing dumb."

"Sounds like you had this all figured out."

"I just had no reason to kill Jolene. All I needed to do was end it with Carla. It's not like it was some love affair. We were just having a little fun."

"But you didn't end it with Carla, did you?"

"What do you mean?"

"You were with her again after Jolene was killed."

Steve shrugged. "Yeah. With Jolene dead, I didn't see the harm. But afterwards, I realized it had gotten too complicated and figured it would be best to end it." Steve tossed the paper back onto the table. It slipped across the tabletop and floated off and down to the floor. "I just never imagined Carla would turn on me like this. She got into my email. Came to you." He shook his head.

"She was afraid."

Steve rolled his eyes. "Right. I'm so terrifying. More like she's playing the vindictive card because I ended our relationship."

"Jolene is dead. I'd say Carla has a right to feel vulnerable, especially if she believes you might have killed Jolene. You did have a motive."

"I didn't kill anyone. Anyway, Carla had as much of a motive as I did to kill her. More."

"How do you figure?"

"Because when I went to the restaurant that night after getting Jolene's email, I told Carla we had to cool it. I told her Jolene knew about our affair, and I didn't want her going to my wife. I said if we stopped seeing each other, she wouldn't be able to prove anything, because I didn't believe she had any tangible proof."

"So why does that give Carla a motive?"

"Because she wanted me to leave my wife."

"I thought you said you and Carla were just…having fun?"

"We were, and I was always up front with her. But I'm not stupid. I know she hoped I'd someday leave my wife and marry her. She figured if she stuck around long enough—did whatever I wanted—I'd eventually leave my wife for her." Steve smiled. "That was never going to happen—but—well, when a young woman is desperate to get in a man's wallet and is looking to board the gravy train—she can be mighty accommodating, if you know what I mean."

Steve started to say something else when he glanced over to the mirror and froze. Standing up abruptly, he pointed to the mirror. "Who's listening?"

"Don't worry, Steve, your wife doesn't have to know…for now. Although, you better pray Carla has a long healthy life."

"What are you talking about?"

"If she's involved in any unfortunate accident, I'll be bringing you in again for questioning. I'll make sure your wife is in the next room, listening."

"YOU REALLY DON'T THINK Steve had anything to do with Jolene's murder?" Brian asked MacDonald after Steve left the station. He and Joe sat with the chief in the break room.

"Is he a killer? It's possible. I'm not ruling it out. But there is one thing I learned about Steve Klein today."

"What's that?" Joe asked.

MacDonald downed his soda and then said, "That guy is a major jerk."

TWENTY-TWO

"This is lovely," Melony told Danielle when she was finally shown up to her room. She turned to face Danielle, who stood in the doorway. "Chris told me on the plane you had a cancellation resulting in a vacancy. It seemed like an unexpected stroke of luck after all the recent unpleasantness. I think I'll be quite comfortable here."

"I'll admit I'm a little surprised you decided to stay here instead of your mother's house."

Melony smiled. "Do you mean because of what my father's business partner did?"

Danielle studied Melony for a moment before asking, "You know what Clarence Renton did?"

"Of course. Even though I rarely spoke to my mother, I do watch the news. Just so you know, I never cared for Clarence. I knew him all my life, he was my father's best friend, but I loathed that man."

"Why are you staying here?" Danielle didn't intend to voice the question; it just popped out of her mouth.

Melony set her suitcase on the bed and then turned to face Danielle again. She sat on the edge of the mattress. "When I heard about my mother, I booked a flight as soon as possible. I wanted to get my mother's estate settled and put it behind me. In my haste, I really didn't consider where I'd be staying."

"I'd just assumed you'd want to stay at your mother's."

Melony shook her head. "Too many unpleasant memories. When I was on the plane, talking to Chris, and he mentioned Marlow House, well, it just seemed right. Coming full circle."

Danielle frowned. "I'm afraid I don't understand."

"I wanted to meet you."

"Meet me? Why?"

Melony stood up. "It's hard to explain." Cocking her head to one side, she studied Danielle for a moment and then asked, "What was your relationship with my mother? I know you knew her."

"Honestly, your mother didn't like me very much."

Melony laughed. "I don't imagine she did. From what I understand, Clarence's little downfall took her with him. Unfortunately, Mother was not very good at accepting personal responsibility."

"I take it you and your mother weren't close?"

"No—definitely not close. To say my mother and I had issues would be an understatement." Melony opened her suitcase and started to unpack. She paused a moment and smiled at Danielle. "I imagine you think I'm awful?"

"Awful?"

"My mother was just killed—murdered, which adds an even more tragic element—and I'm not showing proper grief. Some would assume that because of those issues, my grief should be more devastating—losing a mother before she and I were able to resolve our issues." Melony let out a sigh and grabbed some of her clothes. She turned and put them in a dresser drawer.

"I was under the impression your mother moved to New York to be with you after your father died."

"True. That's what she told everyone. But it wasn't the case." Turning back to the bed, Melony looked up to Danielle. "You see, I came to terms with my mother years ago. Counseling helped. I learned I didn't have to like—or love—my mother simply because she was the woman who raised me."

DANIELLE FOUND LILY, Walt, and Chris downstairs in the parlor.

"Is Melony all settled in?" Lily asked.

"She's unpacking." Danielle turned her attention to Chris, who sat on the sofa next to Lily. Walt stood by the bookshelf, a cigar in hand. "I figured you'd have gone to your place and get unpacked yourself."

Chris flashed her a smile. "Plenty of time for that. And Marlow House feels like home." He leaned back in the sofa and propped one ankle casually over the opposing knee.

"Don't get too comfortable," Walt grumbled.

"Aw, come on, Walt, admit it, you're happy to see me. Someone else to talk to." Chris grinned.

"I'll take that as my cue to go." Lily stood up.

"What do you mean?" Danielle asked.

"I always feel weird sitting in on these conversations with Walt." Lily looked to where the source of the cigar scent drifted from. "No offense, Walt."

"None taken, Lily." Walt puffed his cigar.

"Anyway, I'm going to see what's taking Ian. Thought I'd let him know you're back." Lily flashed Chris a smile and started for the door. She paused at the doorway and looked back. "Welcome home."

"Glad to be home!"

When Lily left, Danielle took her place on the sofa next to Chris. "Melony seems nice, but I felt a little uncomfortable up there when she was talking about her mom. I didn't like Jolene, but it felt strange listening to Melony talk about her—so detached."

"Apparently they had some issues," Chris said.

"No kidding," Danielle scoffed.

"I had no idea her mom was the woman you told me about on the phone. Do they have any idea who murdered her?"

"I think you might ask our other guest," Walt said, strolling from his place by the bookshelf and taking a seat facing Danielle and Chris.

"You talking about that lady I just met?" Chris asked.

Walt looked to the open doorway. In the next moment, the door closed, seemingly on its own volition. Neither Chris nor Danielle seemed surprised.

"Hillary Hemingway, that's her name," Danielle explained. "I told you about her. She's a mystery writer. I guess sort of famous. She's one of Ian's favorite authors."

"What did Walt mean?" Chris asked.

"On the night Jolene was murdered…" Danielle began. She then went on to tell Chris about the writer's notes Walt had read and then told him what she knew about Jolene's murder. By the time she finished filling him in on what had been going on, he sat next to her, silently shaking his head.

"You don't think your writer had anything to do with Jolene's death, do you?" Chris asked.

"Like I told you, MacDonald suspects Hillary witnessed the murder but didn't say anything. He said that's not uncommon. Witnesses are often reluctant to come forward. But he plans to show her those notes I gave him and see what she says. Of course, he figures she'll probably tell him she wrote that after she read the article in the paper about finding Jolene's rings off the pier. But maybe he can get her to step up and do the right thing. And if the killer finds out Hillary saw him, she could be in danger."

"But maybe the chief is wrong," Chris suggested.

"Wrong how?" Walt asked.

"Are you both forgetting your guests know each other. Don't you think that's a little odd?"

Danielle frowned. "That's right. I meant to ask Melony how she knew Hillary, but when she started talking about her mom up there —well—I started feeling like a voyeur."

Walt cocked his brow at Danielle and asked with a chuckle, "Voyeur?"

"It was just weird." Danielle shrugged.

"Melony is a very nice woman," Chris said. "I enjoyed talking with her on the plane."

"She's quite beautiful, too," Walt observed.

"I suppose she is. But I prefer brunettes." Chris flashed Danielle a smile.

"I prefer not to judge a woman by her hair color," Walt countered.

Danielle couldn't help but laugh. "That's very—*enlightened*—of you, Walt."

Walt flashed Chris a smug smile and took another drag off his cigar.

"Oh, I haven't told you." Danielle looked at Chris. "There was a break-in at the Gusarov Estate. Everything's okay, but some homeless guy was living there. We found him the day of the murder."

Chris frowned. "We who?"

Danielle went on to tell Chris the part of the story she had forgotten to tell him—about the wine bottle with Adam's fingerprints and how she had gone to the estate with Joe, Brian, and Adam.

"I'm just glad you didn't go over there yourself and run into that guy," Chris told her after she finished recounting the events. "That could have been dangerous."

"I don't think he was a dangerous guy. Just some poor homeless man."

"But if he admitted to taking the wine bottle down to the beach, how can the chief be so sure he isn't the killer?" Chris asked.

"For one reason, he was in the ER at the local hospital during the time of Jolene's murder. It couldn't have been him."

"My next question—why would Adam spend so much on one bottle of wine? A case of beer would make me happy."

"That's pretty much what I told him," Danielle said.

Walt stood up and waved his hand. The cigar vanished. "I'll let you two catch up in private. I suppose you don't need me hanging around." In the next moment, Walt vanished.

Chris looked from where Walt had been sitting, back to Danielle. "How's it been going with you two?"

"Going? What do you mean?"

Chris shrugged. "I don't know. I guess I just wondered if Walt was glad to get me out of his hair for a while. Have you to himself."

ON THE SECOND FLOOR, Walt watched as Hillary approached Melony's room. Its door was ajar. She peeked in. Curious, Walt moved to the door, standing next to Hillary. Looking into the room, he could see Melony standing by her bed. He watched as she closed her suitcase and then lifted it from the mattress before placing it in the closet.

Tentatively, Hillary knocked.

"Come in," Melony called out, her back to the door.

Hillary stepped into the room. "Are you all settled in?"

Walt followed her into the room and listened.

Melony turned to face Hillary. "Yes. It's been a long time, Hillary. How have you been?"

"Good. Working on a new book."

"Yes, you mentioned something about your muse. He brought you here?"

Hillary smiled. "I suppose. In a manner of speaking."

"How long are you staying?" Melony asked.

"I planned to stay at least a month. I've been here a few weeks already. And you?"

"Just long enough to get my mother's estate settled."

"I'm sorry about your mother. I knew you were from Oregon, but had no idea you were from Frederickport," Hillary told her.

"I find that hard to believe. You have a way of knowing everything."

When Hillary didn't respond, Melony asked, "Why are you really here?"

"I told you, my muse—"

"Enough with that muse crap, Hillary. If I had my way, you'd be in a mental institution, writing your damn books."

Walt thought Hillary looked as if she had been slapped. "I…I can't believe you just said that," she stammered.

"And I can't believe you're here!" Melony snapped.

"Melony, I know this must be hard on you; you just lost your mother."

"You don't know anything about me!"

"No…I suppose I don't. But you really know nothing about me either."

"Don't I?"

Hillary turned from Melony and rushed from the room. Walt watched as she retreated into her bedroom. He heard a clicking sound—Hillary had locked her door.

Walt was still standing by Melony's doorway when she walked through him and slammed her door shut. Walt glanced down, watching as Melony again walked through him, returning to her bed. She sat down and began to cry.

With a shake of his head, he looked to the crying woman and back to the closed door. "I have to say I don't believe you two are friends."

TWENTY-THREE

"It doesn't prove you didn't kill Jolene," Bill told Adam. The two sat in a booth in the diner, waiting for their lunch order to arrive.

"What do you mean it doesn't prove I didn't kill her? I told you that guy who broke in admitted he took the wine bottle down to the beach and left it there. His fingerprints were all over it."

"And they also found your fingerprint." Bill picked up his glass of iced tea and took a swig.

Adam frowned across the table at Bill. "From when I put that bottle in the house."

Bill shrugged. "Still doesn't prove you didn't kill her. You threatened to kill her once."

"Lord, that's ancient history. And I was drunk."

"It was right before she left town. I seemed to remember you saying something like, *'If you ever come back to Frederickport, I'll kill you.'* And she did just move back."

"Shut up. You're just being a jerk."

Bill laughed and took another drink of his iced tea. "Yeah, I am. You just better hope MacDonald doesn't hear about your little threat to Jolene. Do you remember who else heard you say it? I can't remember who was all there."

Adam shrugged. "Hell, I was so drunk that night, I barely remember saying it."

Bill shoved his glass of tea aside and glanced toward their waitress, who was taking an order on the other side of the room. "The food is taking long enough today."

"That would be one hell of a coincidence. Picking up an empty bottle on the beach that I happened to buy before it was stolen and left there. And then I use it as a murder weapon. That's quite a stretch."

"Or incredibly crappy luck. Especially if you thought you'd wiped off all your fingerprints—except for one you left when you first bought the bottle. Now that would be crappy luck."

"Oh, shut up."

"Have you heard from Melony?"

Before Adam could answer, a server arrived with their food. After they were alone again, Bill picked up his sandwich. Before taking a bite, he looked across the table and asked, "Well, have you?"

"Have I what?"

"Talked to Melony?"

Adam frowned, picked up a French fry, and popped it into his mouth. Bill watched, waiting for an answer. Adam picked up a second fry. Feeling Bill's eyes on him, he glared across the table. "No. I haven't talked to Melony, and I doubt I will. I wouldn't even be surprised if she didn't come back to town."

"Not even to settle her mother's estate? I'd think she'd want to sell her mom's house." Bill smiled at Adam. "Hey, I bet she'll have you list the property."

Adam rolled his eyes and chuckled. "Now that would make Jolene roll over in her grave."

"When is the funeral, by the way?"

"I heard there isn't going to be one. She's being cremated." Lifting his sandwich to his mouth, Adam paused a moment and said, "So I guess she won't be rolling around in her grave. But if I listed her house, she would probably come back and haunt us. That, I could definitely do without."

"I have to admit that woman had balls. With the history of you two, for her to go to your rental and try claiming those gold coins." Bill shook his head at the thought.

"Like I said, all that is old news. Happened a long time ago. Hell, as far as I know, I didn't threaten to kill her. You probably told me that to be a jerk."

Bill chuckled. "No, you said it. You were pretty drunk, but you said it."

A few minutes later Adam's cellphone vibrated, signifying an incoming text message. Setting his half-eaten sandwich back on his plate, he picked up his phone and looked at it.

"It's from Chris. He's back in town. I thought he was going to be gone for a few more days."

"Did you replace the wine yet?" Bill asked.

Adam shook his head. "No. They don't sell that wine locally. I haven't had a chance to replace it. I'll probably do what Danielle suggested."

"What's that?"

"Pick up a couple cases of beer for him."

Bill laughed. "Well, that would have saved you a hell of a lot of money if you had done that in the first place. Not to mention you probably wouldn't have been hauled down to the police station."

The phone vibrated again. Adam picked it up from the table and looked at it. "He got a car."

"Who?"

"Chris. Told me to stop by and see it." Adam then laughed.

"What's so funny?" Bill asked.

"He told me not to forget to bring him a case of beer to make up for the wine."

BEFORE HEADING over to Chris's house, Adam stopped by the grocery store and bought a couple cases of beer. It was much cheaper than the bottle of wine he had originally purchased. Chris obviously knew about the stolen bottle of wine, which Adam assumed Danielle had told him about, along with how much he had spent. He figured since it was the thought that counted—or so his grandmother was always telling him—as long as Chris knew he had spent a fortune on a thank you gift, the pricy purchase wasn't a complete waste.

When Adam drove down Beach Drive, he noticed a new car parked in front of Marlow House. It had dealer's plates. He guessed it was Chris's new car. Just to be sure, he drove down the street to Chris's house. There was no car in Chris's driveway, and by the looks of the closed blinds, he suspected Chris was still visiting with Danielle. Making a U-turn, Adam headed back to Marlow House.

When Danielle answered the door a few minutes later, Chris was by her side. Adam pointed over his shoulder and said, "I have some beer in the car I'm trying to deliver."

Chris let out a laugh and shook Adam's hand in greeting. "I heard about the wine. Thanks for the thought."

"I figured Danielle would tell you." Adam followed Chris into the house.

"I guess a lot's been going on since I've been gone." Chris closed the door.

Adam paused a moment and looked back at the closed door. "I was serious. I have some beer in the car for you."

"I'll get it in a minute and toss it in my car. Thanks. You'll have to stop by and help me drink it."

"As long as it doesn't get ripped off first, like the wine." Adam then smiled at Danielle and said hello. He and Chris followed her into the living room.

"We have a new guest. Someone you know," Danielle told Adam when she sat down on the sofa.

"Someone I know?" Adam asked as he took a seat.

"Yeah. Chris met her on his flight. When he found out she was coming to Frederickport, he suggested she stay here."

Adam frowned. "Who is it?"

"Melony—Jolene's daughter," Danielle told him.

"Melony? She's here?" Adam glanced at the door leading to the hallway. He stood up.

"She's upstairs."

"I guess I can understand why she doesn't want to stay at her mom's." Adam glanced at his watch. "You know, I really need to get back to the office." He looked at Chris. "Is your car unlocked? I can just put the beer in it. Or maybe stop by later and give it to you."

Chris stood. "I'll go out with you. I wanted to show you my new car anyway."

Just as they stepped back into the hallway, a woman's voice called out, "Adam? Adam Nichols? Is it really you?"

Danielle silently watched from the living room doorway as Melony approached Adam. If she was Adam's old friend, one he was excited to see, his blank expression didn't give away his feelings.

"Melony…" Adam put out his hand in greeting.

She accepted his hand and then pulled him in for a brief hug and whispered, "Come on Adam, a handshake?"

"I didn't consider you two probably knew each other," Chris said when the brief hug ended. He stood with Adam, Melony, and Danielle in the foyer.

"Yeah, Adam and I grew up together," Melony explained. "On our first day of kindergarten I made him cry."

Adam laughed. "I didn't cry."

"Sure you did." Melony smiled. She glanced at Chris and then Danielle. "I hope you don't mind if I steal Adam away. I'd like to talk to him a moment in private."

Danielle pointed to the door leading to the parlor. "You can have some privacy in there."

"I really need to get back to the office," Adam stammered.

"Don't be silly. This will only take a minute. I can't believe you haven't time for an old friend." Melony grabbed hold of his hand and began leading him to the parlor.

"Shall I see what she wants to say to him?" Walt asked when he appeared the next moment. He flashed a smile at Danielle and Chris and then followed Adam and Melony into the parlor.

The moment they entered the small room, Melony closed the door and turned to face Adam. Her smile vanished. "Did you kill her?"

"I wasn't expecting that," Walt murmured. He took a step away from the pair and leaned back on the edge of the desk, watching.

"Seriously, that's the first thing you ask me after all these years? Did I kill her?"

Melony shrugged and then walked farther into the room. Turning to face Adam, she plopped down on the sofa and looked up. "Well, it did cross my mind. Mother called me, by the way, after she found that gold in your grandmother's house. She told me how angry you were. Reminded me of how you'd threatened her."

"I was drunk, Mel. That was a long time ago."

She shrugged again. "I suppose…an ocean's gone under that particular bridge."

With a sigh, Adam took a seat on a chair facing the sofa.

"How have you been, Adam?"

He studied her a moment and then laughed. "You haven't changed, Mel. One moment asking me if I killed your mother and the next casually asking how I've been."

"I only asked because I wanted to know if I should thank you."

"Whoo…that's cold, Mel. Even for you."

"After I left Frederickport, our relationship didn't improve."

"Funny, when I ran into your mother that time—" Adam paused a moment and let out a wry chuckle "—when I supposedly threatened to kill her—at least according to Bill—she told me how you two had worked it all out. Ironic, I've a spotty memory regarding what I actually said to her, but I can clearly remember everything she said to me."

"Mother was never very good at telling the truth. How is Bill, by the way? Is he married, a bunch of kids?"

"Bill?" Adam laughed. "No, he's never been married. He has a handyman service in town and does a lot of work for me. Hasn't really changed since high school, maybe smokes more."

"What about you? Mother told me you were still single. Why's that?"

Adam shrugged. "I was in a serious relationship a while back. She died."

Melony's smile softened. "I'm sorry."

Walt narrowed his eyes and studied Adam. "Are you talking about Isabella?" he asked aloud, knowing neither party could hear him. "Yes, she died, like a year after you two broke it off."

"Did your husband come with you?"

"No. We're getting a divorce."

TWENTY-FOUR

When Walt eventually left Melony and Adam, he found Danielle and Chris in the living room. "Those two have a history," he announced.

Rolling her eyes, Danielle shook her head and said, "I can't believe you followed them in there."

Walt raised his eyebrows and smirked. "That means you don't want to know what I heard?" With a wave of his hand, a lit cigar appeared. He took a puff.

"Of course I want to hear," Danielle confessed.

Chris chuckled. "What kind of history are we talking?"

"To begin with, the first thing she asked Adam when they went into the room was if he killed her mother."

"She thought he killed her mother?" Danielle's eyes darted to the open doorway.

Walt shook his head. "I don't think it was a serious question. But from what was said, it was obvious there was no love lost between Jolene and Adam, and Melony mentioned something about Adam once threatening Jolene."

"That's still an odd thing for her to ask Adam," Chris said with a frown. "Even if she was joking, that humor is a little dark considering her mother was just murdered."

"When they took him in for questioning after finding his fingerprints on the wine bottle, Marie did allude to some past between

Melony and Adam, something that might make him appear guilty. I asked Adam about it, but he pretty much told me to mind my own business."

"I suspect there was something romantic between those two." Walt watched the smoke from his cigar curl and drift to the ceiling.

"Why do you say that?" Chris asked.

"When Melony asked him why he hadn't gotten married, he told her he had been in a long-term relationship, but she died."

Danielle shrugged. "That's true. He dated Isabella for a long time—a long time for Adam."

Walt looked at Danielle and shook his head. "He made it sound as if their relationship ended with her death. Completely different implication. And then, when she was asking him if he was seeing anyone—questioning him on the possibility of marriage in the future—"

Danielle interrupted Walt with a laugh. "Marie would love that. Sometimes I suspect it's what keeps her going; she's determined to see her grandson married. But Adam practically breaks out into hives when that topic comes up."

Walt smiled. "According to what Adam just told Melony, he can't imagine ever getting married because he lost the love of his life."

"Isabella?" Danielle frowned. "He called Isabella the love of his life?"

"He didn't mention her by name," Walt told her. "But that's who Melony assumed he was talking about."

Danielle started to say something, but grew silent when she heard the door to the parlor open and then heard Melony's and Adam's voices coming in their direction.

"Are you still going to show me your house?" Melony asked Chris a few moments later when she reached the doorway to the living room. "Adam said he would give me a lift down there."

"You don't need to get back to the office?" Chris asked Adam.

"No. I'm the boss."

Chris looked over at Danielle. "You coming with us?"

"I suppose." She glanced over to Walt.

"Looks like a nice day out," Walt told her. "Have fun."

MELONY STOOD on Chris's back patio and gazed out at the ocean. White puffy clouds, without a hint of gray, dotted the blue sky. Closing her eyes a moment, she took a deep breath—drinking in the cool, salty air. The sound of waves washing up on the nearby shore filled her head. The momentary sensation of isolation was broken a moment later when she heard the sliding glass door open.

"It's an amazing view, isn't it?" came Danielle's voice.

Melony turned toward the house and smiled at Danielle, who had just stepped out onto the patio. "I always said if I ever moved back to Frederickport, I'd have to get a house on the beach." She turned back to face the ocean.

Danielle shut the sliding door behind her. She walked to Melony and asked, "Did you ever consider moving back? I imagine living in New York was a huge culture shock after growing up here." She stood beside Melony. If they took just two more steps, they would be standing on the beach.

"I suppose it would have been had I moved directly from Frederickport to New York. But I moved from here when I was fourteen. I didn't move to New York until after I finished college."

Danielle glanced to Melony. "I thought your family lived in Frederickport until your father died."

"My parents did. Let's just say I was considered a bit of a wild child in my youth. My parents sent me off to a boarding school in France."

Danielle studied Melony, who continued to gaze out to the ocean. "France?"

"I imagine my mother later regretted spending all that money shipping me over there, considering how she ended up losing everything."

Danielle thought Melony sounded amused as opposed to regretful over the observation.

"So you never lived in Frederickport again?" Danielle asked.

"I never even came back for a visit. This is the first time I've been back since I left at age fourteen."

"Wow..." Danielle muttered under her breath, unsure what to say.

"Funny thing..." Melony let out a deep sigh before continuing. "This place still feels like home—the good parts of home I remember. I never realized how much I missed it until just now."

Danielle studied Melony for a moment. "I thought you were friends with Chief MacDonald's late wife."

Melony turned to Danielle and smiled. "You know Eddy?"

"Eddy?" Danielle choked out, suppressing a laugh.

"I guess he's not called Eddy anymore?" Melony asked with a smile.

"Umm…no, not really."

"His wife and I were roommates in college. She was a good person. They always say the good ones die young."

"I assumed you were friends from Frederickport."

Melony shook her head. "No. It was one of those small-world things. My roommate ends up moving to my hometown after she gets married. But we always kept in touch. Once a year we'd meet up someplace for a girls' weekend. I miss that."

"The chief is a good guy. We've become close friends."

Melony looked at Danielle and cocked her brow. "Close friends? I…well, I sort of assumed you were the one Chris was talking about."

Danielle frowned. "I'm not sure what you mean."

"When you said you and Eddy were close friends, did you—"

"No!" Danielle interrupted with a laugh. "Not that kind of friend. I consider the chief a good friend, but strictly platonic. In fact, he's dating a nice lady named Carol Ann."

Melony shrugged. "Well, he's a great guy. I just want to see him happy." She studied Danielle a moment and then asked, "So you and Chris, I was right? You two a couple?"

Danielle glanced to the sliding glass door and then back to Melony. "Honestly, I'm not sure what Chris and I are exactly. It's sort of complicated."

Melony looked back to the ocean and laughed. "Isn't it always?"

"I suppose it is." Danielle smiled.

"I'm in the middle of a somewhat amicable divorce." Melony glanced at Danielle for a moment. "You ever been married?"

"Yes. He was killed in a car accident over a year ago."

"Oh, I'm sorry."

With a wry chuckle, Danielle said, "That relationship was also complicated."

Melony laughed and then glanced briefly to the closed sliding door. "What are the guys doing, anyway?"

"I think Chris is still showing Adam his car."

"Still? What is there to show?"

Danielle shrugged. "The last time I looked, Chris was opening the hood so Adam could look at the engine."

"You want to take a walk down on the beach? I'm dying to get my feet wet."

"The water's cold," Danielle warned.

"Which is why my feet are the only things getting wet." Melony slipped off her shoes and tossed them aside.

When they reached the water's edge, Melony began asking Danielle about the *Eva Aphrodite*. She had read about its mysterious appearance and then departure and understood it had washed up on the north side of town. Danielle pointed to the area where the ship had beached itself—*with Jack's help*.

The two women stood by the shore's edge. Water from the incoming waves washed toward them, threatening to soak their feet. So far, they remained dry. The topic of conversation shifted when Melony started telling Danielle about a family friend who lived along this stretch of the beach, when a woman's shout distracted Danielle. "You came!"

Turning to the ocean, toward the shout, Danielle found herself staring into the face of Jolene Carmichael. As she had at the pier, Jolene ignored Danielle, this time focusing her attention on her daughter.

Oblivious to her mother's ghostly presence, Melony prattled on, speculating as to which house along this stretch of the beach had belonged to their friend.

"I was just trying to protect you!" Jolene cried out to Melony. She hovered over the water, less than four feet away. Outstretching her arms, reaching for Melony, she begged, "Please don't ignore me!" In the next instant she vanished.

"Do you know?" Melony asked.

Danielle blinked her eyes and glanced around, looking for Jolene.

"Danielle?"

Giving herself an internal shake, Danielle looked to Melony and smiled sheepishly. "I'm sorry, I didn't hear what you said. I…I thought I heard a woman shouting. It must have been my imagination."

"I was just asking if you knew if Pete Rogers still lives in this neighborhood."

"Pete?" Danielle frowned.

"Yes. He was the family friend I was just telling you about. When I was a kid, we used to have cookouts on the beach behind his house. I wondered if he still lived in Frederickport."

"Yeah, Pete's still here. When the *Eva Aphrodite* washed up on shore, the historical society wanted to see about keeping it here as some sort of historical exhibit. Pete was not thrilled with the idea. Fortunately, that problem took care of itself when it washed back out to sea and sank."

"I saw the pictures online. I can't say I blame him. It would be a shame to spoil this view." Melony turned toward the row of houses and pointed to one. "I think that's Pete's house."

"You're right. It is."

Melony grinned. "I thought it was. Do you mind if we walk over and say hi?"

A few minutes later, Melony and Danielle stood at Pete's back door. After knocking several times, they decided he wasn't home.

"I can walk over later and say hi," Melony said.

As they made their way back to Chris's, Melony asked, "Do you know Pete very well?"

"Not really. When the *Eva Aphrodite* washed up, he thought I should pay to haul it off since it was once owned by Walt Marlow."

Melony laughed. "That sounds like Pete. He was always kind of tight. I just appreciated the cookouts he'd have behind his house. Those are some of the good memories I have about living in Frederickport."

TWENTY-FIVE

Max's purr reminded Walt of the electric fan Joanne sometimes used in the kitchen. Lazily stretched out across the attic windowsill—eyes closed—Max's chin rested on his front paws. Spittle dribbled down from his mouth, ignored by the woman absently stroking his back.

Hillary gazed out the glass pane, not noticing the hefty cat might at any second roll off his narrow perch. Her attention fixed on Danielle, who was down on the sidewalk, approaching Marlow House's front gate.

Walt studied Hillary as she stared out the window. He had found her standing by his spotting scope after Danielle had left the house with Chris, Melony, and Adam. He had been surprised to discover she had invaded his private space. He could only recall one or two times she had wandered up here. Walt had no idea what she was thinking, but when she stopped stroking Max, he observed the cat lift his head, open his eyes, and stare intently at the woman for several minutes. He knew exactly what the cat was thinking.

"Don't you dare bite her," Walt warned.

Blinking once, Max turned his golden eyes to Walt and let out a loud meow.

Hearing the cat's cry, Hillary glanced down and smiled. Her hand moved over his silky fur. Max settled his chin back onto his paws and began purring again.

Walt shook his head and chuckled. "Max, you can't go around biting our guests just because they stop petting you. You'll get Danielle in trouble."

Ignoring Walt, Max continued to purr. Enjoying the back rub, he stretched lazily and turned to one side. Misjudging the width of the windowsill, he promptly rolled off its edge and slid downward. Scrambling from his unexpected exit, Max managed to right himself and land on all four paws. Now disgusted, the displaced feline let out a loud meow, gave his body a shake, and strolled panther-like to the sofa bed. There, the cushions were wider and softer than the windowsill.

Hillary turned back to the window and looked out. She could no longer see Danielle and assumed she had probably come inside.

"I WAS up in the attic. I love the view up there," Hillary explained a few minutes later when she met Danielle on the second-floor landing.

"Yes, it is nice." Danielle glanced to the ceiling, wondering if Walt was in the attic.

"Where is everyone?" Hillary asked.

"We took Melony to see Chris's house. And then Adam offered to take Melony to her mother's place so she can pick up Jolene's car. Chris stayed at his house. I imagine he's unpacking. I assume Lily's with Ian. I thought you'd be writing."

"I needed a little break. I thought I heard something in the attic, so I went up there. Your cat was sleeping on the windowsill."

"Max likes to look out that window." *So does Walt.*

"It's quite the view of the neighborhood. If I was you, I'd consider converting it into my bedroom. You'd have an ocean view."

"Hmm, I hadn't thought of that." *I wonder how Walt would like that idea?*

"It would also make an excellent guest room, with that view. Have you ever considered renting it out?"

"Actually, we did rent it out over Christmas when we were booked up. The sofa up there makes into a bed. But it's a bit of a pain since there's not a bathroom up there." *And I imagine Walt would have a fit if I made it a habit of renting out his attic.*

"I suppose I should get back to work." Hillary flashed Danielle a smile and then turned, heading back to her room.

Hillary was just opening her bedroom door when Danielle called out, "Can I ask you a question?"

Hillary paused and looked back at Danielle. "What?"

"I was curious. How do you happen to know Melony?"

Hillary's smile vanished. "You didn't ask her?"

Danielle shook her head. "No. I didn't."

"Actually, Melony was my attorney."

Before Danielle could respond, her cellphone began to ring. Hillary turned back to her bedroom door while Danielle pulled her phone from her sweater pocket and looked at it to see who was calling. Hillary retreated to her room.

"Hey, Chief."

"I'm trying to get ahold of Hillary Hemingway, but I don't have her cell number."

Danielle glanced to Hillary's now closed bedroom door. "I assume it's about those notes?" Danielle asked in a whisper.

"Yes. I considered coming there again, but I'd rather she come down here."

"She's in her room. I'm out in the hall. If you hold on, I'll get her for you."

A few moments later Danielle knocked on her guest's door. When Hillary opened it, Danielle handed her the phone. "Chief MacDonald has been trying to get ahold of you."

"SHE DOESN'T SEEM the least bit nervous," Joe noted as he observed Hillary through the two-way mirror. The older woman, dressed in tan slacks and a smock-like thigh-length blouse adorned with embroidered birds and flowers, sat alone at the table in the interrogation room while he, Brian, and the chief watched.

Hillary glanced around the room curiously, and then she reached down and picked her purse up from the floor. Opening it, she removed a notepad and pen.

"What's she doing?" Joe asked.

"Looks like she's writing something down," MacDonald said.

"Taking more notes for a future story. Impressions of a small-town interrogation room?" Brian chuckled.

"I really don't know why you had her come," Joe said. "I'm sure she wrote those notes after she read the newspaper article. This seems like a waste of time."

"Danielle was certain that trash can was filled the morning of the murder—before we found Jolene's rings," the chief lied.

"Danielle does seem to know her trash," Joe said with a dry chuckle.

"I would have liked to have seen that." Brian laughed.

"I was tempted to snap a picture with my phone, but I figured there wasn't enough light."

"Your phone has a flash," Brian reminded him.

Joe dramatically snapped his fingers and said, "Damn, you're right."

MacDonald shook his head and walked to the door. "I'm going to talk to her."

"Are you sure you don't want one of us to do it?" Brian asked. "I know you've got other more important things to do."

"No. I'd rather do it."

WHEN MACDONALD WALKED into the interrogation room, Hillary quickly shut her notebook and then set her pen down. She smiled up at him. "I'm not sure why you wanted me to come down here. But this place provides wonderful story fodder. Do you think perhaps you might be able to give me a tour later? I'd love to see where you keep the prisoners."

MacDonald tossed the folder he had been carrying onto the table and sat across from Hillary. "I think I can arrange something."

Hillary pointed to the mirror. "That isn't a two-way mirror, is it?"

MacDonald glanced to the mirror and back to Hillary.

"Or did you just hang a regular mirror there to intimidate the people you interrogate?" Hillary leaned across the table and added in a dramatic whisper, "Make them think someone is watching them."

MacDonald cocked a brow. "Do you think someone is watching you?"

Hillary glanced warily to the mirror, looked at it a moment, and then looked back at the chief. She studied him a moment and then laughed. "You're being funny."

MacDonald leaned back in the chair and looked at her for a moment. "Ms. Hemingway, why do you think I asked you in here today?"

"I imagine you're hoping I remembered something since the last time we spoke that might be able to help you. But I'm afraid I have nothing more to tell you. I wish I saw something—anything—that could help you. But I really didn't." She smiled sweetly.

"I'd like to show you something. It might jog your memory."

"Why certainly!" She beamed.

Opening the folder, MacDonald pulled out the crumpled sheet of legal-sized paper Danielle had given him. Yet now it was encased in transparent plastic. He slid it across the table to Hillary.

Eagerly, Hillary picked it up and looked at it. Her smile vanished. She stared blankly at the page. Finally, she set it on the table and looked at the chief.

"Did you write that?" he asked.

Hillary nodded. "Yes. Where did you get this?"

"That's not important right now. I would like you to tell me how you happened to write that?"

Licking her lips nervously, she stared down at the paper. "I really would like to know where you got this. I never let anyone see my notes—my story ideas—when I'm this early into a project. I knew I should have torn it up before I threw it in the trash."

"So you admit you threw it away."

She looked up, her expression no longer friendly. "Of course. I didn't need it anymore. Just random thoughts—my ideas. When I'm working on a new book, I find the ideas flow freer when I write them out longhand. Sometimes I don't even read the notes after I write them. It just helps me form thoughts, develop my storyline."

"Did you throw these away right after you wrote them?"

"I threw them away yesterday afternoon."

"Are you sure you threw them away yesterday?" MacDonald asked.

"Yes. I don't know why it matters. But you can ask Joanne. She came to my room and asked me if I had any trash to go out."

JOE LOOKED at Brian and shrugged. "I told the chief this was a waste of time. Danielle had it in her head Ms. Hemingway tossed those notes before the article came out yesterday morning, which obviously didn't happen. Might as well let her leave. I don't imagine there's anything unusual about an author jotting down notes after reading a news article."

"Can you tell me when you wrote this?" Joe and Brian heard MacDonald ask Hillary.

"Waste of time," Joe mumbled as he and Brian turned from the window.

"That night," Hillary said.

"What night?" MacDonald asked.

"Late Tuesday night. Technically it was Wednesday morning. I don't know. I didn't really pay attention to the time."

Joe and Brian froze. They looked at each other and then turned and hurried back to the window to listen.

NIBBLING ON HER UPPER LIP, Hillary fidgeted with the edge of the plastic holding her notes hostage.

"You wrote that before we found the body?"

Hillary nodded. "Yes. It was still dark outside."

"You do realize what you wrote describes exactly what happened."

Hillary picked up the paper and reread it before tossing it back on the table. "I don't know about that. It's possible there were several killers instead of a lone man like in my story. Or maybe the killer was a woman. It's just a coincidence. I write murder mysteries. It's not really that unusual for one of my stories to resemble a real-life crime. After all, what is it they say, there's less than ten plot lines?"

"So you're telling me you came home that night around the same time Jolene Carmichael was murdered, and you sat down and wrote out a crime scene that just happens to match what happened?"

"No." Hillary shook her head. "I came back from Pier Café and stayed up for a while. Then I went to my room and went to bed. I woke up in the middle of the night, couldn't sleep because I had some ideas rattling around in my head. So I brought out my notepad and just started writing." She pointed to the paper. "And I wrote this. No big deal."

"I would say it is a major big deal. How would you have known about the killer tossing those rings off the pier unless you saw him do it? We assumed he had taken Jolene's jewelry, that it was a robbery. But it wasn't. Whoever killed her wanted to get rid of those rings. You either saw someone toss those rings off the pier, or you threw the rings off yourself."

TWENTY-SIX

If Hillary still wanted a tour of the police station, she did not mention it. The moment MacDonald told her she could go, she left; yet not before trying to take her notes with her.

"Witnesses who don't come forward generally stay quiet out of fear. She didn't seem afraid. Annoyed that you had her notes, but not afraid of the killer," Joe said as he and Brian walked into the chief's office.

"Sometimes they stay quiet because they don't want to get involved," Brian reminded him.

"No matter what her reason, she obviously witnessed the murder," Joe said. "How else would she have known about the rings being dropped off the pier?"

MacDonald sat behind his desk and leaned back in the chair. "Had she not told us when she supposedly wrote that, I suppose I could have chalked it up to a coincidence, even if it had been written before we found the rings."

"Why did you let her go?" Joe asked. "If nothing else, I'd say we have enough to hold her on as a possible suspect, considering what she admitted to writing before Jolene's body was found. Not that I think she had anything to do with the murder, but if she did write that when she claims to have, she has to be a witness."

MacDonald let out a sigh. "I can't figure out why she'd admit to writing that before the body was found, yet insist she hadn't seen anything."

"Now what?" Joe asked.

"I don't want to rush into anything. Insinuating she was the one who threw the rings off the pier didn't seem to ruffle her. As for her being the killer, we have no motive. From what I know, the two women had never even met before. All we have are the notes written by a bestselling murder mystery author, which just happens to be identical to our murder scene," MacDonald explained.

With a snort Brian said, "If you did lock her up, I imagine she'd be thrilled."

"Why do you say that?" Joe asked.

"Think about it. What great publicity for her books. People love that sort of crap. Her books would be flying off the shelf."

"From what I understand, they already do," Joe said.

"True," Brian conceded. "But the chief is right, there's nothing to hold her on. And if we did arrest her, we would end up looking foolish, and she'd just sell more books."

"I'm surprised she didn't try to lie about when she wrote the notes," MacDonald murmured.

"Is she taunting us?" Brian suggested.

"What do you mean?" Joe asked.

"Think about it. She is a mystery writer. It's entirely possible this is all a publicity stunt."

"How do you figure that?" MacDonald asked.

"Maybe she did lie, but not about seeing the murder. Maybe she wrote that after she read the article in the paper. And later, if we hold her—she would come out and say she'd gotten her days mixed up, she had written it after the article. Of course, that would be after the national news got ahold of the story and she got free publicity," Brian theorized.

"You forget, she wrote about Jolene being covered in sand; that wasn't in the paper," the chief reminded him.

"Heather lives down the street from Marlow House, and she found the body. It's entirely possible she's told people about Jolene being covered in sand, and Hemingway heard about it," Joe suggested.

"Your theory would mean Hemingway wanted Danielle to find those notes," MacDonald reminded him. "Not quite sure how she manipulated Danielle to go through the trash cans late at night or how she arranged to have her pages stick to the paperwork Danielle was looking for." While MacDonald knew Danielle didn't accidently find Hillary's notes—he also didn't believe Hillary was attempting to pull a publicity stunt. Yet he couldn't tell Brian or Joe that.

"We need to find those fishermen," Brian said. "Maybe one of them saw Hillary on the pier that night."

"Or the killer," Joe added.

DANIELLE STOOD AT THE SINK, washing up a few stray dishes that she hadn't been able to fit into the dishwasher, when Walt appeared in the room. Grabbing a dishtowel off the counter, she wiped her hands and turned to face him. "The chief called a few minutes ago to let me know Hillary's on her way back here. Or at least, he assumes she's coming back to Marlow House."

"What did she say about the notes?"

"Strangely, she admitted to writing them that night—after she left Pier Café. Although, according to her version, after she got home she went to bed and then woke up later and jotted down the notes."

Walt considered that scenario a moment and then said, "That's possible. I stayed in the parlor and watched television after she went upstairs. She could have gone to bed first and then woke up before I got up there. I only assumed she had never gone to bed."

"I called Lily right after the chief called me. I was hoping she'd be here when Hillary gets back." Danielle glanced uneasily to the doorway leading to the front hall.

"I assume Joanne's gone?" he asked.

"She's not coming back until the morning." Danielle tossed the now damp towel back on the counter. "I'm counting on you, Walt."

"What do you mean?"

"If Hillary tries to smash me over the head with something for giving the chief those notes, I expect you to stop her."

Walt smiled. "I promise. But I have to assume that if the chief let her go, he doesn't feel she's dangerous."

"He believes she witnessed the murder, but for whatever reason, refuses to admit it."

"If she didn't want the world to know she witnessed the murder, why write about it?" Walt asked.

"Maybe she didn't think anyone would ever see those notes."

"What about when her book comes out?" he reminded her.

Danielle wandered to the kitchen table and sat down. "Maybe she doesn't intend to use any of that in her new book. Perhaps she witnessed the murder; she got scared and being a writer—wrote about it. Then she threw the notes away, never imagining anyone would ever see them."

Walt took a seat at the table. "The only problem with that—the scene is in her new book."

Danielle frowned. "How would you know that?"

Walt looked at Danielle and sighed. "Did you honestly believe I wouldn't be keeping a closer eye on her after reading those notes—after learning of Jolene's murder?"

"What have you done?"

"I haven't *done* anything," Walt snapped. "Other than spending some time reading over her shoulder while she hammers away on her typewriter. The book she's writing, the murder scene, it's the same one you took to the chief."

Fifteen minutes later, Walt and Danielle retreated to the living room, waiting for Hillary's return.

Danielle stared at the empty doorway. "I wonder if she's going to check out."

"It would probably be more comfortable for you if she did."

"I can't believe the chief would be thrilled if she left Frederickport right now—and just disappeared."

"That is not really your problem, Danielle. You did what you had to do."

Danielle considered her situation when a thought occurred to her. With a gasp, she looked at Walt and said, "I forgot to tell the chief Melony and Hillary know each other."

"I would think that would only be a critical issue if Hillary was a suspect. Didn't you say he believes she simply witnessed the murder?"

"Yes." Danielle considered the possibility of Hillary being the killer. Finally, she said, "I find it hard to imagine for a moment Hillary killed Jolene, even if she had a motive. Jolene was a tall woman, and unless she was leaning down, I don't see how Hillary would be capable of hitting her over the head with sufficient momentum to kill her."

"Not to mention the fact Hillary doesn't move around very well.

Like I said, I've been keeping an eye on her and she sometimes struggles to climb the stairs. While it has been a long time since I've walked on the beach, I recall walking in the sand can be difficult, especially for a clearly arthritic woman of Hillary's age."

Danielle started to say something and then paused. She glanced to the open doorway. With a whisper she said, "I think she's back." Snatching a magazine off the coffee table, Danielle leaned back in the chair and pretended to read while Walt wandered to the fireplace and summoned a cigar.

A few moments later, Hillary's voice came from the doorway. "Danielle, are you alone?"

Looking up from the magazine, Danielle forced a smile. "I'm in here."

Hillary stepped into the room. "Is Melony or Lily here?"

Setting the magazine on her lap, Danielle shook her head. "No. They haven't come in yet."

"I think we need to talk," Hillary said calmly as she walked toward the sofa facing Danielle. She sat down.

Danielle could feel the rapid acceleration of her heartbeat. Nervously she glanced to Walt.

With a wink he said, "Don't worry, Danielle, I won't let that little old lady hurt you."

"Anything in particular?" Danielle asked uneasily.

"I think you know. You're the one who gave my notes to the police, aren't you?"

"I want you to know I never went into your room. I promise. I would never go through a guest's things."

Hillary studied Danielle. With a calm and steady voice, she asked, "But you go through your guests' trash?"

"It wasn't like that," Danielle insisted. "I accidently threw some paperwork away, and the trash had already been set out on the curb. I had to try to find it before the trash man came. It was dark out, so I couldn't see what I was doing very well. I found some papers in the bottom of the bin and thought they were what I was looking for."

"Did you find your papers?" Hillary asked.

"Umm…no…I mean yes. Yes, but they were stuck to one of your papers."

Walt shook his head. "Danielle, sometimes you are absolutely the worst liar in the world."

"So I suppose you read what I wrote?"

Danielle shrugged apologetically. "I'm sorry, I was just curious."

"Worst liar ever," Walt muttered.

Hillary considered Danielle's version of events for a moment and then let out a deep sigh and smiled. "I suppose I understand. If I stumbled across something like that, I couldn't resist reading it either."

Walt frowned at Hillary. "Well, I'll be damned. I believe she bought your cockamamie story."

"I imagine what I wrote scared you—being so similar to what happened to Jolene." Hillary let out another sigh and settled back in the sofa. "It isn't the first time my imagination has gotten me in trouble."

"Are you in trouble?" Danielle asked.

Hillary shrugged. "I was called down to the police station and interrogated. And Chief MacDonald did tell me to check with him before I leave town."

"Are you leaving town?"

"Eventually." Hillary smiled at Danielle and then stood up. "I wonder, do you have any of that wonderful cake left? I'm ravenous."

"Umm…yeah…in the refrigerator."

Hillary started for the doorway and then paused and looked back to Danielle and asked, "You don't mind if I have a piece, do you?"

"Umm…no…help yourself." Just as Hillary turned back to the door, Danielle called out, "Hillary, can I ask you something?"

Pausing again and looking back to Danielle, Hillary smiled. "What's that?"

"You aren't mad at me for giving your notes to the chief?"

Hillary considered the question for a moment and then shrugged. "I confess I was initially annoyed. I was quite serious when I said I don't like anyone reading anything I've written until—well, until I'm ready for them to read it. But considering the circumstances, I can certainly understand how my notes might have been upsetting. You did the right thing. I don't blame you at all." Hillary flashed Danielle a departing smile and then headed for the kitchen to cut herself a piece of cake.

With a furrowed brow, Danielle murmured, "Wow. I really thought she'd be checking out."

"She still didn't explain why her notes were identical to Jolene's murder," Walt reminded her.

"True. But I didn't quiz her." Danielle continued to stare at the now empty doorway.

"I'm surprised she bought your story."

Danielle rolled her eyes at Walt. "You're funny."

"How so?"

"You said I was a lousy liar. But you've told me before I'm pretty good at it."

Walt shrugged. "It's true, sometimes you're an expert at covering your tracks when your gift complicates things. And other times, like a minute ago, you seem awful transparent." Walt let out a sigh and sat down. "Perhaps I'm just getting so I can read you better than other people can."

With a startled gasp, Danielle looked back to the open doorway.

"What is it?" Walt asked.

"You said I have a gift. Maybe Hillary has a gift. Perhaps she's clairvoyant?" Danielle suggested.

"Clairvoyant, what do you mean?"

"Maybe the murder scene just came to her—maybe she's one of those people who can just see things that have happened."

"I seriously doubt your Hillary Hemingway is clairvoyant."

Danielle looked from the doorway to Walt. "Why do you say that?"

"For one thing, she bought your story about how you happened to find her paper in the trash. A clairvoyant person would have seen through your story at your first stumbled 'umm.'"

TWENTY-SEVEN

A locked screen door separated Danielle from Sadie. Tail wagging, the golden retriever impatiently waited for Ian or Lily to come open the door so that she could give Danielle a proper greeting. It was Ian who came to the door a minute later.

"I thought Chris would be with you," Ian said as he let Danielle into his house.

"I left him down at his place, unpacking." She followed Ian into the living room while Sadie nuzzled her with a wet nose and leapt playfully at her feet, demanding sufficient attention.

"Go lie down," Ian told his dog. Reluctantly, Sadie complied.

In the living room Danielle found Lily sitting on the sofa. She noticed Ian's laptop sitting open on the coffee table.

Lily briefly glanced out the window. "I see Hillary is back. What did she say? Is she staying?"

"It would have been nice if you'd come back and given me some support," Danielle said as she plopped down in a chair.

"Oh, I knew you would be okay." *You had Walt.* "Anyway, Ian wanted to look some stuff up."

Ian walked to the sofa and sat next to Lily. "What did Hillary say when she got back from the police station?"

"Lily told you about the notes we found?" Danielle asked.

Ian nodded. "Yes. I just figured it was something she wrote after the article came out. But when Lily told me she admitted to writing it the same night Jolene was killed…I wasn't sure what to think."

Danielle went on to tell Lily and Ian what had transpired between Hillary and herself. She understood Lily had fed Ian the fabricated story about finding Hillary's notes after the previous night's trash can fiasco.

When Danielle finished bringing them current on recent events, Lily said, "Ian's been doing a little research on Hillary."

Danielle glanced to Ian, who sat next to Lily, his arm casually draped behind her shoulders. "What kind of research?"

"Lily's never read any of Hillary's work—"

"Neither have I," Danielle interrupted.

"I wanted to show her the list of Hillary's books and the crimes critics claim they were based on. Of course, Hillary has always denied using real crimes as inspiration. I've always wondered why she's so adamant about insisting she doesn't borrow from real life—all writers do. And it's obvious she's doing that, considering the release dates of her books in relationship to the crimes."

"What do you mean?" Danielle asked.

"Hillary publishes a new book every six months. If you look back and compare the release date of one of her books with the crime some critics claim that particular book is based on, you'll discover it occurred six months before that book's release."

"But what's even more bizarre, in my opinion, some have claimed Hillary has been in the general vicinity of each crime when it was committed," Lily added.

Danielle glanced from Lily to Ian. "Seriously?"

"It's possible that's an urban legend. Hillary's never confirmed or denied that accusation—but she has denied borrowing details from those crimes," Ian said. "There are a couple instances where she was undoubtedly in the general vicinity of the crime when it was committed. But I don't know if that holds for all of them."

"So in six months, the book Hillary publishes will be based on Jolene's murder?" Danielle asked.

"It sounds that way, considering the notes you found. But let me clarify, the actual stories are not about the real murder victims, just the particulars of the crime scene. Which I suppose is one reason many readers and critics believe Hillary. This has been an ongoing debate on a number of her fan sites."

"What do you mean when you said her books aren't about the real victims?" Danielle asked.

"Let me give you an example," Ian said as he turned his attention to the laptop sitting on the coffee table. His fingers moved quickly over the keypad. One of Hillary's book covers appeared on the screen.

Danielle moved from the chair to the sofa. She sat on one side of Ian while Lily sat on his other side. She looked at the monitor.

"In each of Hillary's books, she starts out with the murder. In this book, the victim's name is Stan. The killer is Gabriel, yet we don't know his name until the end of the book. The story starts out with Stan sitting at a bar, drunk. Gabriel comes in and starts talking to Stan. The readers are led to believe Gabriel and Stan are friends, but at the end of the book we learn they never knew each other. Gabriel is actually a hit man hired by Stan's wife to kill him while she's visiting her sister in another state."

"Not a terribly original murder scenario," Danielle noted.

"Ahh…" Ian smiled at Danielle. "It's about how Stan is killed, not the murder motive. Rather than putting drunk Stan in his bed, the killer drags him down to the basement laundry room and leaves him on the floor, where he passes out from the booze. Then the killer puts on some sort of gas mask before filling the laundry sink with a combination of ammonia and bleach. He leaves Stan passed out in the basement, with the door closed."

"Yikes. That's a toxic combination. That would kill poor Stan."

Ian nodded. "It did."

"So what happened to the real Stan's wife? Did she go to prison?" Danielle asked.

"The guy who was really killed in that basement, he wasn't married. It wasn't even his house. It was vacant; no one was living there. But in the real story, like in Hillary's, the victim left a bar with someone he apparently knew, but the police were never able to identify the man who left with the victim."

"They never found out who killed Stan?" Danielle asked.

"Some speculate he wandered into that basement drunk and mixed the bleach and ammonia himself, but his fingerprints weren't on the empty bottles."

"You mean the crime wasn't solved?"

Ian shook his head. "No. None of the real crimes have been solved."

Danielle cringed. "You're saying Hillary's been using unsolved murders in all her books?"

"Just the murder scenes. The rest of the stories never bear any resemblance to the actual murders. I assume that's why Hillary is so adamant in her claim she doesn't borrow from real life, she probably doesn't see it that way," Ian suggested.

Danielle leaned back in the sofa and propped her feet up on the edge of the coffee table. "So, in essence, crime scenes get her creative juices flowing."

"That's what I suspect," Ian said.

"Reminds me of my grandmother's doodles," Lily said.

Both Danielle and Ian glanced over to Lily, waiting for an explanation.

"When I was little and would visit my grandma," Lily began, "she would make a squiggly doodle on a piece of paper and give it to me to make a picture out of. I used to do it sometimes with my students. It was a fun rainy-day project when they couldn't go out on recess."

"What I find disturbing," Ian said, "it looks as if she witnessed the murder. I hate to think one of my favorite authors, someone I've looked up to, would be so callous as to witness a murder, refuse to help the police, and then use the details in a book."

Lily leaned forward and looked past Ian to Danielle. "Dani, in the story about the drunk, the description of the bar and murder scene in Hillary's book matched the real-life house and bar exactly." Lily pointed to a link displayed on the computer monitor. "You can read about it."

"HI, EDDY," Melony greeted as she peeked into the chief's office.

MacDonald looked up from the paperwork on his desk. Melony stood at his open doorway, grinning. He stood abruptly and tossed his pen onto his pile of papers. "Melony!" he greeted her, then rushed around the desk to give her a welcoming hug. After the brief exchange, MacDonald returned to his place behind the desk while Melony sat in one of the chairs facing him.

"I heard you were here," he said.

"I got in late this morning. I just picked up my mother's car.

Thanks for taking it back over to her place and not having it impounded."

"I didn't want to put you through that. Figured you'd need to use it when you came into town. Apparently you found the keys okay."

"Yes. They were just where you said you left them."

"I heard you were staying at Marlow House."

Melony settled back in her chair. "News always traveled fast in this town. So tell me, anything new on my mother's murder?"

"Nothing I can share at this point. But we're working on a few leads."

"Adam told me you brought him in for questioning."

"Adam…when did you see him?"

"He stopped by Marlow House. Gave me a ride to Mother's."

"That's right…you probably knew each other when you lived here."

"Adam and I grew up together. We go way back."

"I suppose he told you how his fingerprints were on the wine bottle."

"Yes. He also told me why they were there."

Picking up his pen, MacDonald looked across the desk at Melony, his expression now somber. "Do you have any idea who would want your mother dead?"

Melony shrugged and shook her head. "I've been thinking about that since you first called. No one benefits financially from her death. I know I'm her sole beneficiary, and unless she wasn't telling me the truth the last few times we spoke, there's nothing left. I doubt I'll be able to list the house for enough to pay off the loans against it."

"Did your mom ever mention a problem she was having with anyone since moving back to Frederickport?"

Melony shook her head. "We only spoke a few times on the phone since she moved back. She never said anything."

"How about someone from New York? Maybe she had a problem with someone back there, and they followed her here? Did she ever talk to you about having a problem with anyone?"

"Sorry, Eddy. I really don't know much about my mother's personal life. We haven't been close for years—if we ever were. And while we occasionally spoke on the phone, those calls—well, those calls weren't much more than, *'Hello, how are you, just calling to let you know I'm alive, goodbye.'* That was pretty much the extent of our relationship. Except, of course, the few times she recently called to rant over Clarence's death and how she had lost everything. But frankly, I think those calls were her attempt to guilt me into sending her some money."

"Like I told you on the phone, we went through your mother's house after the murder, but we couldn't find anything that might help us. When you go through her things, if you come across anything we missed that you think might be of importance, please let me know."

"Of course." Melony stood up. "I think I'm going to head back to Marlow House. The last couple of days have been crazy. I'm exhausted."

MacDonald stood up. "How long do you think you'll be staying?"

"Not sure. I reserved a room at Marlow House for the week."

"Does Frederickport seem much different to you? I know you haven't been back since you were a teenager."

Pausing at the doorway, Melony turned to face MacDonald. "Not really. Although, it is a little strange staying at Marlow House. When I was a kid, we'd dare each other to run up the walk and peek into the windows. The house had been vacant for years. We were convinced it had to be haunted."

MacDonald smiled. "Really? Haunted? Have you seen any ghosts over there?"

Melony laughed. "No ghosts. Oh…but I do know the other guest staying there."

MacDonald raised his brows. "Hillary Hemingway?"

"Yes. I was surprised to see her."

"I assume when you say you know her you mean because she's a well-known author."

"That too. But I know Hillary personally."

TWENTY-EIGHT

The plain white legal-sized envelope had been addressed to him, yet the actual street address was for the Frederickport Police Department. He could tell by the postmark it had been mailed locally. The top seal flap portion of the envelope had been tucked into the back portion, securing the envelope's contents. The sender had been careful not to deposit DNA via saliva when sealing the envelope. Not that MacDonald would seriously consider having it tested for DNA—*or would he?* Picking the now empty envelope up off his desk, he noticed its stamp was the sticker type. *No saliva DNA there. Do they even make stamps you lick anymore?*

MacDonald set the envelope down and picked up the letter. He reread it. When he had first opened the envelope and read the letter, he realized what it was. He had immediately slipped on a pair of latex gloves to protect the evidence. Like the envelope, the letter had been typed. He didn't think it looked like something printed from a computer. No, the sender had used an old-fashioned typewriter, he would bet on it.

A light knock came at the chief's door. He looked up from the letter and saw Joe standing in his doorway.

"I may have a lead on the fishermen," Joe told him.

MacDonald waved him into the office with his gloved hand.

Noting the latex gloves, Joe frowned. "What's going on, Chief?"

Holding the sheet of paper, he said, "This came in the mail today."

Joe took a seat facing the desk. "What is it?"

"It's a letter from someone who claims to have witnessed Jolene's murder."

"Really?"

MacDonald pointed to the door. "Close it, and I'll read it to you."

A moment later, the door to the office was shut, and Joe was again sitting in the chair. MacDonald began to read. *"I witnessed the murder under the pier. I fear for my life, but I have to do the right thing. I was walking on the beach when I heard two people arguing, a man and a woman. When I got closer, I realized who it was, Jolene Carmichael and the bank manager, Steve Klein. She accused him of having an affair with a waitress and told him if he didn't approve her loan, she would tell his wife. He got angry, and the next thing I knew, he picked something up off the beach and hit her over the head. I was terrified. I watched as he removed her rings and then covered her with sand. I stayed hidden in the shadows until he left. I saw him go back up on the pier. Steve Klein killed Jolene."*

Joe let out a low whistle. "Now what?"

"I need to find out who wrote this letter."

"We know Steve was having an affair with Carla and that he was being blackmailed. Whoever wrote that letter knew about the loan Jolene was trying to get Steve to approve. That letter has to be legit. How else would someone know all that unless they overheard them talking?"

MacDonald studied the letter in his hand. "After Steve's interview, I thought he was a complete jerk, but I didn't think he was a killer. I believed him when he said he planned to tell his wife about Jolene's blackmail attempt and paint her as the crazy one. Frankly, I thought that would work. There was no reason for him to kill Jolene. But after reading this, I might have been all wrong."

"The killer didn't arrive on the scene with a murder weapon. He used a bottle he just happened to find on the beach. I don't believe he went down there with the intention of murdering Jolene. It sounds like a crime of passion. The letter said they argued, and he then picked something up and hit her."

MacDonald sighed. "True."

"Unfortunately, without testimony from whoever wrote that letter, all we have is circumstantial evidence," Joe said.

"I agree. But I think I know who wrote this letter. And if I could just get her to do the right thing..."

"Hillary Hemingway?" Joe asked.

"Yes. According to Danielle, Hillary has a typewriter. She brought it with her. I'm 99 percent positive this is typed and wasn't printed off on a computer."

"What do you want to do?"

"I could just ask Hillary again. But I imagine she'll deny it—*again.* I suspect she figured the best way not to get involved while attempting to do the right thing was to write this anonymous letter and send it to me. But I need more than this letter to bring any charges against Klein."

"If you can prove the letter came from Hillary's typewriter, can she seriously keep denying she saw anything?" Joe asked. "We have her handwritten notes, now this."

CHRIS SILENTLY THANKED the vagrant for stealing the expensive bottle of wine Adam had bought him. If that hadn't happened, he wouldn't have a refrigerator full of beer, and he would have to go to the store right now. Exhausted from his recent travels, all he wanted to do was grab a cold beer, sit on his back patio, and enjoy the view.

He felt a momentary stab of guilt when he remembered Melony's mother had been murdered with the stolen bottle, yet he suspected the killer would have found another way to murder Jolene, even without the bottle. After all, they were alone under the pier together, and she was an older woman.

Wearing jeans and a light jacket over his T-shirt, he snatched a can of beer from his refrigerator and headed for the back patio. He didn't bother slipping shoes on his stockinged feet. Outside, Chris took a moment to rearrange his patio chairs so that he could sit on one while using a second one as a footstool. Once he sat down, he leaned back in the chair, rested his feet up on the second chair, and popped open his beer.

Chris gazed out past the confines of his patio to the breakers washing up along the shore. Smiling, he let out a satisfied sigh and congratulated himself on selecting the ideal property. He was halfway through his can of beer when his solitude was interrupted.

Standing between him and the pristine shoreline was a tall, older woman with platinum blond hair. Startled by her sudden appearance, he quickly sat upright and placed his stockinged feet on the patio.

"Can I help you?" he asked.

The woman glanced around nervously. "I'm looking for someone. I thought I saw her come in here."

Chris shook his head. "No. It's just me."

"She's an attractive young blonde, I saw her walking on the beach," she explained. "I'm certain she walked this way."

"There was someone who fits that description who was here about an hour ago. Who is it you're looking for?"

Instead of answering his question, the woman studied him a moment. "Who are you? I don't remember seeing you here before."

"I haven't lived here long, and I've been gone for the last couple of weeks. Do you live in this neighborhood?"

"My house isn't far from here."

Chris smiled. "Have you lived in Frederickport long?"

"I grew up here," she explained.

"Really? My name's Chris Johnson, by the way. You are?"

"I just want to find Melony," she snapped.

Chris frowned. "Melony?"

"The woman I saw on your patio earlier."

"Well, one of the women who was here is named Melony. You didn't tell me your name." Chris stood up.

The woman looked to her left and hissed, "What is he doing here?"

"Who?" Chris asked just as the woman vanished.

In the next moment, Chris's neighbor Pete Rogers stepped into view. He smiled at Chris and said, "You're back!"

"Umm…hey…hi, Pete." Chris glanced around. The woman was nowhere in sight.

"I thought I heard you talking to someone."

Chris patted his pocket and said, "I was talking on the phone."

"Ahh, well, that explains it." Pete laughed. "Thought for a moment there you were talking to your imaginary friend." He laughed again. "Welcome home!"

"Thanks."

Pete started on his way when Chris said, "Hey, Pete, I met

someone you know on the flight from New York. She drove with me here from the airport."

Pete paused and turned back to Chris. "Yeah, who?"

"Melony Jacobs. She said you were an old family friend. She was here earlier, stopped by your house to say hi, but you weren't home. You knew her as Melony Carmichael."

"Melony?" Pete smiled softly. "Haven't seen that girl in years. So she really came back? I figured she might—imagine she'll have to deal with her mother's house and all."

"I never met Jolene Carmichael. But Melony seems awful nice."

"She was a sweet kid, from what I remember. Back in those days, the neighbors would get together a lot and have bonfires on the beach. Good times." Tucking his hands into his jacket pockets, Pete gazed out to the sea. "She went through a rough patch when she hit high school—a lot of kids do. I always figured she'd eventually come back to Frederickport, but I guess she moved on."

"She's here now to take care of her mother's estate."

Pete shook his head. "Shame about Jolene. Real shame. Can't believe something like that happening in Frederickport, but according to the newspaper, they don't think it was a robbery. Sounds like Jolene made an enemy when she moved back."

"Any idea who'd want her dead?" Chris asked.

Pete shook his head. "Not really. Jolene could be kind of pushy—she liked to have her way—but can't imagine why anyone would want to see her dead."

"She have any enemies in town?" Chris asked.

Pete chuckled. "Well, I did hear she had a bit of a run-in with your friend Danielle Boatman. I guess those two weren't the best of friends."

"Yeah…I heard about that."

"So you say Melony is staying at Marlow House?" Pete asked.

"Yes. She didn't want to stay at her mom's house. I can't say I really blame her."

"It's probably better for Melony not to be alone right now. I'll have to go over and say hi. Do you know when she's having her mother's funeral?"

"From what she told me, there won't be one."

Pete frowned. "No funeral? Well, that seems like a shame. There should be a funeral. Jolene grew up in Frederickport, I'd think a lot of people would like to pay their last respects."

Chris shrugged. "I guess Melony doesn't plan to have one. Maybe it was her mother's wishes; I have no idea."

"Hmm, no funeral?" Pete shook his head. "Well, I need to get my walk in. I miss one of my walks and these old bones get stiff."

"Have a nice walk."

"No funeral…imagine that…" Pete muttered as he continued on his way.

Chris stood at the edge of his patio and watched as Pete continued down the beach. When the neighbor was out of earshot, he pulled his phone from his jacket pocket and called Danielle.

"Hey, Chris, I thought you'd be sound asleep," Danielle greeted him when she answered the phone.

Holding the phone to his ear, Chris looked down the beach and then said, "I think I just met Melony's mother. She was here a few minutes ago, looking for her daughter."

TWENTY-NINE

When Danielle opened the front door of Marlow House and found Chief MacDonald dressed in his uniform, standing on her front porch, she wondered for a moment if her psychic powers extended beyond communicating with ghosts. Just moments earlier she had been contemplating calling him and asking him to stop by on his way home from the station. Now, here he was.

"Wow, I'm good," Danielle muttered as she opened the door wider to let him in.

"That's one of the strangest greetings I've ever received." MacDonald removed his baseball cap as he stepped inside Marlow House.

"I was just thinking of calling you. We need to talk." Danielle pointed to the parlor and shut the door behind him.

"I don't even get a hello, or why are you here?" He followed Danielle into the front room.

"Hello, why are you here?" Danielle asked as she waited for MacDonald to enter the parlor so that she could shut its door.

"We have to keep this between the two of us," MacDonald began. In the next moment his nose twitched, teased by the distinct scent of cigar smoke. He turned to where he believed it originated. "Afternoon, Walt. I will rephrase. We need to keep this between the three of us."

Walt chuckled and took a puff off his thin cigar.

"Can't pull anything over on you, Chief." Danielle grinned and took a seat on the sofa. "Go ahead and tell me what you came here for, and then I'll tell you what I found out."

"I suspect Hillary witnessed Jolene's murder."

"Yeah, I know that's what you've been saying." Sitting on the sofa, Danielle pulled her bare feet up on the cushion, tucking them under her.

"It explains those notes she wrote. I believe she saw Steve Klein murder Jolene."

"Steve? I find it difficult to imagine Steve as a killer."

MacDonald removed a photocopy of the anonymous letter he had received from the supposed witness to the crime. He handed the folded piece of paper to Danielle. "I received this in today's mail. It was sent to the station, but addressed to me." After Danielle accepted the paper, MacDonald took a seat on one of the chairs facing her.

As she unfolded the page, Walt moved to the sofa, standing behind it, looking over Danielle's shoulder so that he could read what appeared to be a typed letter.

After reading it, Danielle looked up to the chief. "I assume you think Hillary sent this?"

"It's the logical explanation. But I really don't have enough to arrest Steve on. If I had a witness, one who was willing to come forward and not hide behind an anonymous letter, I could bring Steve in."

"What's your plan?"

"I need to convince her to do the right thing. Whoever wrote that letter didn't print it off from a computer. I've already had the original letter examined—it was typed on an old-fashioned typewriter with ribbon ink."

"What about fingerprints?"

He shook his head. "None. Of course, I wouldn't expect a mystery writer to leave her fingerprints on a letter if she intended to remain anonymous."

"She also wouldn't use her own typewriter," Walt said. "I imagine you can identify the machine this was typed on."

Still holding the letter in her hands, Danielle glanced over her shoulder at Walt.

"I plan to show this letter to Hillary, tell her I know she wrote this, and do what I can to convince her to do the right thing. I'll remind her it will be fairly easy to prove whoever typed this did so on her typewriter," MacDonald explained.

Walt shook his head. "But it wasn't."

"What are you saying, Walt?" Danielle asked.

MacDonald looked from Danielle to where he imagined Walt must now be standing.

Walt took the letter from Danielle. From where MacDonald sat, it looked as if the letter floated up from Danielle's hands and was now suspended over her head.

"Not sure I'll ever get used to this," MacDonald muttered under his breath.

"This wasn't typed on the machine upstairs in Hillary's room," Walt said. The letter seemingly floated back down into Danielle's hands.

"Walt says this wasn't typed on Hillary's typewriter," Danielle explained.

"What do you mean? Of course it was," MacDonald insisted.

Walt shook his head and took a seat on the sofa next to Danielle. "It's not the same type style."

"Walt says it's not the same type style," Danielle told MacDonald.

"How would he know that?" MacDonald asked.

Danielle glanced to Walt and flashed a smirk. "Because Walt can be nosey. He's been reading over Hillary's shoulder while she types her book."

"Don't blame me. I initially did it to help—but she's a good writer. And the story's getting interesting."

Standing briefly, Danielle handed the letter back to MacDonald and then sat back down. "If Walt is right, then you're wasting your time trying to get Hillary to admit she was the witness. And if she didn't write this, you obviously have another witness out there. Or perhaps it's a hoax?"

"If the anonymous writer hadn't mentioned the part about Jolene blackmailing Steve over an affair with a waitress—something only Jolene and Steve would know—or someone who overheard their argument before Jolene was killed, I wouldn't give much credence to that letter."

"You forget the waitress," Walt reminded them.

Danielle looked to Walt. "What do you mean?"

"The chief just said only Jolene and Steve knew about the blackmail. You forget the waitress knew."

"Are you suggesting Carla might have sent that letter?" Danielle asked.

Walt shrugged. "If Carla is the waitress."

"Carla?" MacDonald muttered. "She did claim to be worried over her safety."

"Walt has a point," Danielle said.

"Maybe she wrote the letter, but that doesn't mean she witnessed the murder. In fact, I'd be surprised if she did, because the first time I interviewed her, she didn't come across as someone who had just witnessed her lover murder someone. Unless she's been a great actress all these years, I've always found Carla to be fairly transparent," MacDonald said.

"Perhaps Carla is the killer?" Walt suggested.

"Carla?" Danielle asked.

"Carla what?" MacDonald asked.

"Walt suggested Carla might be the killer. Maybe she's throwing her lover under the bus for this one."

"Steve told me Carla had more of a reason to kill Jolene than he did. I don't buy that," MacDonald said. "Yet I could see her sending something like this if she thought he was guilty and wanted him locked up because she feared for her life."

"I suppose the first thing you need to do is find out what typewriter was used. And then figure out if whoever wrote this was actually a witness," Danielle said.

MacDonald refolded the paper and placed it in his shirt pocket. "I'm still not buying into the suggestion this wasn't written on Hillary's typewriter."

"I can settle that once and for all," Walt said as he removed the letter from the chief's shirt pocket.

MacDonald looked down and watched as the folded piece of paper floated from his shirt pocket, unfolded itself, and hung in midair. "What is he doing?"

"Tell the chief I'm memorizing this letter."

Danielle shrugged. "He says he's memorizing the letter. Why? I have no clue."

"I'm going upstairs to type the same letter on Hillary's typewriter. You can then compare the two letters and see I was right."

"You know how to type?" Danielle asked.

"As a matter of fact, I do. We did have typewriters back in my day."

"I know. But didn't you have secretaries to do menial things like typing?" she asked.

"Haven't you learned by now, I'm a liberated man," Walt boasted.

Danielle laughed. "Liberated man? I betcha back in your day you didn't use phrases like *liberated man*."

"What are you two talking about?" MacDonald asked.

"Walt's memorizing this letter so he can type a duplicate using Hillary's typewriter, and then you can compare the two."

"Sounds like a good idea, but won't Hillary get a little suspicious when her typewriter starts typing by itself?"

Danielle laughed. "I'm pretty sure I can lure Hillary downstairs to the kitchen with the promise of chocolate cake. You can join us. And if Walt proves the letter wasn't written on Hillary's typewriter, then no reason to mention the letter to her."

"While you two decide what you plan to say to Hillary, I'm going upstairs to see what she's doing. I'm also going to check in on Melony and make sure she's still sleeping. Then I'll let you know if it's a good time to get her to come downstairs."

"Walt just left to check on Hillary and make sure Melony is still sleeping in her room. She went up earlier to take a nap."

"I suppose we should wait here until Walt returns?"

Danielle glanced up to the ceiling. "Might as well."

"While we're waiting, why don't you tell me what you wanted to talk to me about? When I got here, you said you needed to tell me something."

"It seems Hillary knows your victim's daughter." If Danielle expected the chief to be surprised at her announcement, she was disappointed.

"Melony stopped by my office earlier. She mentioned she knew Hillary."

"And you didn't find that an interesting coincidence?"

"When I asked her how she knew Hillary, she said professionally. I asked her if Hillary knew her mother, and she said no."

"She told you Hillary had been her client?"

"*Her* client?" MacDonald frowned. "No. Hillary was her soon-to-be ex's client."

"Is that what Melony told you?"

"No. I just assumed that's what she meant when she said she knew her professionally. Melony's husband is some sort of an entertainment attorney. He works with authors, people in the movie industry. He handles some pretty famous clients, from what I recall. I just assumed she meant he was Hillary's attorney."

Danielle shook her head. "No. According to Hillary, Melony was her attorney. She never mentioned anything about Melony's husband."

"Melony is Hillary's attorney?"

Danielle shrugged. "Technically speaking, I believe Hillary said Melony *was* her attorney.

The chief let out a low whistle. "Well, that's interesting."

"Why is that interesting?" Danielle asked.

"Because Melony is a criminal attorney. She's handled some high-profile cases over the years."

"Criminal attorney?" Danielle asked.

"Yes. And we're not talking penny ante stuff—like burglary or fraud."

"Burglary and fraud are penny ante?"

"Compared to capital offenses, yes. I imagine, had Clarence Renton hired his old business partner's daughter as his attorney when he was arrested for Cheryl's murder, he might have gotten off. Melony is that good."

"Why would Hillary have needed a criminal attorney?" Danielle muttered.

MacDonald shook his head. "I have no idea."

Danielle shivered and glanced up to the ceiling, thinking of who was on the second floor. "Makes the rest of what I wanted to tell you seem even creepier."

"Creepy how?"

Danielle told the chief what Ian had told her about Hillary's other books—how each of her murder scenes was identical to a crime that had taken place six months prior to that particular book's release—and each real-life crime remained unsolved.

"I see what you mean." MacDonald glanced to the ceiling. "Jolene's murder scene will be featured in Hillary's next book… which I imagine will be released in about six months."

THIRTY

She hadn't changed her clothes, but she had slipped off her shoes before climbing into bed. Wearing dark blue leggings and her hip-length sweater, Melony hugged one pillow while her head rested on a second one. She had climbed under the sheets and had managed to fall asleep within minutes.

But an hour had since gone by, and Melony—who rarely took midday catnaps—shifted restlessly on the bed and began to wake up. Groggily fluttering open her eyes, it took her a moment to get her bearings. *Mother's gone—I'm in Frederickport—staying at Marlow House.*

With a yawn, she closed her eyes again, hugged the pillow tighter, rolled onto her side, and told herself, *I'll sleep a few more minutes*. She lay there in the silent room, but unlike an hour earlier, she couldn't fall asleep. Just as she decided she might as well get up, she froze. Instead of opening her eyes, she held firmly onto the pillow, afraid to move.

Someone is standing over me.

Too afraid to open her eyes and discover her hunch was correct, she lay perfectly still, practically holding her breath. While she hadn't seen anyone in her room, she felt it. The inescapable sensation gripped her. The beating of her heart seemed to accelerate and she wondered if she were to scream, would anyone hear her?

She then remembered Hillary had been in the next room typing her book when Melony had first come up the stairs. For a brief moment Melony imagined it was Hillary who had invaded her room and now stood over her. That thought terrified her. But then she heard it, the faint tapping of the keys of a typewriter. She could barely hear it through the wall separating her room from Hillary's.

Maybe I'm imagining things.

Mustering her courage, Melony opened her eyes and bolted upright in the bed, prepared to fight. To her amazement, she was alone. Dazed, she looked around the room and then leaned back against the headboard. Again, she heard the faint rapping of the typewriter keys.

She sat there a moment, took a deep breath, and chastised herself for being so edgy. After considering the events of the last few days, she decided she was being too hard on herself. Who wouldn't be out of sorts under similar circumstances?

She lay there a few more minutes and then finally climbed out of bed and stretched. Walking over to the dresser, she looked into the mirror. Leaning closer to her reflection, she used the tip of one finger to gently wipe away a smudge of mascara under one eye.

Grabbing a brush off the dresser, she ran it through her hair to smooth out the tangles caused by her recent nap. Tossing the brush back onto the dresser, she murmured, "I wonder if I can talk Danielle into a sandwich."

Melony stepped out into the hallway from her room and looked around. All the other doors on the second floor were closed—except for Hillary's, which was slightly ajar. She could hear the continued tapping of the typewriter.

Heading toward the stairs, Melony paused by Hillary's doorway and curiously peeked in. She expected to see Hillary's back, as she sat at the desk in front of the typewriter. Yet when Melony looked in, she was surprised to find the desk chair empty.

Curious, Melony eased open the door and glanced around. There didn't appear to be anyone in the room. *But what is that noise? It sounds just like a typewriter.*

Without making a peep, Melony tiptoed into the room. Her first thought: *Does crazy Hillary have a recording of a typewriter playing?*

Stealthily approaching the desk, Melony suddenly froze, her eyes fixed on Hillary's antiquated manual Royal typewriter.

Inserted in the typewriter was a sheet of white paper. The keys busily moved over the page as the carriage moved from side to side, the piece of paper slowly making its way up the roll as freshly inked words appeared on the page.

Melony's eyes widened as she let out a scream and then turned abruptly, running from the room.

WALT TURNED from the typewriter and let out a sigh. "Well, I guess *someone* woke up."

Danielle heard the scream from downstairs. She knew immediately what had happened. She had been sitting at the kitchen table with MacDonald and Hillary when Melony tore into the room a few moments later. They all stood up.

Hillary was the first to speak. "What happened? Is there a fire?"

"No. It's…it's…I know this is going to sound crazy," Melony said in a panic.

Gently, MacDonald placed an arm around Melony and said, "Calm down. What happened?"

"You're going to think I'm crazy, but that typewriter in Hillary's room, well, it was typing all by itself."

Hillary's expression of concern quickly faded. "It was what?"

"Just what I said. I woke up from my nap and heard the typing. I decided to come downstairs, and on the way down I noticed Hillary's door was open, so I looked in. And…and…the typewriter was typing."

Danielle let out a chuckle and grabbed hold of Melony's hand, giving it a squeeze. "Don't you see what happened?"

Melony looked blankly into Danielle's smiling face and shook her head, still confused.

Danielle patted Melony's arm and ushered her away from MacDonald, leading her to a kitchen chair. "It's pretty obvious to me. You've been asleep for over an hour. Understandably, you're exhausted, and I can't even imagine the stress you're going through with your mother's death and all the unanswered questions." Gently, she nudged Melony down into a chair.

Dazed, Melony looked up into Danielle's dark eyes. "What are you saying?"

"Hillary was typing upstairs not ten, fifteen minutes ago. You probably heard her earlier. You obviously weren't totally awake when you came downstairs."

"Are you saying I was dreaming?"

"I certainly don't imagine Hillary's typewriter was typing on its own, and I'm fairly certain you're sane. But I also know you've been through a great deal lately, so it's not that unusual to have strange dreams."

"Can we at least go upstairs and look? Just to make sure?" Melony asked.

Smiling, Danielle gave her a quick hug. "Sure we can."

Just as Danielle released Melony from the hug, Walt appeared in the room. He stood behind Melony, wearing a sheepish smile.

"Sorry about that," Walt told Danielle. "I looked in on Melony right before I went back into Hillary's room. I was certain she was sound asleep. I managed to type about half the letter, which should be more than enough for a comparison. I put the letter in the top drawer of the parlor desk."

Danielle took Melony's hand. "Come on. Let's go upstairs. I'll show you it was all just a bad dream."

WHEN THEY ALL came back downstairs ten minutes later, Danielle led Melony to a chair at the kitchen table and brought her a piece of chocolate cake. Hillary's piece of cake was still on the table—only one bite eaten—as were the pieces Danielle had cut for herself and MacDonald.

Still dazed, Melony shook her head and said, "It was all a dream."

"Chocolate fixes everything," Danielle announced cheerfully as she set a glass of cold milk on the table in front of Melony.

Picking up her fork, Melony took a quick bite of cake and then laughed. After washing down the bite with a sip of milk, she said, "I imagine you think I'm crazy."

Instead of sitting back at the table with Melony and Hillary, Danielle and MacDonald stood by the table, eating their cake.

"Of course not," Danielle said. "Stress does crazy things to people."

Hillary looked up from her cake; her eyes met Melony's. "I agree. Stress can make people see and imagine all sorts of things."

Just as MacDonald put his last bite of cake into his mouth, Danielle snatched his plate from him and set it with hers in the sink.

She turned to Melony and Hillary, who continued to sit at the kitchen table, and said, "If you ladies will excuse us. There was something I promised to show the chief earlier."

"IF THEY ASK, what are you going to tell them you had to show me?" MacDonald asked as he followed Danielle into the parlor.

"I have no idea. I'm exhausted from trying to make up crap." She shut the door behind them.

"I felt so sorry for poor Melony," MacDonald said. "It must have been quite a shock watching that typewriter type on its own."

"It wasn't really typing on its own," Danielle reminded him.

MacDonald let out a snort. "I don't imagine learning a ghost was doing the typing would be an especially comforting consolation."

"I don't imagine it would be." Danielle walked to the desk to retrieve the paper Walt had placed in its drawer.

MacDonald glanced around the room. "I don't smell any cigar smoke. Is Walt in here with us?"

Danielle opened the desk drawer. "No. He stayed in the kitchen. I imagine he's eavesdropping on Hillary and Melony." Taking the paper from the drawer, she handed it to MacDonald.

He placed the paper on the desktop and then removed the photocopy of the original letter from his pocket. After unfolding it, he set it on the desk next to what Walt had typed.

"Well, I'll be damned," MacDonald said, staring down at the two pieces of paper.

Standing next to MacDonald, Danielle compared the two pages and then shook her head. "Walt was right. There's no way your anonymous letter writer typed that on Hillary's typewriter."

"Now I'm back to square one. I need to figure out who sent me that letter."

WALT CASUALLY LEANED against the kitchen counter and puffed his cigar. He eyed the piece of chocolate cake slowly disappearing on Hillary's plate and tried to remember how chocolate tasted.

"Did you know Chief MacDonald when you lived in Frederickport?" Hillary asked Melony after she finished her last bite of cake.

Wiping her mouth on a napkin, Melony shook her head. "No. He moved here after I was gone. I haven't lived in Frederickport since I was a teenager. Eddy didn't grow up here."

"I just got the impression you two were friends," Hillary said with a shrug.

"We are, actually. His wife and I were college roommates. We were best friends."

"Are you still friends?" Hillary asked.

Melony stood up from the table. She picked up her fork and now empty plate along with Hillary's and carried them to the sink. "No. She died. He's a widower. But we've stayed in touch over the years. I consider him a good friend."

"Then you know about him questioning me regarding your mother's murder," Hillary asked her.

Standing by the sink, Melony turned to face Hillary. "Adam told me Eddy interviewed everyone who was at Pier Café the night Mother was killed. He mentioned you were there. I have to assume you didn't see anything, or I would have heard about it."

"Then he didn't mention my notes?"

With a frown Melony asked, "Notes? What notes?"

Picking up a napkin from the table, Hillary wiped imaginary crumbs from the edge of her mouth. She looked up at Melony. "It happened again. My crime scene for the book I'm writing."

Melony stared at Hillary, her expression unreadable. She began to shake her head. "No…"

THIRTY-ONE

According to the background information on Tom Fowler, he and his wife had moved to Frederickport the past summer, after he retired from his job as a high school track coach in California. Wearing faded jeans and a gray sweatshirt, he sat at the table in the Frederickport Police Department's interrogation room and warily glanced around. Officer Brian Henderson sat across the table from him, thumbing through a file folder.

"My wife told me I had to come in," Tom began.

Brian closed the folder and set it down. He looked across the table at Tom. "I'm glad you did. Why didn't you come in right away?"

Tom shrugged. "Didn't see any reason to. It's not like I saw anything that night."

"You might have seen something that can help us find the killer."

"Yeah, that's what my wife said too. And then she heard on the radio you were looking for whoever was fishing on the pier that night; I figured she was right. I better come in."

"Were you down there alone?" Brian asked.

"Yeah. My wife doesn't like to fish, and I really don't know too many people in town yet."

"Why don't you start by telling me everything you remember about that night, starting with when you arrived at the pier. Try to remember people you saw that night or anyone you might have talked to."

Tom sat quietly for a moment, composing his thoughts. With a sigh, he leaned forward, resting his elbows on the table. "When I arrived, I remember the parking lot had about half a dozen cars. But I didn't see anyone walking around. When I got up to the pier, I only saw one other guy fishing. I figured the cars must have belonged to whoever was in Pier Café."

"About what time was that?"

"I got there late. Around nine thirty or ten."

"What did you do when you got to the pier?"

"Like I said, there was one other guy fishing. I started to go ask him if he was catching anything, but he was cussing, fighting with his line."

"Fighting with his line?"

"Yeah. It was all tangled. By the way he was handling his pole, it was obvious he didn't know what he was doing. I moved to the other side of the pier."

"So you didn't talk to him?"

"No. Looked over at him a few times during the night. Seemed like he spent more time screwing with his line than actually fishing."

"Did you move around on the pier that night or stay in one spot?"

"Pretty much stayed at the same spot all night. Started catching fish right away. So I didn't see any reason to move."

"Whereabouts were you?"

"Same side of the pier as the row of shops. About twenty feet from the café entrance."

"So you could see who was coming and going from the café?"

"I suppose, when I was looking that way."

"Did you notice any other fishermen?"

Tom shook his head. "Nahh. Just that one guy. It was pretty quiet that night."

"Do you remember anyone else on the pier, aside from that one fisherman?"

"Yeah. I was just reeling in a fish and this guy walks by. People tend to stop when you're bringing in a fish, want to see what you got. That's one reason they come down to the pier. But this guy didn't seem very interested. Just kept walking."

"Which way was he walking?" Brian asked.

"To the end of the pier."

"Do you remember what time it was?"

Tom shook his head. "Not really. I'd probably been down there at least an hour. Maybe more. I started catching fish right away, but they were all small, tossed them back. This one was a nice size. Gave me a good fight."

"But you don't remember the time?"

"No. I didn't look at my watch."

"Did you notice what the guy did at the end of the pier?"

"I saw him walk that way and thought it was funny that he didn't seem remotely curious about what I was bringing in. In fact, he didn't even pause, just kept walking. But then I was dealing with the fish and didn't notice him after that."

"What did he look like?"

"Can't really say. Average height. Didn't get a look at his face. He had some sort of hat on. Big jacket, jeans, maybe. Had his hands in his pockets, never really looked my way."

"Any idea how old he was?"

"Sorry. He might have been twenty or fifty. Like I said, I didn't see his face. He just walked by, and I was pretty focused on the fish I was bringing in."

"Do you know where he came from, from the café maybe?"

Tom shook his head. "I didn't notice him until he was there, walking by me as I was reeling in the fish. He could have come up from the beach, parking lot, café, I have no idea."

"Did you see anyone else that night on the pier?"

"Yeah. After I landed that fish, a young couple came by to see what I'd caught. We talked for a minute. He works at the gas station by the grocery store."

"How do you know that?"

"I saw him the next day when I went to fill up for gas. I remember thinking he was the kid I'd talked to on the pier."

"Did you see anyone else on the pier that night?"

"Not that I remember."

"What time did you go home?"

"I'm not sure what time I left, but I remember it was a little past midnight when I got home. So I imagine I must have left here sometime after 11:30."

"It takes you thirty minutes to get home?"

"No. But it takes time to pack everything up and get it in my car. Maybe I left after 11:45." Tom shrugged.

Brian opened the folder and removed a photograph. He slid it across the table to Tom. "Have you ever seen this woman?"

"That's Hillary Hemingway, sure!" Tom smiled.

"You know her?"

"Not personally. But I've read every one of her books. When my wife said she was staying in Frederickport, I didn't believe her, but then I saw her that night."

"The night of the murder?"

"Yeah."

"You didn't mention seeing her on the pier," Brian said.

"I didn't see her on the pier. When I went by Pier Café, I looked in the window and saw her sitting at a booth. I was sure it was her, especially after my wife said she was staying in town."

"Was she alone?"

"She was when I saw her."

"Did you see her again that night?" Brian asked.

"Yeah. I was tempted to ask her for an autograph, but I didn't have anything for her to sign."

"When was that?"

"I don't know the time. I think it was after I reeled in that fish—might have been before. But I saw her leaving the restaurant, and she took off in the opposite direction, heading for the street."

"You didn't see her walking on the pier that night."

"No. I'm sure I would have noticed. I only saw her leaving the restaurant and heading down to the street."

JOE MORELLI FILLED two cups with coffee. Turning from the coffee maker, he walked to the table and handed a cup to Brian and then sat down with him. The two officers sat alone in the Frederickport Police Department's break room.

"He seemed pretty confident Hemingway didn't walk down the pier that night," Brian told Joe as he sipped the coffee.

"If he's right, then how could she have seen anyone toss those rings off the pier?" Joe asked.

"Or how could she have tossed the rings herself?" Brian added.

"If the killer is the one who threw those rings off the end of the pier, then that takes Hemingway off our suspect list—in spite of what she wrote."

"What about your fisherman? Did you get anything?" Brian asked.

"His story isn't much different from Fowler's. He remembers the young couple—they stopped and talked to him too. He thinks he remembers at least two—maybe three other people on the pier that night aside from the other fisherman. One of which was Steve Klein. He recognized Klein from the bank."

"Did he talk to Klein that night?" Brian asked.

"No. Said he started to say hi to him, but he seemed preoccupied. Watched as he walked down to the end of the pier."

"Klein did admit to walking on the pier that night. Did your fisherman happen to see Klein throw anything off the pier?"

"No. It was dark. And he wasn't the only one on the pier, just the only one he recognized," Joe said.

"So what do we have here?" Brian set his mug on the table and leaned back in the chair. "We've already interviewed our young couple, who like your fisherman, recall seeing three men on the pier that night, along with the two fishermen. Your fisherman is the only one who could identify any of the men on the pier—Steve—who already admitted to being there. None of them saw Hillary on the pier that night."

Joe's cellphone began to ring. He picked it up and looked at it. Before answering it, he said, "It's the chief."

Brian sat quietly, listening to Joe tell the chief what he and Joe had learned in their interviews with the two fishermen they had finally tracked down. When Joe got off the phone a few minutes later, he told Brian, "If Hemingway typed that letter, it wasn't done on her typewriter. The chief's stopping by Pier Café and then returning to the station."

"Why is he stopping there?" Brian asked.

"I guess he wants to talk to Carla again."

CARLA SAT across the booth from Chief MacDonald, staring at the photocopy of the letter he had received. After a few moments, she looked up at him. "Where did you get this?"

"You don't know?" he asked.

Setting the paper on the table, she shook her head. "Steve really did kill her?"

"I don't know. I was hoping you might be able to tell me who wrote that letter."

Carla frowned. "Why would I know who wrote this letter?"

"Whoever wrote that either witnessed the murder or knew about Jolene blackmailing Steve and wanted to implicate him for some reason. You knew about Jolene blackmailing Steve, and I imagine you weren't happy with the fact Steve was so casual about ending your relationship."

"Are you suggesting I wrote this letter?" Carla gasped.

"I don't know who wrote that letter."

With a shove, Carla sent the letter moving the rest of the way across the table to MacDonald. "If I witnessed a murder, I would come to you; I certainly wouldn't send a letter like this. And if you recall, I did come to you and tell you I suspected Steve. Why would I do that if I actually saw him murder that woman?"

"But if you didn't witness the murder, yet suspected he might have been the killer—and you knew he had a motive, and you felt unsafe, then I could see how you might write a letter like this. Who else knew about the blackmail?"

"I don't know. Aside from you, I never told anyone about the blackmail."

"Do you own a typewriter?"

"Typewriter? Who has a typewriter these days?"

"So I take that as a no?"

"I don't own a typewriter. I have a printer for my computer."

"Do you know anyone who has a typewriter?"

Carla shook her head. "Like I said, who has a typewriter these days? But I suppose this letter proves one thing."

"What's that?"

"I was right. Steve Klein murdered Jolene Carmichael." Folding her arms across her chest, Carla slumped back in the booth seat and glared off into space while muttering, "Damn, I certainly know how to pick them."

THIRTY-TWO

Danielle stood a moment at the attic doorway, silently observing Walt, who gazed out the window, watching the last hour of daylight.

"I'm going now," she said in a soft voice.

Turning from the window, Walt smiled at Danielle. His eyes swept over her, noting she had changed into leggings and a mauve sweater. Her hair, fashioned into a fishtail braid, was still damp from her recent shower.

"You aren't going to a restaurant?" he asked.

"No. Cookout on the beach. Have a bonfire, maybe roast some marshmallows."

Walt turned back to the window and looked out. "It's been a few years since I've been to a cookout on the beach."

Danielle walked to Walt and looked outside. "Hillary's downstairs in her room, still at her typewriter. I expect her to be there until we get back."

"Did she have dinner yet?"

"She went out after the chief left, grabbed a burger, and brought it back here. Went right to her room with it," Danielle explained.

"Something odd about that one—especially after what I overheard—but she's obviously a dedicated writer."

"I'd love to know what the deal is with her and Melony. Maybe I'll learn something tonight."

"Who's all going to be there?"

"Lily and Ian, and Adam and Melony."

"And you and Chris?" Walt asked in a soft voice.

Danielle shrugged. "Just some friends getting together."

Still staring out the window, Walt said, "I like Chris, Danielle. He annoys the hell out of me—but I like him."

"He likes you too."

Walt sighed and then said, "That's not what I'm talking about."

Danielle looked curiously to Walt. "What are you talking about?"

"We already know you and Chris are friends. But being friends doesn't mean something more can't develop. In fact, it's best to begin as friends."

"Are you trying to play matchmaker, Walt?"

Walt looked at Danielle and smiled softly. "I want you to be happy. That's all. And I think you might be happy with Chris."

"Who says I'm not happy now?" she asked defensively.

Walt's serious yet sweet expression instantly transformed into a mischievous smile. "Plus," he added, now grinning, "you really aren't getting any younger."

KNEELING ON HIS KITCHEN FLOOR, Chris moved cans of beer out of the open refrigerator and placed them in the ice chest. He glanced up at Danielle, who leaned back casually against the kitchen counter, absently toying with the glass of wine he had just poured her. She had been the first to arrive.

"Are you okay?" he asked as he stood up and grabbed some ice from the freezer.

Danielle glanced over at Chris and smiled. "Umm… sure…why?"

Chris dumped the ice into the open chest. "I don't know; you just seem a little preoccupied."

Rubbing a finger around the rim of the wineglass, she watched Chris. "I think Walt just gave me his permission to…" Instead of finishing her sentence, she took a sip of wine.

Chris placed the lid on the ice chest and stood up. "Permission to what?" Wiping his damp hands on the sides of his jeans, he turned to face Danielle, waiting for her to finish her sentence. When she didn't, he said, "Permission to what? What did Walt give you permission to do?"

Nervously flicking the tip of her tongue over her lower lip, she looked into Chris's blue eyes. "For you and I…to…well…be more than just friends."

Chris cocked his brows and smiled. "And you needed Walt's permission for that?"

"No," Danielle said quickly and then took another sip of wine. "It's just that he said he liked you…"

"And I like Walt. He drives me crazy sometimes. But he's a good guy."

Danielle chuckled.

"What's funny?" Chris asked.

"He said practically the same thing about you."

"Did he?"

Danielle took another sip of wine and then said, "Actually, it's not the first time he's said something like that."

Chris took several steps to Danielle. Standing before her, he reached out and gently took the wineglass from her hand and then set it on the counter behind her. Her eyes followed the departing glass and then looked up into Chris's eyes. His hand moved from the wineglass to Danielle's chin and tipped it up slightly, toward his face.

She started to say something, but just as she opened her mouth to speak, his lips brushed over hers. Closing her eyes to enjoy the kiss, the doorbell rang.

"Damn," Chris whispered against her lips.

Now smiling, Danielle opened her eyes. "Your company has arrived."

"Whose idea was this cookout anyway?" Chris grumbled as he moved away from Danielle.

"Yours." She picked her wineglass back up and watched Chris walk to the front door.

"ADAM AND MELONY." Chris shook his head. "I didn't see that one coming."

Chris stood with Danielle by the sliding glass door, looking outside. Just beyond the patio, Adam helped Ian build a bonfire while Melony and Lily stood nearby chatting. Chris and Danielle had come back inside the house to get the cooler of beer and another bottle of wine.

"They're just childhood friends," Danielle said. "I like Adam, but come on, him and Melony? Maybe Melony is from Frederickport, but she's definitely a Park Avenue girl. No way would she wear a scrunchie."

"What is that supposed to mean?"

"Did you ever watch *Sex and the City*?"

"Yeah, what does that have to do with a scrunchie?"

"There was this episode where Carrie is talking to a guy she's seeing—he's another writer—and in his book he has his female character—a New Yorker—wearing a scrunchie. Carrie is adamant that she and her friends would never wear one."

"Next question. What is a scrunchie?"

Danielle laughed. "It's a fabric rubber band thingie used to hold a ponytail."

"Ahhh…well…I don't know if Melony would wear a scrunchie or not, but there's some chemistry going on between those two."

"Maybe you're right." Danielle started to open the sliding door but then paused. She glanced over to Chris. "Do you think Jolene will show up again?"

"It's entirely possible, since Melony's here."

"If she does, I wish there was some way to get her to tell us who killed her. But I don't see that happening with an audience."

"When I saw her, I don't think she realizes she's dead yet," Chris told her.

"But she showed us where her rings were," Danielle reminded him.

"True, but she probably followed her killer and watched him dump them in the water. She was just trying to get them back. But did she understand she's dead? I don't think so. Not from how she acted with me."

LILY AND IAN'S contribution to the dinner was the steaks they had purchased before coming over to Chris's house. Adam and Melony had picked up some salads at the deli and French bread from Old

Salts Bakery. Danielle brought marshmallows, chocolate bars, and graham crackers to make s'mores for dessert. Chris provided the beverages and grilled the steaks. After dinner they all sat around the bonfire, roasting marshmallows.

Instead of beach chairs, they had spread blankets around the blazing fire. Sadie napped on the blanket she shared with Lily and Ian. Danielle glanced over to Melony, who shared a blanket with Adam. By the way the two continually exchanged whispers and private jokes, she suspected Chris might be right.

Removing a marshmallow from the fire, Danielle blew on it a moment, trying to cool it down before slipping it from the stick. Just as she pulled the gooey marshmallow off, Chris reached over and snatched it from her, popping it into his mouth.

"You brat!" Danielle cried out. Unable to maintain the proper amount of outrage, she smacked him with her now empty stick.

Chris started to say something, but he was distracted when Jolene suddenly appeared, hovering over Melony.

"I'd stab him with your stick," Lily said with a laugh.

Danielle, like Chris, was now distracted. Mesmerized, they watched Jolene, waiting to hear what the spirit had to say. The others—Melony, Adam, Ian, and Lily—prattled on, discussing marshmallow thieves and appropriate punishment, oblivious to the new arrival.

"What are you doing with him!" Jolene shouted, pointing to Adam. Jolene then turned her attention to Adam. "I told you to stay away from my daughter! You've ruined her!"

Sadie woke up, jumped up from her place by Ian, and began barking at the intruding spirit. In the next moment, Jolene vanished. Danielle and Chris exchanged quick glances.

"Sadie!" Ian snapped. "What are you barking at?"

Sadie let out a *woof*, glanced around and then reluctantly returned to her place on the blanket. After making several perfunctory circles, she plopped down with a grunt.

Ian scowled at his golden retriever, shook his head, and reached over and ruffled the fur on her back. "Crazy dog," he muttered.

Chris stood up and stretched while surveying the area, looking for any sign of Jolene. Walking a few feet from the bonfire, he glanced down the beach. "Hey, looks like we aren't the only ones having a bonfire tonight."

"Oh yeah?" Ian asked. "Who's having a bonfire, and why weren't we invited?" They all laughed.

"Looks like it's at Pete Rogers's house," Chris told them.

"Pete Rogers?" Melony looked to Adam. "Hey, you want to walk down there with me? I'd love to say hi to Pete."

MOONLIGHT LIT the way for Adam and Melony as they walked down the beach from Chris's house to Pete's. It wasn't a far walk, yet when they were about twenty feet from Pete's bonfire, they paused a moment and watched. They hadn't expected him to be alone. Nor had they expected him to be standing by his blazing fire, ripping pages from a book and feeding them to the flames.

"What is he doing?" Melony asked in a whisper.

Adam shrugged. "It's tax time. Maybe he prefers fire to a shredder."

They continued on their way, and when they were about six feet from Pete, Melony called out, "Hello, Pete!"

Startled, Pete looked in their direction and squinted, trying to see who it was. At the same time, he shoved whatever he had been ripping pages out of into a sack by his feet.

When they reached him, Melony said with a smile, "I bet you don't know who I am."

Pete's eyes widened and recognition dawned. "Melony!" He then greeted her with a warm hug and then stepped back to have a better look. "Still a pretty thing. But now a young woman, all grown up."

Melony laughed. "Not so young anymore."

"Oh peshaw! From where I'm sitting, you're just a babe."

Pete gave Adam a quick greeting and then turned his attention back to Melony. His expression grew serious and he reached out, taking her hand in his. "I'm real sorry about your mother."

"Thanks, Pete. I know you and my parents were good friends."

Pete nodded. "We had some fine times back then."

"I remember those cookouts on the beach." Melony glanced at Pete's fire. "I didn't really expect you to be alone when I noticed your bonfire. Thought you'd be out here with all your friends."

Pete shook his head. "So many folks have either moved away or died."

"Pete, do you know if Mother had a problem with anyone since she moved back to Frederickport?"

"I heard Danielle Boatman decided not to make a donation to the museum because of some problem she had with your mother." Pete looked over to Adam and arched his brow. "And I understand Adam here had a bit of a ruckus with your mom over some treasure she was trying to claim."

THIRTY-THREE

Before going to Marie Nichols the next morning, Danielle stopped at Old Salts Bakery and picked up freshly baked cinnamon rolls. When she arrived at Marie's, the coffee was already brewed, and Marie had set cups and napkins on the kitchen table.

"Do you want to know what one of the best things about being my age is?" Marie asked.

From what Danielle recalled, Marie was approaching her ninety-first birthday. "What's that?"

The two women sat at the kitchen table. Marie pulled a cinnamon roll out of the sack and set it on the napkin in front of Danielle, and then she took a roll for herself. "I don't fret about calories anymore."

Danielle laughed.

"Of course, that annoying doctor of mine keeps harping about salt."

"Sugar isn't terrific for us either," Danielle said as she took a satisfying bite of the sweet roll.

"Nothing delicious ever is." Marie sipped her coffee.

Danielle nodded and took another bite of her roll.

Setting her cup on the table, Marie looked over at Danielle and asked, "Have you heard anything about Jolene's case? Have they any new leads on her murder?"

Danielle picked up a napkin and wiped her mouth. "I think they have a few leads, but they're keeping quiet until they learn more. Did you know Jolene's daughter, Melony, is staying with us?"

Marie nodded. "Yes, Adam told me."

Danielle set her half-eaten roll on the napkin and looked over at Marie. "Can I ask you something?"

Marie smiled. "You want to know about Adam and Melony?"

"How did you know?" Danielle grinned.

"I heard you all got together last night at Chris's for a bonfire. I remember when I was younger, we used to do that a lot."

"I just wondered if they…well…did they used to date or something?"

"Just between the two of us?"

Danielle nodded. "Promise. I won't even tell Lily."

Marie took another sip of her coffee and then said with a chuckle, "I imagine you will." Setting her cup back on the table, she said, "Adam and Melony ran away together when they were kids."

"Ran away?"

Marie nodded. "They weren't gone long, a couple days." Marie shook her head. "Adam's folks were sick about it, and of course, Jolene was furious, kept blaming Adam, said she was going to have him arrested. But those two were the same age—both minors—wasn't like some older boy leading her astray. And quite frankly, Melony always had a mind of her own. I doubt Adam, or anyone, could get her to do something she didn't want to do."

"What happened?"

"They found them after a couple days, and her parents sent Melony off to boarding school."

"Did Adam and Melony ever see each other again?"

Marie shook her head. "Not as far as I know. And then when Melony eventually married, Jolene couldn't wait to tell Adam—rub it in. Silly woman, it had been years since those two ran off; they were just kids. But one thing about Jolene, she knew how to hold a grudge."

"What happened?"

"This was just after Doug had died, and Jolene was preparing to move. From what I understand, Adam was at some cocktail lounge with friends in Portland and had a bit too much to drink. He happened to run into Jolene and her party as they were leaving the restaurant. Jolene sees Adam, marches up to him, tells him Melony is on her honeymoon and then starts telling Adam what a loser he is and starts going on about the wonderful man her daughter just married."

"From what I understand, Melony is getting a divorce."

Marie picked up her roll. "Yes, Adam mentioned that."

"So what did Adam say to Jolene?"

"Like I said, he'd had too much to drink. Foolish boy, he threatened to kill her."

"Oh my…" Danielle tore off a piece of her roll and popped it into her mouth.

"When Jolene moved back to town a few months ago, Adam seemed to be over all that—didn't give Jolene a second notice. Of course, then Jolene pulled that stunt at my Beach Drive house." Marie took a bite of her cinnamon roll.

"No wonder you were upset when they brought Adam in for questioning."

"The idea of Adam killing Jolene after all this time, well, it's ludicrous. The boy has moved on. He wasn't harboring some grudge against Melony's mother. Holding grudges was Jolene's forte."

"Well, we had a nice time last night. It was fun. But I imagine Melony is busy today dealing with her mother's estate."

"So she's really not having a funeral?" Marie took another bite of her roll and then set it down, reaching for her coffee cup.

Danielle shook her head. "No. I guess not."

"Well, not sure Jolene had many friends left in town anyway. Seems like she'd ruffled the feathers of all the historical society's board members, from what I hear."

"There is Pete Rogers. I guess he's one of her old friends."

Marie nodded. "Yes, Pete. What made you think of him?"

"Melony mentioned he was a good friend of her parents. She said they used to have bonfires over at his place. In fact, she and Adam walked down there last night and said hello to him."

Marie sipped her coffee and then set the cup back down. "Yes, I remember, Pete was always cozy with the Carmichaels and that whole group."

"Did there used to be a Mrs. Rogers?" Danielle asked. "I've never heard him mention a wife before."

"Yes. He's a widower. Never remarried. In fact, his house belonged to her parents. Well, the house that used to be there.

Burned down a few years after his wife died and he built what's there now."

"Does he have kids? I've never seen anyone visit him."

Marie shook her head. "No. In fact, his wife—or more accurately his bride—died before their first wedding anniversary. Rather a tragic love story. Charlotte Michaels, she was a pretty thing. Sweet, but a mite timid, from what I recall."

"How sad. What happened?"

"She got ill just months after they were married. Lingered miserably. It was so sad. When she died, there was a ruckus about her estate. Her parents had left both her and her sister, Angeline, well off. Charlotte had inherited their property in Oregon, while Angeline inherited their property in Washington."

"What kind of a ruckus?"

Marie picked up a napkin, dabbed her mouth, and then set the napkin back on the table. "Doug Carmichael was Charlotte's attorney before she ever married Pete. After she died, Angeline informed Pete that Charlotte had left everything to her, including the Beach Drive house. Pete was furious."

"I can understand, since they hadn't really been married that long. But what happened, did he buy the Beach Drive house from his sister-in-law?"

Marie shook her head. "The will had been prepared by Doug Carmichael—and according to its date, it had been revised several months after Charlotte got ill. Apparently, up until Charlotte's marriage, Angeline was her heir. Right after she married Pete, she changed the will to leave everything to her new husband, including all the Oregon properties. But then, she changed her will again, leaving her sister everything."

"She wrote her husband out of her will?"

"Yes. But not until after she got sick."

"So how is it that Pete has the property now?"

"Apparently there was a later will; it left everything to her husband. According to Doug, while Charlotte had changed her will, leaving everything to her sister again when she first got ill, she later came to him and said Angeline had pressured her to write Pete out of the will, something he wasn't aware of when he had made the changes. Charlotte had a change of heart and instructed Doug to revise her will—again. She was pretty sick by this time, but the courts later ruled she was still fully capable to make this decision. In the final will, she left everything to Pete. According to Doug, Charlotte wanted to do this because Pete had so steadfastly stood by her side and taken care of her during her illness."

"That's horrible for Angeline to try to manipulate her dying sister like that."

Marie shrugged and picked up her half-eaten roll. "I suppose that depends which side you listen to."

"What do you mean?" Danielle sipped her coffee.

"In court, Angeline claimed Pete neglected his wife during her illness—that he was cold and mistreated her. Practically accused him of abusing his sick wife. Of course, she had nothing to substantiate her claim, and then there was the will Charlotte's own attorney had presented."

"So he inherited everything?"

Marie nodded. "You may not realize it by just looking at Pete, but he's a very rich man. Over the years he's sold most of the properties he inherited from his wife and reinvested the money. Apparently, he's very good with managing money—and tight as a tick."

Danielle chuckled and shook her head.

"What's funny?" Marie asked.

"I was thinking about how upset Pete was when the historical society was talking about keeping the *Eva Aphrodite* on the beach as some sort of tourist attraction and how Pete freaked, worried about his property values. The way he went on, I assumed his entire financial world was wrapped up in that house. While I can understand not wanting that monstrosity blocking his view, it's kind of funny, when you think about it."

"Like I said, he's tight as a tick."

"THANKS FOR COMING WITH ME, ADAM," Melony said as she and Adam walked through her mother's house.

"Where's all the furniture?" Adam asked.

"When Mother moved to New York after Dad died, she took all her furniture with her. And then when she moved back, she sold it all. She couldn't afford to ship it back."

"Why didn't she sell the house or rent it out?" He glanced around the sparsely furnished living room.

"I suspect she didn't want to sell the house because it had

belonged to her parents. And then, well, she didn't need the money at the time. As for renting it, I don't think she wanted strangers in it. Mother liked to hold onto what she believed belonged to her, even if she didn't need it and someone else did."

"Sounds like your mom," Adam muttered under his breath.

They moved from the living room to the kitchen. Melony opened the refrigerator and looked in. "I need to hire someone to come over and clean this out."

"Hey, Mel, can I ask you something?"

Melony shut the refrigerator. "Sure, what?"

"Why didn't you come back for your father's funeral?"

Melony shrugged. "I didn't see the point."

"The way your mother talked, she moved back to New York to be with you and your new husband."

Melony let out a harsh laugh. "Yeah. I suspect the only reason she decided to move to New York was to give people that impression. She was pretty angry with me for not coming to Dad's funeral and for eloping."

"You two never mended fences?"

Melony turned to Adam and leaned back against the kitchen counter. "Can I tell you something in confidence?"

"Certainly, Mel."

"Remember when we were in high school, and Dad always wanted me to be a lawyer like him?"

"Sure. Which was one reason I always figured your folks were so furious with me. I'd led their straight A student astray, off the path they'd planned for her."

"If you will remember, it was my idea to run away," Melony reminded him.

"I know. And I never understood why. Back then, it just sounded like a good idea to me. Running off with a hot chick who I was crazy about."

Melony chuckled. "Yeah, well, you were always pretty easy to manipulate."

Adam scowled. "Not sure I like the way that sounds."

"Oh, come on, admit it, Adam. Teenage girls are always more savvy than boys the same age, while the boys are just—well, horny."

Adam shrugged. "Maybe."

Melony laughed. "No maybe about it."

"So what did you want to tell me—that I can't tell anyone else?"

"The real reason I ran away back then."

Adam frowned. "The real reason?"

"Yes. The reason I never told you."

"Which was?"

"My father fell off his pedestal. If you'll remember, back then I started working weekends in my father's office."

"I remember."

"I learned far more than I wanted."

"What do you mean?"

"He was crooked, Adam. My father, the man who I loved and looked up to, was nothing but a crook."

THIRTY-FOUR

Melony arrived at Marlow house a few minutes after Danielle. After parking Jolene's car along the front of the house, she walked down the drive toward Danielle, who was busy taking groceries out of the back of her car.

"Hey, need some help?" Melony called out.

"Thanks, but I think I got this." Picking up the last of the groceries, Danielle juggled the bags while she slammed the back hatch shut.

Melony held open the kitchen door for Danielle. Once inside the house, Danielle set the sacks on the counter and turned to Melony. "Did you have a productive morning?"

"I went over to my mother's house. I got Adam to go with me. I didn't feel like going over there alone."

"That was nice of him. Have you decided what you're going to do with her house?"

"I'm having Adam run a comparative market analysis on it. Mother took out some loans on the property, and I suspect it's upside down. We'll have to see. I might have to walk away from it."

Danielle shook her head sympathetically. "Sorry."

Melony shrugged. "It is what it is."

"Is there a lot of stuff to go through? I had to do that after my parents were killed—and then with my cousin, Cheryl. One of my least favorite things to have to do." As Danielle talked, she continued to put away her groceries.

"She really didn't have much here. Got rid of most of her things when she moved back to Frederickport from New York. There was one thing I looked for; I thought it might help Eddy."

Folding a now empty grocery bag, Danielle turned to Melony. "What was that?"

"Mother always used a day planner. Figured if we could look through her schedule, we might have a better idea what was going on these last few weeks. You know, track her steps—see what kind of appointments she set. And knowing Mother, if she argued with anyone, she'd jot down something about it."

"It wasn't in her house?"

Melony took a seat at the table. "No. Wasn't in her car either."

"Maybe it was in her purse? Did you check with the chief? I know they have her purse."

"I already asked. When Eddy described the purse they found with her, I realized the type of day planner she typically used wouldn't have fit in it."

Danielle paused a moment and pointed to the covered cake plate on the kitchen table. "There's some chocolate chip cookies under there, help yourself."

"Thanks." Melony smiled. She lifted the lid off the plate and grabbed two cookies. "So how did you spend your morning?" She paused a moment and then added, "I guess that's a silly question. Grocery shopping."

"Actually, I spent most of the morning visiting with Adam's grandmother." Danielle paused a moment and folded the sacks she had emptied. "And then I stopped at the store."

"Adam mentioned you two were friends."

Returning to her groceries, Danielle said, "Yes, Marie was a friend of my aunt—great-aunt, really—the one who left me Marlow House."

"Oh, that's right…Clarence was her attorney…"

They were both silent for a few moments, and finally Melony said, "I'm really sorry about your cousin, by the way. I knew Clarence was a crook; I just never realized he'd be capable of murdering someone."

Danielle paused and looked at Melony. "You know, your mother blamed me for her financial problems."

Melony sighed. "That doesn't surprise me. Mother was never big on personal responsibility—at least not for herself."

"I imagine it was a shock for her to discover her husband's business partner—the man she believed was his best friend—would do something like this. Which ended up wiping her out. I suppose I can understand why she resented me."

"Danielle, that would only be true if my parents had no idea what Clarence was up to."

Danielle stared at Melony. "Are you saying your mother knew?"

"I'm not saying she knew about Clarence killing your cousin—but everything else—embezzling from clients, I'd be surprised if she didn't know."

"Why do you think that?"

"Because, I'm sad to say, my father was cut from the same cloth as Clarence Renton. They were best friends for a reason."

Before Danielle had time to respond, Hillary barreled into the kitchen. "Oh, you're back, Danielle!" Hillary greeted her cheerfully, and then she spied Melony sitting at the table. Her smile vanished.

"Hello, Hillary," Melony said stiffly.

"Melony," Hillary returned, equally stiff.

Danielle glanced from Melony to Hillary and back to Melony.

"Melony, I'm sorry about your mother. And if it would make you more comfortable, I will find someplace else to stay," Hillary told her.

"I don't imagine Eddy would be thrilled if you left town right now, considering everything," Melony returned.

"You know I had nothing to do with your mother's death."

"I don't know anything anymore, Hillary." Melony stood up and faced Danielle. "If you will excuse me, I think I'll go upstairs and lie down."

After Melony left the room, Hillary took a seat at the kitchen table. With a sigh, she lifted the cake plate lid and snatched a cookie. Returning the lid atop the plate, she leaned back in the chair and took a bite.

"Hillary," Danielle began as she took a seat at the table. "What's the deal with you and Melony? When she first arrived, you told me she was your attorney. Yet you two act like you can't stand each other."

"Lawyers don't always like their clients," Hillary said as she took another bite of her cookie.

Danielle glanced at the empty doorway and then back to Hillary. "No, I guess not."

"Plus, she thinks I'm crazy." Hillary shoved the rest of the cookie in her mouth, quickly eating it.

"Why does she think you're crazy?"

Hillary cocked her head to one side and looked at Danielle inquisitively. "I would have thought by now you would wonder why Melony represented me. I was quite open with you. I told you she was my attorney."

"You mean because she's a criminal attorney?"

Hillary smiled. "I was beginning to wonder if you didn't know what kind of law she practiced."

"I didn't at first."

"She's an excellent criminal attorney. Although, I'm surprised she's still practicing. She hates her job."

"She told you that?"

"I can tell. She expertly defends her clients—gets them off—yet deep down, she believes they're guilty. Which makes her feel guilty for putting a criminal back into society. Although in my case, she believes I'm insane and would like to see me locked away."

Danielle had to ask, "What were you charged with?"

"Murder." Hillary then lifted the cake plate lid again and grabbed another cookie.

"Are you saying you were really guilty?" Danielle asked in a quiet voice.

Biting down on the cookie, Hillary smiled at Danielle. Shaking her head, she chewed and then swallowed the bite and said, "I didn't kill that woman. I didn't kill any of them. There really was no evidence, and Melony, being a master at what she does, kept it all out of the press. Although, I imagine it would have done wonders for my book sales, although I don't really need it. I do well enough without having to kill people to get in the press." She took another bite of the cookie.

"So you're saying Melony cleared you of all charges?"

"Yes, in a way." Hillary licked the cookie crumbs off her lips.

"And you didn't kill anyone?"

Hillary shook her head. "No, I promise you. I never killed anyone. Never."

"But Melony thinks you may have?"

Wrinkling her nose for a moment, Hillary considered the question and then shook her head. "I think she wonders if I was an accomplice, but there was no real evidence. Then she decided I was crazy."

"Crazy?" Danielle asked in a whisper.

Hillary looked into Danielle's eyes. "I think she may be right. I might be crazy."

"Did you have anything to do with my mother's murder?" Melony asked from the kitchen doorway.

Hillary looked to Melony. "I thought you went up to take a nap?"

"I heard everything you told Danielle," Melony said.

"It's true," Walt announced when he appeared the next moment. "I've been watching Melony while she's been lurking in the hall, eavesdropping."

Danielle glanced from Walt to Melony.

"Why would Hillary kill your mother?" Danielle asked.

"Because she's—"

"Crazy," Hillary finished for Melony. "She thinks I'm crazy. Didn't I just mention that?"

"And you just admitted you might be!" Melony snapped.

Danielle pressed the palm of her hand to her forehead. She was getting a headache. Glancing from Hillary to Melony, she asked, "Does this have anything to do with the fact all Hillary's murder mysteries are based on unsolved crimes?"

"They aren't!" Hillary insisted.

"And that Hillary's notes for this new book match Jolene's crime scene?" Danielle finished, ignoring Hillary's interruption.

Melony stepped into the kitchen, but stopped by the sink and did not approach the table. "Yes. When the crime scene from one of her books included facts only known to the police, they began to look into Hillary and discovered it wasn't the first time she'd been so eerily close to the truth—or in such close proximity to a crime scene. Of course, she insisted it was all a coincidence, and since each crime occurred six months before the book's release, I argued she could have easily read about the crimes in the paper—and used them for her inspiration. As for the facts she included that were not public knowledge, I argued it was no more than a coincidence; after all, she is a mystery writer, with an active imagination."

"But that wasn't the truth," Hillary told her. "I didn't read about those murders in the paper."

"Which is why it's probably a good thing I didn't let you say anything. Fortunately for you, they didn't file any charges, and we kept it out of the press."

"But you think I'm crazy. And now you ask if I murdered your mother!"

Danielle studied Hillary for a moment. Finally she asked, "Hillary, if you didn't get your ideas from the newspaper, where did you get them?"

Melony rolled her eyes and let out a harsh laugh before saying, "From her muse!" Melony turned and marched from the room. By the sound of her pounding up the stairs, there was no doubt she had gone to her room this time.

"It's true," Hillary insisted. She closed her eyes briefly and then looked up at Danielle. "Maybe Melony is right. Maybe I am crazy. But it's my muse who tells me these things."

Walt took a seat at the table. "I have to hear this. Danielle, ask her to explain her muse."

WALT, Danielle, and Hillary sat at the kitchen table. Yet Hillary didn't know of Walt's presence, in spite of the hint of cigar smoke drifting in the air.

"About eleven years ago, I was at a crossroads in my career. I wrote romance back then, and I was simply burned out. To be honest, I didn't feel like writing romance anymore. Maybe it was my age. And then one night, I had a dream. A man came to me, told me he knew I was having a hard time figuring out what to write and asked me to come with him."

"Were you dreaming about someone you knew in real life?" Danielle asked.

Hillary shook her head. "No. I had never seen him before. And frankly, there was something frightening about him. But I went with him anyway."

"Where did he take you?"

"He took me to an alley where a woman was being murdered. I was terrified—woke up screaming. I couldn't get that murder scene out of my head, so I started writing about it. And before I knew it, an entire story came to me. It was my first murder mystery, and it made *The New York Times* Best Sellers list," Hillary said proudly.

"Then what happened?"

"He came to me again, showed me another murder. And again I wrote about it."

"He's your muse?" Danielle asked.

Hillary nodded. "I explained it all to Melony when she asked me how the stories came to me."

"And she thinks you're crazy?"

Hillary sighed. "I think she might be right."

THIRTY-FIVE

By late afternoon, Hillary was back in her room, typing away on her book, and Melony was on her way to Adam's office to discuss the comparative market analysis he had prepared on her mother's house. Danielle wasn't sure where Lily was, yet assumed she was with Ian, since her car was parked in front of Marlow House, while Ian's car was not in his driveway. She thought it possible it was in his garage, yet his living room blinds were drawn, and he usually left them open when he was at home.

Danielle found Walt in the library, reading a book, with Max curled up on the sofa by his side, sleeping soundly.

"Is it a good book?" Danielle asked as she walked into the room and took a seat across from him.

Looking up at Danielle, he smiled and set the book on his lap. "To be honest, I haven't been able to get into it. Other things on my mind."

"Such as?"

Walt closed his book. "What Hillary told you in the kitchen about the muse."

"I've been thinking of that too."

"From what Hillary said, she seemed to recall each dream vividly," Walt reminded her.

"Yes." Danielle leaned back in the chair and crossed her legs.

"Come on, Danielle, you haven't been wondering what I have?"

Danielle frowned. "What are you talking about?"

"To use your coined expression—a dream hop."

Danielle stared at Walt, her expression blank. "Are you suggesting her muse is actually a spirit who's showing her these murders?"

Walt shrugged. "It's the only explanation that makes sense to me."

Danielle cringed. "That's kind of creepy."

"Yes. Especially considering these murders have all gone unsolved. I would have to assume the spirit witnessed them when they happened. I don't believe it would be possible to recreate a scene like that without being there."

"No, you're right. I remember when you took me to the speakeasy in a dream hop, you could only show me what happened when you had actually been in the room."

"It might be argued the spirit didn't actually witness the murders—perhaps he likes to hang around with homicide cops and was there when they discussed the details of the crime. But that would not explain—"

"Jolene's murder," Danielle finished for him.

"Exactly. From what I can piece together, Hillary went to bed and fell asleep when I was still downstairs the night of the murder. By the time I went upstairs, she had woken up from the dream and started writing about it."

"Jolene's body wasn't found until hours later."

They sat quietly for a few minutes, considering Walt's theory.

"You know what this means," Danielle asked.

"What's that?"

"Whatever spirit's been visiting Hillary knows who murdered Jolene—and probably the rest of them."

"I imagine he does. But so?" Walt asked.

"If I could talk to the spirit—"

Walt stood abruptly. The book that had been on his lap now rested on the couch cushion he had seemingly been sitting on a moment before. "Absolutely not!"

"But, Walt, this guy knows who killed Jolene!"

Walt angrily glared at Danielle. "What kind of spirit perversely shares gruesome murder scenes—like a twisted voyeur—yet does nothing to expose the guilty party? How many other murders could have been prevented had he behaved differently?"

Danielle studied Walt for a moment. "He's a ghost, Walt. You more than anyone should understand how someone from your realm typically views death different from someone who is still alive. Spirits I've encountered—including you—often see death as less permanent—less tragic."

"I agree, a person's death no longer affects me in the same way it once did—but you, Danielle, are still alive, and you should not expose yourself to that type of energy."

"I suppose it's a moot point anyway. Not sure how I could hook up with Hillary's muse. I don't think his spirit has been lurking around the neighborhood—there haven't been any signs of another spirit aside from Jolene, who both Chris and I saw."

"Where is Chris, anyway? I thought you two would be together today."

Narrowing her eyes, Danielle studied Walt. "Why is that?"

Walt shrugged. "I don't know. Figured now that he's back, you two would be spending all your time together. Did you have a nice night last night?"

Danielle didn't answer immediately. Finally, she said, "It was a nice evening. I didn't tell you…we saw Jolene."

"Jolene? I wonder why she's hanging around Chris's house. She's still not saying who killed her?"

Danielle sat up in her chair. "No. The moment she appeared, she started yelling at her daughter—and at Adam. But then Sadie jumped up and started barking at her, and she disappeared."

"She yelled at Adam? Why?"

Danielle went on to tell Walt what Marie had told her about Melony and Adam's past relationship.

"Interesting…" Walt murmured when she was done.

"As for where Chris is today, he's over at the Gusarov Estate, making a list of what he needs to do to turn that place into his nonprofit headquarters."

DANIELLE SAT on the front porch swing, watching the sunset, when her phone rang. It was Chris.

"How did it go today?" Danielle asked as the toe of her right shoe gently pushed against the ground, keeping the swing in motion.

"I forgot how big that place is. Not sure what I was thinking when I bought it."

"Buyer's remorse?"

"Nahh, not really. How was your day?"

Danielle went on to tell Chris about her visit with Marie, what Hillary had told her about her muse, and Walt's dream hop theory.

"A dream hop? Possible," Chris murmured.

"Walt also told me if anyone tries to communicate with the muse ghost to get information on any of the murders—he says it should be you."

Chris chuckled. "Of course he did. But not sure how either one of us can do that. A spirit doesn't need to be in close proximity to enter your dream. He could be haunting somewhere in the UK or already crossed over to the other side."

"That's true about a general dream hop. But not in this case. If he'd crossed over, I don't think he would've been able to witness Jolene's murder. And if he did witness her murder, we know his spirit's been in the neighborhood."

Chris let out a sigh. "I suppose you're right. Plus, if those murders she's dreamed about really happened when she was near the crime scenes, as you suggested, then it seems this ghost is sticking pretty close to Hillary."

"Wherever he's been haunting, I certainly haven't seen a hint of him, and neither has Walt or Max."

"Danielle, see if you can get Hillary to describe her muse."

"You're suggesting we might have walked right by him and never realized it was a spirit?"

"Exactly."

MELONY AND ADAM stood under the pier. The evening's sunset painted the blue sky in swirls of orange and red. But their attention was not on the picturesque sunset hanging over the ocean, but on the damp sand beneath the pier. The tide had since washed away any evidence of a crime scene.

"I thought I would feel something, anything," Melony told Adam.

"What do you mean?" he asked.

Melony shrugged. "I don't know. It just feels like we're standing under the pier. I don't feel any chill going down my spine. No sense of dread." She looked at Adam. "Does that make me a horrible person?"

"It just looks like it always does down here." Adam glanced around.

"I wonder why Mother came down here in the first place. I just don't picture her taking late night walks on the beach alone. I have to assume she came down here willingly and met with her killer. If someone had forced her down here, wouldn't someone on the pier have heard something?" She looked up at the bottom of the pier. "After all, there were a couple of guys fishing up there that night."

Adam glanced around again and then looked at Melony. "You want to get going?"

"Would you mind if we walked down the beach a bit? It looks like a beautiful sunset."

Adam shrugged. "Sure." Together, he and Melony started walking north along the shoreline.

"So do you want to list it? There's some equity in the house," Adam asked a few minutes later. They walked barefoot on the sand, each carrying their shoes.

"You know, I sort of expected to have all those old negative feelings about the house, but it doesn't feel the same."

"Probably because none of the furniture is there from when you lived in it."

"It kind of feels like a blank canvas. It's a beautiful house…and I've missed the Oregon coast."

"A beautiful house with a hefty mortgage—in spite of the equity," he reminded her. "If you're looking for a vacation home here, you'd be better off selling your mother's house and paying cash for something smaller with the equity."

Melony laughed. "You really are a real estate salesman, aren't you?"

"Hey, I'm not making that suggestion just because it would mean a commission for me—assuming you use me as your agent—on both properties. But now that you mention it, it would be a nice perk."

"Actually, I'm considering something other than a vacation property."

Adam glanced over to Melony as they continued to stroll down the beach. "What do you mean?"

"I wouldn't mind moving back here. I'm a little weary of living in the city," she confessed.

"What about your job? Aren't you some hotshot criminal attorney?"

"I'm a little weary of that too—at least some of the cases I take. And from what I understand, since Renton's incarceration, Frederickport could use another attorney." Their conversation drifted from her job to Adam's and what they had each been doing over the years.

Just as they reached the stretch of beach in front of Chris's house, the wind began to gust up. Brushing her blond hair behind her ears, Melony squinted as the sand swirled around them.

"We should go back," Adam shouted over the wind. "Or we can just cut over to Marlow House, and I'll walk down and pick up the car." They had left Adam's car at the pier parking lot.

"No, I'll go with you," Melony shouted back as she turned toward the direction of the pier. A sheet of paper, blown by the wind, landed on her bare feet, and in the next moment the air grew still.

Startled by the abrupt absence of wind, Adam glanced around. "Where did that come from?"

"It was like a little twister," Melony said as she reached down to pick up the sheet of paper from her feet. Not wanting to litter and toss the paper aside, Melony looked at it briefly, intending to crumple it and shove it in a pocket to be tossed in the trash when they returned to the pier. Instead, she stared blankly at the page, saying nothing.

Adam noticed the black edges of the paper. It looked as if it had been scorched in a fire. "What is it, a treasure map?" he teased.

Gripping the paper in her hand, Melony looked to Adam, her expression dazed. "This is my mother's, Adam. It's from her day planner."

THIRTY-SIX

MacDonald wasn't wearing his police uniform. He had already gone home for the evening, changed into denims and a T-shirt, and was fixing dinner for his boys when the call had come in from Melony, telling him she needed to see him. It was urgent. Fortunately, the teenager who lived next door to him and who often babysat his sons was able to come over and stay with his boys so he could leave.

"I'm really sorry to have to drag you over here," Melony told him for the third time. She sat alone with McDonald in the parlor of Marlow House. Not completely alone. Walt lounged by the bookshelf, lit cigar in hand, eavesdropping on the conversation. While Melony didn't know they had company, MacDonald did.

Sitting on the sofa, holding the burnt-edged paper Melony had found on the beach, MacDonald glanced up at her as she restlessly paced the room. "Where exactly did you find this?"

"On the beach not far from Chris's house. Like I told you, a gust of wind came up and that flew into me."

"More like a spiritual gust," Walt mumbled as he puffed the cigar. "How much you want to bet your mother caused that burst of wind."

"What makes you so sure this is hers?" MacDonald asked.

Melony stopped pacing and took the paper from MacDonald. "For one thing, Mother had distinct handwriting. And for another"—she pointed to a phone number jotted down along the singed edge of the paper "—that's my cell number."

MacDonald took the paper back from Melony and looked at it while she took a seat on a nearby chair. "Perhaps your mother had the book with her when she was killed, and whoever killed her took it with him and then decided to burn it. There's nothing incriminating on this page, but who knows what was on the other pages in that book."

"I thought about that. But honestly, Eddy, I don't really see Mother carrying that book around with her, especially when she's walking down under the pier at night. It's not like that book would have fit in her purse, and I don't see her bringing it with her to make an appointment with her killer."

MacDonald shrugged. "So how do you explain this?"

Melony let out a sigh. "I suppose she could have had it in her car, and he found it there. Maybe he was afraid something was in it that might incriminate him, and he took it."

"Now that I think about it, I can't see the killer stopping along the beach to burn this. Typically, killers don't want to draw attention to themselves, and a fire would," MacDonald noted.

"You're right. And I don't see the killer coming back to burn it. That makes less sense."

"There is another explanation," MacDonald suggested.

"What's that?"

"Yes, I'd like to hear that," Walt said.

"If your mother went to the pier to meet her killer, he might have been concerned she had something with her that might incriminate him. Maybe he checked out her car, found the book, and after looking through it, dumped it along the beach. It's possible someone found it, figured it was trash and used it for kindling."

Melony stared at the rumpled page. "I wish we could find the rest of it."

"Even if we did, I doubt it would help us now. If the killer did take this out of her car, he probably destroyed any incriminating pages from the book."

Melony stood up and started pacing again. "Then perhaps we need to discuss something else."

MacDonald watched Melony pace. "What's that?"

She stopped and turned to him. "Hillary Hemingway."

"I'm not sure what else there is to discuss." After Melony's confrontation with Hillary in the kitchen earlier that day, Melony had called MacDonald before going to the pier with Adam, and had told him about her professional history with Hillary—and how Hillary had confessed to her regarding the notes that Danielle had passed on to him.

What MacDonald didn't tell Melony was that Danielle had also called him, telling him what she suspected about Hillary's muse. It wasn't something he could share with his old friend.

"I think she's crazy," Melony insisted. "Don't you find it bizarre she's here at the same time my mother is murdered?"

"And her motive?"

"An insane person doesn't need a motive. If Hillary had anything to do with my mother's murder, I'm the one responsible for bringing her here. I was hoping you might think of some reason to take Hillary into custody."

"Melony, you're an attorney. You know better than that. I've no legitimate reason to bring her in. I have nothing to charge her with."

With a frustrated sigh, she dropped back in her chair and looked to the floor.

Standing up, MacDonald walked to her side and took her hand. "I can't tell you everything I know, Melony, but I want you to listen carefully to what I have to say."

She looked up into his face.

"I want you to know this. If I thought for a moment Hillary was a danger to anyone, I would do something. I can't tell you what I know, but I can promise you that you're safe at Marlow House. Hillary's not a danger."

MacDonald looked from Melony to where the scent of cigar smoked drifted from and smiled.

"Yes, yes," Walt said impatiently, knowing MacDonald couldn't hear him. "I'm keeping an eye on things. If we're all wrong about Hillary, I'll step in."

MAX SLUNK through the darkened hallway. They had all shut their doors. He stopped at Danielle's room, faced the closed door, sat down, and began beating his paws boxer-like against the barrier.

After a few minutes of persistent battering, light replaced darkness beneath the door.

"Get in here, Max," Danielle said in a hushed whisper as she opened the door a few inches. "You're going to wake the house!"

Walt was just coming down the stairs from the attic when he noticed Max slip into Danielle's bedroom, and the door quietly shut. In the next moment, the light coming from under her door went out. Walt continued on his way and stopped in front of Hillary's bedroom. Effortlessly, he moved through the wall into the room.

Moonlight streamed through the curtains, casting a golden glow across the bed where Hillary slept. A gasping sound broke the silence. Walt moved quickly to the bedside and looked down at the woman. Clad in a flannel nightgown, Hillary lay sprawled on her back, her arms outstretched and her mouth wide open. A snort replaced the gasp—followed by another gasp—a snort…

Walt shook his head and let out a sigh. Focusing his attention on Hillary, he harnessed his energy and watched as she rolled to her side. The snoring stopped. He stayed by her bed a few minutes longer and then moved through the wall back to the hallway.

His next stop was Lily's room. He found her sleeping, curled up under a quilt. Red hair spilled over her pillow as she hugged a second pillow. Smiling down at her, his right hand brushed over her cheek. The corners of her mouth lifted slightly in a sleeping smile.

From Lily's room Walt moved to where Melony was staying. To his surprise, she wasn't sleeping, in spite of the fact the lights were out. Dressed in jeans and a sweatshirt, Melony sat on the side of her bed, lacing up her shoes. With a frown, Walt glanced around the room. He had seen her an hour earlier going from the bathroom to her bedroom. Then, she had been wearing pajamas. *Why did she get dressed?* he wondered.

When she finished lacing up her shoes, Walt watched as Melony grabbed her jacket and then eased open the bedroom door, careful not to make a sound. She peeked into the hallway and then slipped from the room.

Walt followed Melony down the stairs to the first floor, wondering where she was going. If she hadn't changed out of her pajamas and put on shoes, he would have assumed she was just going downstairs to get something to eat.

Once downstairs, Melony went into the library and turned on

the light. Walt silently watched as she went through the room, opening and closing drawers.

"What are you looking for?" he asked aloud. Whatever she was looking for, she didn't find it. Melony turned off the overhead light and moved back into the darkened hallway. Walt followed her to the kitchen. She turned on the lights and began searching through the drawers and cupboards.

Whatever she was looking for, Walt assumed she found it when she let out an "Aha!" In her hand, she now held a flashlight. He watched as she clicked it on and off; he assumed to test to see if it was in working order.

Melony turned off the kitchen lights and moved back into the hallway with the flashlight. He followed Melony down the hallway to the front door. She slipped outside and gently closed the door behind her.

Walt looked out the side window by the front door and watched as Melony disappeared into the night. "Where is she going?"

HUGGING THE JACKET AROUND HER, Melony walked briskly down the sidewalk. Overhead, the moon lit her way. When she was across the street from Chris's house, she hurriedly moved to his side of the street and continued on down the road to Pete Rogers's house. Like Chris's house, Pete's was dark.

Moving quickly, Melony cut between Pete's house and his neighbor to the north, heading toward the beach. Just as she reached the sand, she glanced around nervously and turned on the flashlight. Keeping it close to her thigh, she walked behind Pete's house, looking for the location of his bonfire the previous night.

After finding it, Melony moved the beam of her flashlight over the fire pit. Kneeling down, she took a closer look. There wedged between the rocks, under a fresh pile of firewood, tucked among the ashes, were slivers of scorched paper. Reaching out, Melony pinched the exposed edges and gently tugged them from their nest to have a closer look.

Directing the flashlight's beam on the bits of paper she now held, Melony let out a startled gasp. Dropping the cindered bits onto the sand, she went down on her hands and knees and scrambled to move the newly placed wood, seeking whatever remnants of paper might still be trapped.

Abruptly light replaced dark. Still on her hands and knees, Melony looked up into the bright light of a flashlight.

"Melony?" the voice behind the flashlight called.

Blinking her eyes, Melony slowly stood, facing Pete Rogers. In one hand she held a flashlight while her other hand fisted tightly, holding the bits of paper she had grabbed on to before being bathed in light.

"Pete…oh, I'm sorry…I didn't mean to wake you," she stammered.

"What are you doing out here?" he asked, now lowering his flashlight to his hip so it was no longer shining on her.

"I…I lost something last night. I…I thought maybe I dropped it over here when I came over to say hi."

Pete flashed the light back along the area she had just been rummaging through. "In the bonfire?"

"It was a necklace," she said quickly. "A gold necklace. I was looking around the area and thought I saw something shiny in the wood."

Pete studied her a moment and then smiled. "You know, I found a necklace out here this morning. I wondered who it belonged to."

"You did?" she squeaked.

"Yeah. Come on in the house, and I'll show it to you. I set it on the counter in the kitchen. It has to be yours. Can't believe two people lost a necklace along here."

"Umm…okay." Melony reluctantly followed Pete and then paused at the back door. "Maybe I better stay out here. I got a little dirty looking for it. You could bring it out for me?"

Standing just inside his house, Pete looked out at Melony, saying nothing. Finally, he smiled again and said, "I'll be right back."

Glancing around anxiously, one hand still fisted tightly, Melony considered running back to Marlow House. *You're being silly*, she told herself. *Pete had no reason to kill Mother. He was probably burning tax papers like Adam said. It's my imagination the paper in his fire pit looks a little like the paper I found.*

When Pete returned to the door, he carried what appeared to be a gold chain in his hand. Melony let out the breath she had been nervously holding. *See, he really did find a necklace—it has all been a coincidence.*

"I'm sure this is yours," Pete said cheerfully, holding out his hand.

Just as Melony moved closer to have a better look, the necklace slipped from his hand and onto the ground.

"No, I'm afraid that's not it," Melony told him as she reached down to pick the chain up.

Pete's flashlight hit the back of her skull just as her hand touched the fallen necklace.

THIRTY-SEVEN

She wasn't dead. The blow to her head hadn't killed her as it had her mother. Pete dragged Melony into the house. Before she came to, he used duct tape to secure her wrists, fasten her ankles together, and cover her mouth. He couldn't have her limbs flailing about as he dragged her to his garage, and he didn't want to hear her questions if she regained consciousness.

Pete had liked Melony, he didn't want to do this, but she obviously knew. He had been foolish to assume Jolene hadn't told her daughter. Perhaps Melony had been estranged from her family in her teen and early adult years, but after Doug had died, Jolene had made it clear that fences had been mended, and she was going to New York to be close to her daughter.

Moving her through the house proved easy enough after he rolled her onto the throw rug and slid the bundled load over the linoleum. Getting her from the kitchen to the attached garage proved more difficult, but he managed to do so. Now all he needed to do was hoist her into the trunk of his car.

CHRIS STUMBLED OUT OF BED, yawned, and scratched his head. He then made his way to the kitchen to get a glass of water. If he stopped to look in a mirror, he would see his hair standing on end and might be impressed he managed to obtain that style without applying a liberal amount of hair wax. But he didn't stop, and even if he had, he probably wouldn't be able to see his reflection, considering the lights were all off.

In the kitchen, he yawned again as he grabbed a glass out of the overhead cupboard and went to fill it with ice and water from the refrigerator door. As he stood before the refrigerator a moment later, holding the glass under the low-pressure waterspout, he yawned again and glanced toward the living room and the sliding door on the far wall, where the moonlight was streaming in.

Still half asleep, he waited patiently for his cup to fill while absently looking at the sliding glass door. His slumber-induced stupor ended abruptly when a woman's face pressed against the glass pane and looked into his house. He managed to maintain hold of the glass, but dropped it a moment later when she stepped into his living room, moving effortlessly through the glass door. It was Jolene Carmichael's spirit.

Glass shattered across Chris's kitchen floor. He made no attempt to clean it up, but instead stood frozen by the refrigerator while Jolene's shadowy form moved toward him. Before she reached the kitchen, the overhead light went on, illuminating the room.

"He has her!" Jolene shouted. "He's going to kill her!"

"Who are you talking about?" Chris asked.

"You must save my daughter!" she begged.

"Melony? Who has Melony?" he asked.

Jolene pointed north. "She's in the trunk of his car. Hurry before he takes her away."

"Who has her?" he demanded.

"Pete Rogers," Jolene said, right before she vanished.

Forgetting what he had just dropped, Chris took a step, landing one bare foot on a shard of glass. Letting out a curse, he pulled up his foot, stood on one leg, and gingerly removed the sliver from his heel. Blood dripped from his foot, but he ignored it and managed to jump over the rest of the glass, hopping into the living room, leaving a trail of blood along the way.

He didn't grab shoes or a jacket before heading outside, but he snatched up the flashlight he had left on the coffee table earlier. He had to find out, was Jolene right—did Pete Rogers have Melony locked in his car trunk?

JOE MORELLI HATED the night shift. The only reason he was working was because they were shorthanded, and since Jolene's murder, everyone was putting in extra hours. There had been an increase of calls coming in, reporting suspicious activities. Several minutes earlier, a call had come in from the woman who lived across the street from Chris Glandon. *No, you have to call him Chris Johnson*, he reminded himself, still finding the situation annoying.

According to the caller, someone with a flashlight was lurking around the neighborhood. Joe turned down Beach Drive. Just as he passed Chris's house, he spied a shadowy figure by the back door leading into Pete Rogers's garage. Turning his headlights on the man, Joe stopped his car and demanded he freeze.

To Joe's surprise, Chris Johnson's startled faced looked in his direction, his wild hair standing on end. Despite the cool evening air, Chris stood shirtless and barefoot by Pete's back door, wearing just boxers, while holding his flashlight limply at his side.

Joe stood beside his now parked squad car, its headlights aimed at Pete's house, and ordered Chris to walk toward him. Chris, now shivering, complied. Just as he reached the sidewalk, Pete's porch light turned on, and the front door opened.

"What's going on out here?" Pete demanded.

"That's what I'm trying to find out," Joe said.

"I'm glad you're here!" Chris said excitedly.

Bemused, Joe looked Chris up and down and said dryly, "I imagine you are."

"What are you doing here?" Pete demanded.

Joe pointed to Chris, who now hugged his own body and shivered, as if just realizing it was cold outside. "Looked like Chris here was trying to break into your garage."

"He has Melony in the trunk of his car!" Chris told him. "Quick, you need to get her out!"

"What are you talking about?" Pete asked. "Are you crazy?"

Walking over to the side of the house, Joe glanced down to the door leading into the garage. "There's no window over here, how exactly do you know Melony is in his garage?"

"She's in the trunk of the car!" Chris explained.

"Have you been drinking?" Pete asked.

"When did you last see Melony, Chris?" Joe asked.

Chris stared blankly at Joe. The truth was, he hadn't seen her since the night before.

"CAN you prove you were in Chicago at the time of Jolene Carmichael's murder?" Joe asked Chris. The two men sat in the Frederickport Police Department's interrogation room. Once reaching the station, Joe had taken pity on Chris and had loaned him a jacket.

"I told you, let me talk to Chief MacDonald. Rogers is going to get away. Melony's life's in danger."

"And I told you the chief is at home, and I imagine sound asleep considering it's almost two in the morning. I'm going to repeat my question; can you prove you were in Chicago at the time of Jolene Carmichael's murder?"

"Actually, I was in New York when she was killed. And yes, I can prove I was there. If you aren't going to call the chief for me, I demand I get my phone call, now!"

With a shrug, Joe stood up, looked down at Chris, and said with a smirk, "Fine. I guess I'll have to bring you a phone. Doesn't look like you have your cellphone with you."

"I'll need a phonebook too," Chris called out as Joe walked to the door.

Joe paused at the doorway a moment and looked back to Chris. "Just want you to know, the chief's number is unlisted."

DANIELLE DIDN'T WAKE up on the first ring. It was the third ring that roused her from slumber. Groggily sitting up in bed, she rubbed her eyes and glanced at the alarm clock. Picking up her cellphone, she looked to see who was calling.

"Frederickport Police Department?" Danielle muttered when she read her phone.

Sitting up in bed, she reached over and turned on the light from her nightstand and then answered the call. "Hello? Who is this?"

"Danielle, it's Chris," he said breathlessly.

"Why are you calling from the police station?" She glanced at the alarm clock. "It's after two!"

"Listen, Danielle, it's important. Melony's life is in danger, and that jerk Joe Morelli might come in here any minute and take the phone from me."

Danielle glanced to the closed door leading to the upstairs hallway, thinking of Melony, who she believed was sound asleep under her roof. "What's going on, Chris?"

He then went on to tell her everything he knew.

Danielle was out of her bed and in the hallway before she got off the phone. Throwing open Melony's bedroom door, she found the bed empty.

"She left a while ago," Walt told her when he appeared in the hallway, standing behind Danielle, who stood in Melony's doorway.

Twirling around to face Walt, the cellphone still in her hand, Danielle paused a brief moment and then raced to the stairs. "Wake Lily! Tell her to get downstairs, quick!"

Walt stood at the top of the stairs and frowned at Danielle, who barreled down the stairs. "Just how am I supposed to do that? What's going on?"

Danielle paused one step away from the first-floor landing and looked back up at Walt. She let out a frustrated groan. "I don't know; you figure it out. I don't have time! Pete Rogers might have gotten away already. He has Melony in the trunk of his car!"

Turning her back to Walt, Danielle continued on, racing for the kitchen door. En route, she pressed the button on her iPhone and summoned Siri. "Call Police Chief McDonald's home phone."

Barefoot and wearing her pajamas, Danielle grabbed her car keys from the kitchen counter and raced out the back door. A moment later, she was backing out of her driveway while talking to a half-asleep Edward McDonald on her cellphone.

In a rush, she told him Chris's story as she backed up into the street and then headed toward Pete Rogers's house.

"Chief, his garage door is open!" Danielle cried into the phone. As she approached, she could see Rogers's car still parked in his garage, yet the backup lights were on, and it appeared Rogers was preparing to leave.

Stepping on the gas, Danielle pulled her Ford Flex into his driveway, blocked his exit, parked her car, and laid on her horn.

THIRTY-EIGHT

The neighbor who had initially called the police stood on her front porch, looking across the street at the commotion. Four police cars were now parked on the other side of the road, and a few minutes earlier the ambulance had driven away. She watched as her longtime neighbor Pete Rogers was led handcuffed into the backseat of a squad car.

Wearing an oversized terrycloth robe over her nightgown, her arms folded over her chest, she wondered what he had done. With a shake of her head, she turned back to her door and went inside. *I'll find out tomorrow*, she told herself. It was after 3:00 a.m.; she needed to get back to bed.

Danielle would discover later that Walt had woken Lily after first visiting her in a dream hop, enabling him to tell her what was going on. The moment she woke up, she threw on her robe and called Ian. Within minutes, Ian's car was parked behind Danielle's, and just minutes after that, a police car arrived.

Joe, who had been instructed by the chief to bring Chris back to his house, was horrified when he discovered Melony had actually been locked in Pete's trunk. If Danielle hadn't thought to park in his driveway and block Pete's escape, he hated to think what might have happened to Melony.

He still didn't understand how Chris knew Pete had Melony, and he also wondered why Pete hadn't driven off immediately. Rogers had had the opportunity to get away between the time when Chris was taken into custody and Danielle showed up.

What Joe didn't know, Jolene had intervened. While the newly departed Jolene hadn't learned to harness her energy, her persistence and will had enabled her to awkwardly interfere with Pete's starter in the same way she had managed to turn Chris's kitchen lights on. Had Danielle not shown up when she did, it was entirely possible Rogers would have gotten the engine to eventually turn over, which would have enabled him to take off with Melony, kill her, and dispose of her body. There was only so much a spirit was capable of doing.

At Marlow House, Edward MacDonald Junior had fallen asleep on the bed in the downstairs bedroom while his younger brother, six-year-old Evan, found the old house far too fascinating to sleep in. Less than an hour earlier, he and his brother had been rousted out of their beds by their father. He needed to go somewhere in a hurry, but he couldn't leave them alone and it was too late to call their regular sitter. Since the chief couldn't take his sons to Pete's house—the man could be armed—he had called Lily, who already knew what was going on and had just sent Ian to Pete's house as backup for Danielle.

After tucking the boys in the bed, Lily had gone out on the front porch to see if she could see what was going on up the street. Hillary had thus far slept through the impending drama, blissfully snoring away in her room on the second floor.

Curious, Evan tiptoed to the door and eased it open. Before stepping into the hall, he looked back at his older brother. Eddy continued to sleep. Slipping into the hallway, Evan closed the door behind him and began his exploration.

WALT STOOD at the attic window and watched. A few minutes earlier the ambulance had driven away, its siren on. He assumed Melony was inside and still alive, or they wouldn't use the siren—*or would they?* He watched as another squad car arrived, driving up the street toward the Rogers house. While the moon lit up the street, it was difficult to see who had been riding in the various police cars that had driven by.

"Who are you?" came a small boy's voice from the doorway.

Walt turned to the intruder. Arching his brows, Walt smiled and said, "You must be the chief's son Evan. I've heard about you."

Evan smiled and walked into the attic, looking around. The overhead light was off, but a lamp—sitting next to the sofa bed—was on, dimly lighting the room. "How do you know who I am?"

"Because you can see me." Walt noticed a flush of confusion flicker over the child's face. He suspected the boy took after MacDonald's late wife. He couldn't see much of a resemblance between the chief and his son, other than the smile—which had just disappeared. *Yes, the smile, what I saw of it, is his father's.*

Evan was more delicate than husky, with enormous brown eyes fringed with thick dark lashes. It looked as if he'd had a recent haircut, yet not short enough to discourage the turn of his light brown curls. Walt found something endearing about the child.

"What do you mean?" Evan frowned.

Kneeling down so that he could look into the boy's eyes, Walt said, "I understand you can sometimes see people that others can't."

Evan's already large eyes widened. "That's a secret," he whispered. "My father says I'm not supposed to talk about it."

Walt nodded. "Yes, your father is right. People often don't understand. And it's best to discuss these things with your father first."

"How do you know about it?" Evan asked.

"Because I'm one of those people others typically can't see."

Evan took a step back, his eyes never leaving Walt.

"Please don't be frightened, Evan. I'm a friend of your father's, and I hope you and I can be friends. But I understand if you want to discuss this with your father first."

Evan shook his head. "No. My father told me he can't see the people I can."

"True." Walt stood up and walked to the sofa, giving Evan more space. He sat down. "But my friend Danielle can see me, and she's told your father about me. We sometimes communicate through Danielle."

"You're Walt," Evan said in awe.

"So your dad's told you about me?"

Evan's smile returned. He ran to the sofa and climbed up, sitting next to Walt. "When my dad brought us over here tonight, he took me aside and told me I might meet someone named Walt when I was here, but not to be afraid. He told me I could trust you, but not to say anything to anyone about seeing you—and if anyone was in the room, to pretend you weren't there."

"He did, did he?" Walt beamed. Leaning back in the sofa, Walt said, "So tell me about yourself, Evan."

"THE TYPEWRITER we found in Pete's garage is the same one that typed that letter," MacDonald told Joe as the two sat alone in his office. "Which doesn't surprise me because Pete admitted to sending that letter and claims he witnessed Steve killing Jolene."

"And his reason for attacking Melony? Hit her over the head, shoved her in his trunk, how does he explain that?" Joe asked.

MacDonald shook his head. "He doesn't. Refuses to say another word until his attorney gets here." He glanced at his watch and stood up. "I need to get over to Marlow House to pick up the boys."

"Get some sleep, Chief. I'm going home myself. I'll fill Brian in on what's been going on before I head out."

"IT'S ALL A HORRIBLE MISTAKE," Pete's attorney told Brian Henderson later that morning. "Mr. Rogers was trying to protect Melony Jacobs."

Absently tapping the end of his pen against the desktop, Brian narrowed his eyes. "How, by hitting her over the head and shoving her in his trunk?"

"He was bringing her to the police station for her own safety."

"I don't quite understand; can you elaborate?" Brian set the pen down.

"He knew Steve Klein killed Mrs. Carmichael. He didn't initially come forward because he was understandably afraid for his own life. But he wanted to do the right thing, so he sent Police Chief MacDonald that anonymous letter. Which, I understand, has been verified that it did indeed originate from Mr. Rogers's typewriter."

"That still doesn't explain what he did to Ms. Jacobs."

"He found her looking through his back porch late at night. He assumed she was foolishly playing detective and snooping around anyone's house who had a connection with her mother. He tried to convince her it was dangerous to play detective, but she wouldn't listen. He admits he acted rashly. All he wanted to do was stop her from going to Klein's house and possibly getting herself killed. He was going to bring her down here."

"So he hit her over the head?"

"I told you he admits to acting rashly, and he is willing to face the consequences, but he wants you to know he only had Ms. Jacobs's best interest at heart. He's very fond of her."

"As you know, Ms. Jacobs is still in the hospital—fortunately, doing well. But I did speak to her this morning, and she didn't say anything about your client warning her away from Steve Klein. According to her, one minute she's bending over to pick something up, and the next thing she remembers is waking up in the trunk of a car."

The attorney smiled. "It's a medical fact that people who suffer severe head trauma often never remember what occurred before being struck. I'm not surprised she has no memory of her conversation with my client."

"We have another little problem here." Brian leaned forward, propping his elbows on the table. "Sergeant Morelli showed up at your client's house, and when Chris Johnson accused Mr. Rogers of having Melony Jacobs locked in his trunk, he denied the fact. If he was so anxious to turn her over to the police, why didn't he do it then?"

The attorney stood up, still smiling, "No, Officer Henderson. Your little problem is a lack of motive. My client had no reason to kill Jolene Carmichael or to harm her daughter. They were old friends. In fact, Ms. Jacobs stopped by his house to see him. What happened when Sergeant Morelli showed up at his house was that my client simply panicked. He knew it looked bad and felt it would simply be better if he brought her to the station himself so there would be no doubt as to his true motive. We agree, he used poor judgement, but he had no sinister intent."

IT WAS past noon when Marie Nichols marched into the Frederickport Police Department and demanded to see Police Chief MacDonald. When she was told he was too busy to see her, she refused to take no for an answer.

Stomping her cane on the floor, she said, "Listen to me, young lady, I don't drive anymore, and I had to talk a neighbor into bringing me down here. If my neighbor went to all the trouble to bring me here, then you tell Edward he better see me! This is important!"

"I understand, ma'am, but the chief just got in about a half hour ago, because he was called out late last night and—"

"Yes, yes, I know about all that. That, young lady, is why I'm here. You go tell your boss Marie Nichols is here, and she knows why Pete Rogers killed Jolene Carmichael and why he tried to kill Jolene's daughter, Melony."

When the receptionist just stared blankly at Marie, the elderly woman let out a frustrated sigh and used her cane to point to the door leading to the inner offices. "Go. Now. Tell him. Or do you want a killer to be set free?"

THIRTY-NINE

MacDonald tried to avoid drinking coffee after noon, but considering his recent lack of sleep, he decided caffeine was necessary. Sipping his coffee, he sat behind his desk and studied Marie Nichols, who had just finished telling him her theory regarding Jolene's death.

"So you really think that's why Pete killed Jolene?"

"It's the only thing that makes sense. And you certainly don't believe that cockamamie story about Pete trying to protect Melony."

MacDonald leaned back in his chair. "You seem to know a lot about what's been going on."

Marie shrugged. "I spoke to Adam this morning when he was at the hospital. He told me about that partially burned page from her mother's day planner he and Melony found, and how Melony remembered late last night about seeing Pete burning pages from a book the night before."

"Yes, Melony told me that too when I stopped at the hospital before coming back in today. Apparently, that's why she impulsively walked down to Rogers's place in the middle of the night, to check out his fire pit."

Marie nodded. "And she found scraps of unburnt paper similar to the page she found."

"Yes, she told me. However, someone soaked the fire pit with water late last night, and if there's any paper left, it's mush."

With a disgusted grunt, Marie said, "And we know who that was."

"Unfortunately, there's no tangible evidence to back up your theory."

Using her cane, Marie awkwardly got to her feet. "Then I'll leave it to you to be creative, Edward. I have faith in you." Punctuating her point, she rapped her cane against the floor.

PETE ROGERS SAT with his attorney in the interrogation room when Chief MacDonald entered.

"I was just explaining to my client how he should be out on bail in time to be home for dinner," the attorney boasted.

"Then I'll just have to arrest him again when we file murder charges," MacDonald said calmly when he took a seat at the table.

Pete bolted up straighter in his chair. "Murder charges?"

"Has Ms. Jacobs taken a turn for the worse?" the attorney asked.

"I was speaking of Ms. Jacobs's mother, Jolene Carmichael."

"Ridiculous," Pete stammered, ignoring his attorney, who was now trying to hush him. "Steve Klein murdered Jolene. I'm a witness. I'm prepared to testify. You should be out arresting him and not harassing me!"

MacDonald looked Pete in the eyes. "We know about the fake will—the one Melony's father prepared for you after your wife died. The one leaving you everything. But your wife didn't leave you her estate, did she? She left it to her sister. And Jolene knew that. She was desperate for money, and she expected you to pay up—again. Didn't she?"

The attorney grabbed his client's wrist. "Don't say anything."

Settling back in his chair, MacDonald smiled lazily and said, "Oh, your client doesn't need to say a thing." He turned to face the attorney. "Remember how you told Brian it's not uncommon for someone to forget what happened right before suffering a traumatic injury such as Ms. Jacob's recent blow to the head? Well, sometimes a traumatic injury can jog a memory, like suppressed memories of a troubled teen, who discovered, when working in her father's law practice, that the man she idolized was not quite as shiny as she imagined."

The attorney frowned and looked from Pete back to MacDonald. "I don't know what you're talking about."

"No. But your client does." MacDonald smiled.

Shifting uncomfortably in his chair, Pete swallowed nervously. "What do you want?"

"I've got a pretty good death penalty case here. Your motive for killing Jolene, the fact you were at the crime scene. The fact her daughter, after finding pieces of her mother's missing day planner in your fire pit, ended up in your trunk. But if we make a deal, I can take the death penalty off the table."

"Even if you manage to convince a jury and I get the death penalty, at my age, I'd probably die of natural causes before they ever stick the needle in me," Pete snapped. "I'd rather take my chances with a jury."

MacDonald shrugged. "Maybe, but the last two executions in our state took place three and four years after sentencing. Are you saying you're in poor health and won't make it another five years anyway?"

IF THE HOSPITAL had rules limiting the number of visitors, MacDonald suspected Melony might have exceeded her quota, considering the crowd he found bunched in her hospital room. Yet it didn't prevent him from entering. After all, he had flowers to deliver.

Melony's blue eyes lit up when she saw him standing in the doorway, a vase of spring flowers in his hands. "Aww, Eddy! Those are beautiful."

MacDonald smiled and glanced around. By the number of flower arrangements sitting on the various shelves and counters, he wondered if he should have instead brought candy. Adam stood by Melony's bedside while Danielle and Lily sat in the room's only two chairs. Chris stood behind Danielle while Ian stood next to Lily.

"I understand they're keeping you overnight for observation," MacDonald said as he found a free spot on the sink counter to set the vase before walking over to Melony and kissing her forehead.

"I just hope the food is good here," Melony joked.

"So we hear Pete confessed?" Chris asked.

MacDonald nodded. "Thanks to Adam's grandmother. Her hunch proved spot on."

"I guess she always wondered if something funny had gone on back then," Danielle said.

"You can't pull anything over on Grandma." Adam chuckled.

Melony looked up to MacDonald. "They told me what you said to Pete. But I really had no idea about his wife's will. What made you tell him I did?"

MacDonald shrugged. "To be fair—I just implied it. But I remembered Cindy once telling me the issues you had with your parents started when you began questioning your father's professional integrity."

"I'll have to admit, I'm surprised Pete copped to a plea," Ian said.

Lily glanced up at Ian. "Why?"

"If the only reason he copped a plea was to get the death penalty off the table, why not take his chances and go for a trial? Considering his age, he'd probably outlive the death chamber, and I'm surprised his attorney wouldn't question if you really had the evidence you claimed," Ian explained.

"I reminded him the last two executions were carried off less than five years after sentencing."

"True, but if I remember correctly, didn't they waive their right to appeal?" Ian asked.

"Yes. Which Rogers's attorney pointed out. But I asked Pete if he wanted to spend the rest of his life dodging a needle. That's a special kind of hell. Did he really want to do that?"

Sitting up in bed, Melony leaned back against the mattress's elevated end. "Well, even if I was clueless about what happened with his wife's estate, I imagine once you claimed the will was forged, Pete probably started wondering what damning information you'd find in the files that were put into storage after Clarence went to prison. They're still there, you know. With Mother gone, I have access to them."

"So it's possible, even if the chief hadn't bluffed, he could've found the evidence he needed in those files to prove Pete had a motive to kill your mother?" Lily asked.

"Very possible. And considering I'm now the only one standing between those files and a search warrant, I don't imagine Pete will expect me to do much to keep them from the police." Melony smiled.

Adam reached out and patted Melony's shoulder. "Then he shouldn't have knocked you over the head."

CHIEF MACDONALD WAS JUST GETTING into his police car in the hospital parking lot when he heard someone calling his name. It was Danielle. She hurried in his direction.

"Where's Chris?" he asked, now sitting in his car, its door open.

"We came in separate cars. He went home to get some sleep. I guess Joe hauling him down to the police station sort of messed up his night."

MacDonald chuckled. "Yeah. I'm still not sure how to explain why I believed Chris's claim. Or how Chris knew in the first place."

Leaning back against the inside of the open car door, Danielle folded her arms over her chest and smiled down at him. "Sometimes there is no rational explanation."

"You've taught me that."

"But I do have a question for you. I didn't want to ask back there because I know you told me to keep it to myself."

"What?" he asked.

"In Pete's letter, how did he know about Jolene blackmailing Steve over his affair with Carla? Or even about the loan she was trying to get? Had she put something in the day planner?"

MacDonald chuckled. "It's really that day planner that brought Pete down. If he never took it, he might have gotten away with murder. He was afraid Jolene left some incriminating evidence behind that would implicate him. So after he killed her, he went through her car and then her house. The only thing he found at her house was the day planner, which he took with him so he could go through it."

"So she did write about blackmailing Steve in the day planner?" Danielle asked.

"No. In fact, according to Pete, there was nothing in there about Steve or Pete, at least nothing that would make someone assume she was blackmailing anyone."

"Then how did he know about Steve?"

"Apparently, when Carla and Steve first hooked up, it was in one of their cars in the Pier Café parking lot. Pete was fishing that night and saw them when he went back to his car to get something. They, well…were getting busy."

Danielle wrinkled her nose. "Eww…gross."

"Pete knew Jolene was trying to get a loan from Steve and had been turned down. He didn't know she knew about Steve's affair or if she was blackmailing him."

"That creep. He was just throwing Steve under the bus—not that Steve doesn't belong under a bus."

"Exactly. He figured it wouldn't take long for us to verify Steve was having an affair with Carla and that Steve was on the pier that night. He was supplying us with a motive."

Danielle shook her head. "I wonder what will happen to Pete's money. Is there some statute of limitations on that? Could his estate go back to his sister-in-law, assuming she's still alive?"

"I really don't know. Plus, there may not be anything in Renton's old files to prove anything. Frankly, I'd be surprised if there was."

Danielle stepped away from the car door so MacDonald could shut it. After he did, he rolled his window down and looked up at Danielle. "By the way, Evan enjoyed his time at Marlow House last night."

Danielle grinned. "Yeah, Walt told me about it. Says you have a great kid there."

"Tell Walt thanks for being so nice to Evan. It means a lot to me. This *gift* of his, well, I'm not really sure how to proceed. They don't actually address this type of issue in any of the parenting books I've come across."

"No, no, they don't. But Walt and I are here for you and Evan. Chris too."

FORTY

No one noticed Hillary lingering in the waiting area on Melony's floor. Of course, Hillary did not make an effort to be seen. She discreetly hid behind a tattered edition of *Good Housekeeping Magazine*. When she was confident Melony was finally alone in her hospital room, she tossed the magazine back onto the coffee table and picked up her purse.

A few minutes later, Hillary stood nervously at Melony's open doorway and lightly rapped on the wall.

Melony looked up from the book she was reading. Her blond hair pulled up into a ponytail and her face free of makeup made her appear much younger than her years.

"Hillary?" Melony greeted her, closing the book and setting it on her lap. Wearing the hospital gown, she reclined on the hospital bed under a blanket while the elevated head portion of the bed kept her in a sitting position.

"I didn't bring flowers," Hillary said as she walked into the room and glanced around at the abundance of floral arrangements.

Melony smiled. "I don't think I need any more flowers."

"I wanted to see if you're okay. You look good." Hillary nervously stepped to the side of the bed.

"I'm glad you stopped by," Melony told her.

Hillary looked surprised. "You are?"

"Yes," Melony said with a nod. "I wanted to apologize to you for how I behaved. I really should never have said those things. Said you were…well, you know…crazy. I can't believe how unprofessional I was. You deserve more than that from your attorney."

"I understand," Hillary said quietly. "You're going through a lot, with your mother's violent death…and considering the murder scene I wrote…I would probably feel the same way if I was you…oh, who am I kidding? I do."

Melony frowned. "What do you mean?"

"I think maybe you're right. I am crazy. There has to be something wrong with me for this to keep happening."

Melony pointed to a chair. "Sit down, Hillary."

Pulling a chair closer to the bed, Hillary sat down.

"When Danielle was here earlier, she suggested something—the reason for your dreams. I think she may be right."

Hillary frowned. "What's that?"

"She suspects you may be clairvoyant."

"Clairvoyant?"

"I never really believed in that stuff before, but it makes sense. Before…because none of the murders that were so similar to your stories were ever solved…I always wondered…"

"If I was involved?"

Melony nodded. "Yes. I hate to admit that. I did wonder. But the fact we know who killed my mother proves you weren't involved."

"True. But that doesn't mean I'm not some sort of horrible person who witnesses people getting murdered and doesn't do the right thing and come forward. I can understand why you might wonder that, since in the scene I wrote the killer threw the victim's jewelry off the pier, just as the real killer did. I understand if you'd wonder if I saw him do that and never came forward."

"No. I talked to Eddy—Chief MacDonald—according to one of the fisherman on the pier that night, he saw you leave the restaurant and head for the beach. You never went back on the pier that night. You couldn't have seen Pete get rid of Mother's rings."

Clasping her hands together on her lap, Hillary stared down at her fidgeting fingers. "Clairvoyant," she murmured. "Perhaps that explains…"

When Hillary didn't finish her sentence, Melony asked her, "Explains what?"

Looking back up into Melony's face, Hillary took a deep breath and then continued. "When Danielle took me to Chris's house, I met his neighbor, that man, Pete Rogers. I thought he looked familiar, but I couldn't place him."

"What are you saying?"

"When I heard that he was the one who killed your mother, it suddenly came to me. The man in my dream, the man who killed the woman under the pier, he looked like Pete Rogers."

WALT RECLINED on the library sofa and kicked off his shoes. They disappeared before they hit the floor. He watched as Danielle poured Chris a glass of merlot. The three were alone in the room, its door shut.

"I thought you'd be home sleeping," Walt asked Chris as he fidgeted with the cigar he held between two of his fingers.

"I tried to sleep." Chris took the glass from Danielle. "But I gave up."

Danielle poured herself a glass of wine and then set the bottle on the library desk. She walked to the empty chair next to Chris and sat down. Just as she was about to take a sip of her wine, she looked over to Walt and noticed that while he held a lit cigar in one hand, he now held a glass of wine in the other.

Danielle watched as he took a sip. "You're drinking wine?"

Walt shrugged. "Not really—but I felt left out. You could have offered me a glass."

Danielle extended her hand, holding the wineglass to Walt. "Did you want some wine, Walt?"

"Why thank you," he said with a cheeky grin and then watched as the wineglass floated across the room, from Danielle's hand to his. Just as it arrived in his hand, the glass he had appeared to be holding vanished.

Danielle frowned. "I didn't think you'd really take it."

Walt shrugged and took a sip. But instead of the wine disappearing into his mouth, as had the wine from the first glass he held, the red wine spilled onto the sofa cushion. Seeing what he had just done, Walt righted the glass and cringed.

"Seriously, Walt, did you just spill wine all over my sofa?"

Chris chuckled. "Appears that way."

"I forgot for a moment how this all works." Walt sighed and

released the glass; it floated—now half full—back into Danielle's hand.

Chris and Danielle watched as Walt got up from the sofa. If they thought he was preparing to clean up the wine, they would have been mistaken. Instead, the stained cushion seemingly moved on its own volition, flipping over, and fitting back onto the sofa, but now upside down, concealing the wine stain. Walt took a seat on the cushion.

Danielle shrugged. "I suppose that works." She sipped what remained of her wine.

"I heard what you said to Melony in the hospital room, about Hillary being clairvoyant," Chris told Danielle.

"I couldn't very well tell her a ghost was probably jumping into Hillary's dreams, sharing real-life grizzly murder scenes with her."

"I wonder who this dream-hopping spirit is…or was?" Chris leaned back in his chair, stretched out his legs, and crossed his ankles.

"I wondered if I should try to contact him—"

"No!" Walt and Chris chorused.

Danielle flashed them each a scowl. "I didn't say I was going to. But I did wonder, what kind of spirit manages to witness one murder after another?"

"Over a dozen murders," Chris interjected.

"Exactly. What kind of spirit does that? And if he's going to share information with someone, wouldn't it be nice if it helped the police solve the crime?"

"Not every spirit is as accommodating as Walt," Chris said as he raised his glass to Walt, giving him a brief salute before taking another sip.

Narrowing his eyes, Walt studied Chris. "Why do I get the feeling you're mocking me?"

"I'd never do that, Walt." Chris shrugged and then mumbled, "Okay, perhaps a little."

"Well, maybe Hillary's dream-hopping ghost didn't help her solve any crimes, but thankfully we know who killed Jolene." Danielle downed the rest of her glass and then stood up. She walked to the desk.

"But it would be nice if Hillary could use her gift for something more than story fodder," Chris said.

Danielle lifted the bottle of wine from the desk and refilled her glass. "Not really sure I'd call it a gift exactly."

Walt sighed. "Whatever you want to call it, I have to confess, I'm curious. Rules of the afterlife are confusing at best—and I've been dead for almost a hundred years! You'd think I would've figured it out by now."

"I imagine whatever you haven't figured out will become clear to you when you eventually move on," Chris suggested.

Walt let out a snort. "I imagine you'll be thrilled when I do."

Chris shrugged. "I'm just saying, we're probably not supposed to have all the answers when we're here—on this plane. At least, that's what Danielle's always saying."

Danielle sat back down in her chair. "Whoever the muse is, he's still lingering on this plane. If he wasn't, I don't believe he would have witnessed the murders."

"We don't know that for sure," Chris reminded her.

Walt stared at the cigar in his hand, rolling it gently between his fingertips as its smoke curled upward. "Who makes the rules? I'm confined to Marlow House until I'm ready to move on. Isabella was able to take a road trip with Lily's attackers. My dear wife is under house arrest at the cemetery for trying to kill me, and that annoying little Harvey was able to visit Presley House each Halloween."

"They are pretty random," Danielle said. "But I suppose there's some sense in it somewhere."

"How is this spirit able to find himself at all these different murder scenes?" Walt wondered.

After a few moments of silence, Chris said, "Perhaps the muse makes them murder scenes."

Danielle and Walt turned to Chris. "What do you mean?" Danielle asked with a frown.

Chris stood up, taking his now empty glass to the desk. "Maybe he wanders around, watching for conflict, and then does something—provokes the situation. Take Jolene, for example. If Pete Rogers hadn't found that empty wine bottle—in the middle of the night under the dark pier—in that heated moment, would he have killed Jolene?"

EXHAUSTED, Hillary took a shower and was heading back to her room when she ran into Danielle in the hallway.

"You working anymore tonight?" Danielle asked.

"No. I didn't get much written today, anyway. Too much going on."

"Well, sounds like Melony will be back in the morning. They're just keeping her overnight for observation," Danielle said.

"Yes, I know. I stopped by the hospital this afternoon and saw her."

"You did?"

Hillary nodded. "Yes. She told me what you said—about maybe me being clairvoyant."

Danielle smiled. "It is a possibility."

"I told Melony something after she told me what you'd suggested…I saw Pete Rogers in my dream."

"You did?"

"Yes. He was the one who killed—well, Jolene—in my dream. I knew I recognized him, but I just couldn't place him. If I am clairvoyant—then maybe I can help solve those other murders."

"Do you remember what the other killers looked like?"

"Yes. That's the strange thing about my muse dreams—why they're so different from my other dreams. If I try to remember, I can distinctly recall every detail."

"Any of the killers from the other dreams, do you recognize any of them?"

"Only one. In the first dream like this I ever had."

"You're saying you know who the killer was?"

Hillary let out a sigh. "Only that I recognized him. It was my muse."

Danielle frowned. "Your muse?"

"Yes. The very first muse dream—where I witnessed a murder, he took me to it. But he was also there. He was the one who killed the first victim."

"Your muse was the killer?"

Hillary nodded. "Yes. I told you he made me uncomfortable in the first dream. He was handsome, yet there was something unsettling about him. He wore this black suit and a red bow tie."

DANIELLE CLIMBED into bed and crawled under the sheets and blankets. Max slept soundly at her feet—she could hear him snoring. Glancing down to the foot of the bed, she smiled at the noisy sleeper and then rolled over and closed her eyes.

When Danielle opened her eyes again, she was sitting on a blanket in a field of wildflowers. Hummingbirds buzzed nearby while chipmunks scampered over the blanket's edge. Overhead, white clouds dotted the blue sky.

"Do you know what is nice about this?" Walt asked.

Danielle turned to her right and found Walt sitting on the blanket with her. "It's beautiful."

"Yes, but do you know what's especially nice about visiting a place like this in a dream hop?" he asked.

Danielle reached out and plucked a flower and then looked at Walt while taking a sniff of the blossom. "What?"

"No bugs." Walt smiled.

"Bugs?"

"Certainly. You go find a field of flowers in Oregon and pitch your blanket. I guarantee you'll be covered with mosquitos, flies, and other annoying insects before you have a chance to sit down."

Danielle laughed. "I suppose you have a point."

Walt reclined on the blanket, propping himself on an elbow, and watched Danielle as she gently brushed the soft petals of the blossom against her cheek.

Danielle glanced up at Walt. "I've missed our dream hops."

He smiled softly. "Me too."

In the next moment the space behind Walt began to blur and grow hazy. When Walt noticed Danielle staring behind him, he frowned and turned to see what she was looking at. "What the…" Walt began, only to be silenced when a man appeared, standing amongst the flowers. He was a handsome man wearing a black suit and red bow tie.

Walt stood. "Who are you? What are you doing here?"

Ignoring Walt, the man looked down at Danielle and smiled. Although handsome, his smile—his expression—gave Danielle a sickening feeling in the pit of her stomach.

"You know who I am, don't you?" he asked in a silky voice.

Danielle said nothing.

Confused, Walt looked from the intruder to Danielle.

"I'm here to warn you, ghost girl. Stay out of my business. I don't want you ever discussing me with Hillary again." He vanished.

Dazed, Danielle blinked her eyes and looked around. He was gone.

"Do you know who that was?" Walt asked.

Danielle nodded. "Yes. I believe we just met Hillary's muse."

THE GHOST AND THE MUSE

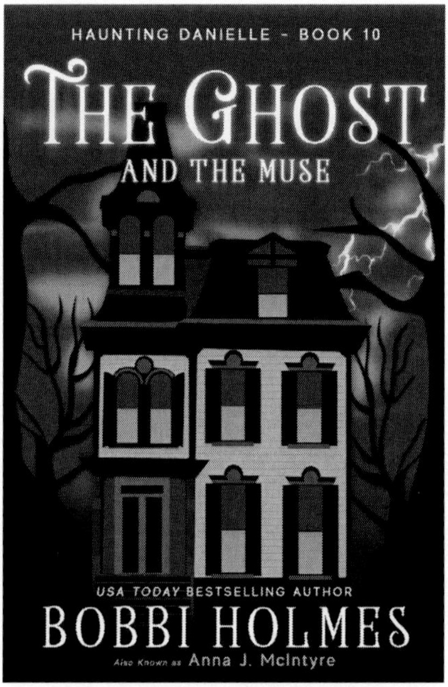

Return to Marlow House in

The Ghost and the Muse

Haunting Danielle, Book 10

Perhaps Danielle's first clue should have been—Hillary's muse is male.

He brings with him restless spirits and murders to solve—if Danielle dares.

She has already been warned to stay away.

NON-FICTION BY

BOBBI ANN JOHNSON HOLMES

Havasu Palms, A Hostile Takeover

Where the Road Ends, Recipes & Remembrances

Motherhood, a book of poetry

The Story of the Christmas Village

BOOKS BY ANNA J. MCINTYRE

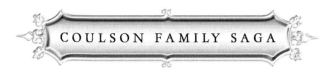

COULSON FAMILY SAGA

Coulson's Wife

Coulson's Crucible

Coulson's Lessons

Coulson's Secret

Coulson's Reckoning

UNLOCKED HEARTS

Sundered Hearts

After Sundown

While Snowbound

Sugar Rush